Abandoned In The Dark

& Other Stories

By
David Boyle

www.AuthorMikeInk.com

ISBN: 978-0-9884468-0-9
Library of Congress Control Number: 2012950741

First Published by *AuthorMike Ink*, 11/27/2012

www.AuthorMikeInk.com

AuthorMike Ink and its logo are trademarked by *AuthorMike Ink Publishing*.

Printed in the United States of America

Table of Contents

INTRODUCTION

Horror is indefinable. Fear is not only engendered by the familiar tormenters (monsters, ghosts, gore, violence, the supernatural) but also by the grimmest aspects of reality, life's frequently ignored machinations which baffle— cripple in fact—the most balanced human psyches. Often I've had nightmares and gut-wrenching daydreams that ruthlessly stole my breath away, rendering me confused, unsettled. What rattled me was not just the sheer repulsiveness of the visions I beheld, but knowing such situations are *real* and could happen to anybody, have happened, and will happen forevermore. The only way I can comprehend life's savagery is to write about it honestly and vividly, channeling my own discomfort into something tangible, and then hoping I can escape the fierce clutch of darkness when it returns to stalk me another time. These stories have kept me awake at night begging for daylight, for my heart to stop pounding, for the warm embrace of safety. But the world has taught me an unforgettable, uncompromising lesson—we're never completely safe, are we? Whenever and wherever horror lurks, we can only temporarily evade its attack, for we must face the abominable whether ready or not. Ask yourself this: Do you dare share my fears?

ABANDONED IN THE DARK

As Karl Stevens ripped himself out of bed, he reached for the remote on the oak night stand. He was in such a rush that he almost knocked the lamp from its perch. He hit the button on the control. The television flickered with life. While Karl got dressed, the babbling Channel 27 news reporter offered only background noise. Karl slid open the louvered closet doors, the rickety wheels rolling noisily in their track and waking his wife, Charlene.

Lucille Kolica kept rambling about environmental issues that troubled the country. Normally, information like that would have captured Karl's attention but he was feeling uneasy about the day ahead of him. He hadn't slept well, had tossed and turned practically all night long, disrupting Charlene's sleep several times. Once or twice she had to nudge him to knock it off.

Charlene rose from the bed and slipped into her robe. "I'm going to make coffee, Karl," she said, wiping her eyes, coming out of an early morning haze. Karl was in a zone, rummaging through his closet for the right suit. "Don't worry about me. I'll get some on the run. I've got a meeting with Huegly this morning and a shitload to do before then. We have to let some people go today. Thanks anyway."

"Does that bother you at all?" she asked, lacing the robe's belt around her waist.

"That's the job. Sometimes you have to lower the boom," he responded, snapping his wristwatch in place. Karl trampled down the spiral staircase tucking his shirt into his trousers, and took a detour to the dining room table to grab one of the new ties he had bought the day before at Lord and Taylor on the way home. Three new spiffy ones were still in the bag.

In the kitchen Charlene was brewing a pot of coffee and fixing toast. She tapped the switch on the space-saver radio underneath the dish cabinet and sure enough another voice was rambling about the environment again. "Too intense for the morning," she mumbled. From behind she heard Karl's footsteps on the linoleum floor. He entered the room and went straight for a granola bar on the counter, then poured a mug of coffee.

Charlene had her attention on a Macy's circular. Her eyes peered over the top for a better view of her husband. "What happened to that 'picking up a cup of coffee on the way' idea?" she asked sarcastically.

As he poured his coffee he turned and smiled at her. "You made it. I might as well have some." He replaced the pot in the stand, sighed, then shook his head. "Can't a guy change his mind from time to time?" He glanced at his Rolex, whistled. "I'm running late." He grabbed his sports coat from the kitchen chair and walked to the door. "See you later. I've got a big day ahead of me." Karl shut the door behind him and stepped out into the beautiful October morning.

Charlene took a bite of her toast. "Yeah…I love you, too," she said under her breath.

Before reaching the heart of the city Karl was able to take in the urban scene as he braced himself for the usual hectic day at Samson Engineering. He made a right on Ridgefield and passed Luke's Bakery. He could almost taste one of their jelly donuts, and he imagined the tempting aroma of their coffee, their special flavor of the day swirling around in his mouth. He wanted nothing more than to pull over. But this morning he was pressed for time, so his hungry imagination would have to suffice for now.

Karl crossed over the town line into the city. He felt better knowing he had avoided the heaviest traffic. Getting an early start this morning certainly helped make life easier. Downtown was relatively quiet for now. The workforce was just starting to get rolling, but within the hour the streets would be crawling with pedestrians— some boarding buses, others hailing a taxi or walking to work. Energetic commuters often rode bikes to the office.

He cruised down Lexington, passing Humphrey Street and Turner Boulevard. At the next block he made a right onto 24th and continued to the intersection of Manor Place. The large corner building housed his 15th floor office. Karl was in a line of cars about five deep waiting to pass through the gate when something struck him as odd. The tires on the security van were flat and not a guard was in sight. Why hadn't somebody reported the problem? It was intolerable irresponsibility. What if somebody needed assistance? Then what? If the employees weren't going to take care of it then he was. As soon as he got settled at his desk he was going to have a nice chat with the head of security about this. Even though it was a sunny day, minimal light found its way through to the parking decks. All the levels stayed dark and cold, making it difficult for drivers to find a space, much less squeeze into it. Karl glided through the first floor, taking the lane headed toward the section of the garage closest to the elevators and security booth. He parked his car in between two larger vehicles. In the rearview mirror he noticed a man wearing a white shirt and an orange vest coming up behind him but couldn't see his face yet. Karl opened the door and stuck his head out. "Hey, is that you, Douglas?"

The security officer stopped in his tracks. "Excuse me, sir?" Then he moved closer.

Karl didn't recognize him. "Oh, sorry, my fault," Karl said. "I thought you were Adrian Douglas, the guard who usually works this shift."

The guard squinted. "Douglas? I don't know any Douglas, sir. I just started here the other day. This is where my boss posted me. I have to work a double today, so if you've got a problem you'll have to speak with—"

"Easy does it, kid. There's no problem at all. I only wanted to report that the security Bronco's tires are flat. That ought to be addressed right away. I'll take it up with the supervisor. It's nice to meet you anyway." He extended his hand.

The guard offered his in return. "Thanks, sir. I'm Todd Fairbanks."

"It's a pleasure to meet you, Mr. Fairbanks. See you around."

"Hopefully not for long, I got college plans," the guard said.

"That's impressive, Todd! Best to you," Karl said.

"Thanks again, sir. Just got approved for a student loan, and my parents were cool enough to pitch in a few bucks too. So I'm taking advantage of all the hours I can get. Later!"

After the men parted ways, Karl hustled to the elevator, one of which was out of order. He approached the non-functioning shaft, stuck his head inside and looked down. A repair company with the head maintenance man, Hutchinson, was working below. The maintenance supervisor glanced up at him, nodded, then went back to work. The crew clearly had their hands full, welding and doing a bit of troubleshooting to the main cables. A "Caution: Men Working" sign stood in front of the elevators. That particular elevator would be out of service until the lunch hour.

Karl boarded the other car and rode it to the 15th floor. When he got off it was business as usual. The typical morning rat race: employees rushing around, answering phones, typing reports and such, carrying on with another day of work. Once he got settled he checked his long list of e-mails and phone messages. He glanced at his watch, wondering where the time had gone. His co-workers strolled past, dropping all kinds of memos on his desk. He knew this morning would be an absolute grind. At least it was Friday, though. Karl opened his desk drawer to pull out his phone message pad. Inside he found an apple. *Who the hell put this here? I hate fruit.* He assumed his secretary had left it there last night; she liked pulling office gags.

Karl was inundated by paperwork and phone calls to clients. To make matters worse, a note on his desk said that his secretary would not be in today. *How unreliable! She has time for gags but not for work? Pain in the ass.* An assembly line of the usual madness had to be completed before he had a chance to take a break, so he jumped into work head first. The few times he'd raised his head to look around he saw the window washers strapped in their harnesses cleaning the large panes of glass around the department. Good thing for them the weather had cooperated. He imagined how much of a chore it'd be if they were dealing with blustery conditions while dangling over the cityscape at hundreds of feet in the air.

The hours passed in a blur. Around eleven o'clock he realized it was time for the big meeting that he had anticipated all morning. He had a sense of how this particular conference would go. He hoped for the best and imagined the worst, knowing how demanding those schmucks from corporate could be. Everything went smoothly up to a point. The conference seemed to chug along swiftly until the end when the room emptied and one of the suits handed Karl a piece of paper. He knew this part was coming. It was inevitable. Karl looked the document over for a minute and then raised his head from the paper, swallowed. "You have five jobs slashed here, Huegly."

Huegly, a paunchy fellow with a thick beard and glasses, had a cigar sandwiched between his lips. He had an intense personality, intimidating actually. "What's your point, Mr. Stevens?"

"We agreed on three job cuts, not five," Karl responded sternly, sliding his fingers through his wavy blond hair, then loosening his tie.

"Well, Stevens. I gave your recommendations considerable thought and I remembered a ways back when you revealed that Hutchinson was deadwood. And don't concern yourself with that security guard either, Adrian Douglas. I had my secretary send him packing yesterday. I brought in a new college kid. They're great. They'll work for less than the average Joe, and I'm doing corporate a favor here. So now…do you recall that little *Hutchinson* chat we had, Mr. Stevens?"

"I…I do, but…but that was six months ago, Mr. Huegly, and I—"

"Pardon me, Mr. Stevens. Last time I checked it was me that controlled the finances of this company. Do we agree on that?"

"Yes sir. It's just—"

Huegly interrupted in a huff. "What is it, Mr. Stevens?"

While biting his bottom lip, Karl took a deep breath. "To be frank with you, sir, the issue I have is that I'm ultimately the one who shoulders the blame for matters like this, and I don't need unnecessary friction between—"

"With all due respect, I am not here to make you feel at ease, Stevens. I'm here to make sure you do your job, which is how you're able to earn the means that you live by. Have I made myself clear?"

Karl looked down at his pad, which outlined the drastic cuts. "Yes, Mr. Huegly."

Huegly rose from the table then walked toward the door with a hand relaxed in his pocket. He turned, faced Karl. "By the way, Mr. Stevens, today I will be sending Thomas Bannister from HR to the respective departments with letters of dismissal for the employees. They'll require your signature, of course, to render them official. Take care of it." As Huegly left the room, he slammed the door.

After the meeting with the upper brass, Karl peeked at his wristwatch: 12:30, well past his lunch time. He was starving. But he was drowning in work, distressed about having to sign off on the termination letters. He knew his boss was right about his recommendation a while back—it had come back to bite him. He wished this mess would go away. Hutchinson had been their head of maintenance and facilities for a long time. Karl was displeased with his attitude over the years. A few of their private confrontations were kept under wraps. Despite Hutchinson's handsome salary, he had become lazy and quite irritable for no reason. The two of them almost fought twice. On one occasion, after having been caught reading a porno magazine on the job and receiving a reprimand, Hutchinson threw an apple core at Karl.

Nothing seemed to remedy the problem, so Karl had left him alone. Over time, he tried to be extra courteous to him. That merely served as a band aid for the wound. Then, when the second in command was fired after being caught smoking marijuana in the supply closet, Hutchinson was given slack until action was taken. The problem was this: Hutchinson knew the place inside and out. To train someone new would require much time and money. So they had held off on moving on things, until now. The whole ordeal would finally be over. Huegly approved the cuts and Karl had to sign off on the changes whether he agreed with them or not. And as he had told Charlene— "sometimes you have to lower the boom."

It had been a stressful day indeed. Somehow Karl was able to keep his attention on his work and complete the bulk of the day's tasks. His boss pretty much avoided him after the meeting except for a brief encounter in the men's room.

The day wore on. It grew late. There were only a few more things to do, a handful of last minute calls to make and then some notes to glance over for another meeting in the morning. After that he was free to go home and even sleep in tomorrow. He could work from his home office as he sometimes had done when things were overwhelming and he needed to catch up.

By 5:30 more of the cubicles had emptied, the offices now darker and quiet. The sun had set minutes ago. The cleaners started to filter in, vacuuming the floors and wiping the desks down—the usual deal. Karl was growing more tired by the minute; it was tougher to push through a day of overexertion. His eyelids were heavy but he battled the urge to rest his head, even for a few moments. That would be counter-productive.

By 6:30 he was extremely lethargic and the office was practically dead. Even the janitor who was mopping the floor earlier had cruised past his desk to remind him that security had to lock up soon. Karl insisted he'd call the guard booth before he left. Fairbanks would let him out in a pinch; he was pulling down overtime.

Seven o' clock approached. Still he wrestled his mind to stay awake, to focus. His body, however, had a different plan. He called home to Charlene to explain his rigorous day and to let her know he was hitting the road soon. She told him that if he was too tired to drive she'd pick him up or call a taxi. Enough was enough already, she explained. After ten minutes of reassuring her everything was okay, he hung up the phone and began winding down.

He organized his papers, filed away stacks of reports, completed odds and ends, made sure that all inquiries were answered and that his desk was free of clutter. Thirsty, he made his way to the kitchen and raided the refrigerator for a cold soda and a snack to hold him over until dinner. His stomach had been growling since he'd forgone lunch to get the job done. Karl opened the fridge door and the interior bulb cut out. Then the lights in the break room fizzled, followed by the fluorescent tubing above the desks in the office. One by one all the overhead lights faded. He put his can of soda on the table and looked beyond the kitchen door to the offices: The power was going down for no apparent reason. His instincts kicked in. He picked up the phone on the wall to report the incident to the security guard on staff. But the line was dead. He pressed the knob on his wristwatch. The glowing dial displayed 7:00 p.m. A power failure in this building was unprecedented. The battery-operated emergency lights perked up, throwing faint light about the office. The backups only cast enough light to navigate certain sections of the room for a brief period of time.

Karl heard a rattling at the front door, which lasted for a few seconds. Then a click. He shouted, "Hey! Hey!" No response. Using the diminishing light to guide his way, he traced the source of the noise to the main office door and looked into the hallway. Everything seemed fine, except for one strange and unforeseen mystery: the main entrance door was chained shut on the outside, the lever and the handle secured with a padlock. This was not a power failure at all…

With his fist he hammered the glass. He yelled again, praying that someone would hear his hoarse voice. But the entire 15th floor was still, desolate. Karl hustled to the nearest window, his gaze hovered above the metropolis. The other buildings were in operation, lights glowing in distant offices just across 24th. At this hour the staff had gone home in each tall structure. Now he was terribly alarmed, unsure how he'd finagle his way out of this horrendous nightmare. Maybe if he stuck it out for a while longer someone would come for him and whoever was responsible would be punished severely. Karl rooted through desk drawers for anything that would help. It was possible some kind of object was stashed there that would be of use. But what?

What the hell can I find?

He knew what he needed to do. He couldn't imagine any other way. He felt himself beginning to panic. He decided that he would have to break the window and take the stairs all the way to the ground floor if he was going to get out. He checked the adjoining door first, the

13

one dividing sectors A and B. It was locked. He ran back to the other side and tapped the glass with his knuckles. The glass was thick, durable. But he felt strong enough to pick up a chair and whale away until he broke through. Karl was ready, eager, and able to think clearly now. He scrambled around the room in search of the perfect chair, something solid enough to break the window. Frantically he grabbed the tops of each chair, sizing them up, feeling what they were made of. First he grasped a wooden chair and threw it at the glass, the collision hardly cracking it. "God damn it!" he hollered.

Then he stumbled upon a paper weight—a plastic globe—on one of the desks next to a tape dispenser and another apple as red and shiny as the one he had found in his desk earlier. He flung it in crazed retaliation at the glass. He heard the globe shatter. He imagined the glass discreetly laughing in his face, daring him to try again, mocking his weakness as a grown man. Karl refused to give in. Not now. He wanted to escape by whatever means it took. Across the room he got a metal desk file. He tossed that at the window with the same force, which produced lots of noise but the same non-result. The glass seemed impervious. *I have to try,* he told himself. It was his only choice, his only method of finding a way out. However, anger and frustration were boiling inside, festering. He continued searching the desks, shoving items aside: papers, pens, and stationery spilling over, littering the floor. Karl began whipping everything at the glass, screaming obscenities, releasing his pent-up hostility one vulgarity at a time. "You mother fucker! Son of a bitch! You wanna mess with me, huh? Whoever you are, you're as good as dead! You hear me?"

Sweat poured off him. His hair hung limp and stringy over his forehead. He finally clawed his way to the corner of the room where he encountered a chair with steel framing. He was relieved to find something stronger than wood. Karl panted heavily now, almost too exhausted to cross the room to try escaping again. But there was no alternative. He removed his tie and undid the buttons on his shirt. Then the emergency lights died, the room blackened, plunging him into deeper trouble. His heart rammed the walls of his chest. He felt dizzy, on the verge of fainting. The darkness played with his mind, manipulated him—pushed him closer to the edge. The nuances of his body were clearer now, especially the *whoosh-whoosh-whoosh* of his heart throbbing behind his breastbone.

At the other side of the office, on the far end, an adjoining door connected the two rooms, the one he'd checked previously. Security locked it at six o' clock. He had watched that Fairbanks kid do it. *Where the hell is Fairbanks now?* He tried to feel his way toward the glass, dragging the chair behind him. As he moved erratically he banged into obstacles in his path, winced in pain; each bump ratcheted up his rage. He heard another *click* in the adjoining office, a noise that forewarned him. He froze, felt something on the floor under his foot. He bent over and picked up the object, a metal cigarette lighter. "Yes!" he hissed. He stood up straight, popped the lid and turned the ridged dial once…a weak spark. Again he flicked it. Nothing.

"C'mon you bastard," he begged. A third time he stroked the dial—a flame jumped from the wick. Satisfied, he lifted his head and stared in the direction of the shackled door to get an idea of where he was, gather his bearings. Karl jumped backwards, dropped the lighter. A figure of a man was leering at him through the pane of glass. He failed to make out the face, since he had only a fraction of a second to get a good look. Karl wanted to scream, to release this accumulation of horror. Whoever that was knew he was alone, helpless. This maniac wanted to play whether Karl was a willing participant or not. He sank to the floor battling a squeamish stomach, shaking like a brutalized soul. The game continued. Someone was lurking, concealed in the thick veil of darkness. Karl knew that if he wasn't miraculously found he'd be forced to confront this menace.

He sat on the carpeted floor thinking of ways to get out, and in the meantime felt blindly for the lighter. A lighter was better than nothing—there was no Plan B. At least the lighter could be used as a weapon if he were to have a showdown with his enemy. He searched on his hands and knees, combed the plush carpet with his fingertips. Seven feet behind him the lighter turned up, sliding between his index finger and thumb. He clutched it in his brittle hand, squeezed tightly. It would never get away from him again—never. He rose to his feet and heard a noise on the far side of the room again, exactly as before.

Click-Click-Click...Keys maneuvered in the housing of the lock, back and forth. A voice came alive in the silence this time. It was faint, a sinister whisper.

16

"Finally...you get what you deserve."

Karl listened to the words, trembled feverishly. His jaw locked, his teeth clenched. He couldn't speak. Seconds later those same words chilled him again. Then the door closed and the spine-tingling voice was gone.

"Hey! Who are you? What the fuck is this?" Karl cried out. "What do you want, you sick animal?"

From the outside the strange man struck the glass where Karl was standing, startling him yet again. He flicked on his lighter but the flame failed to reveal a recognizable image. Tired of being taunted, he picked up the chair and drove it as hard as he could at the window, screaming ferociously with each swing, putting all the strength he could muster into each strike. A resonant *pop*...the window buckled from the abuse. Splits formed. Web-like fissures caused by his aggressive lashing weakened the glass. After five or six attempts Karl needed to catch his breath. His heart was racing faster than before. His hands were wet, slippery. He sucked in air and exhaled—repeatedly—and with each breath tried to ease his pulse.

"Fuck you!" he bellowed.

Once more he clutched the chair and pounded the sturdy window. This time the chair drilled its way through. Shards of glass spread on the floor. The chair tumbled against the other side of the wall and then got lost in the blackness. Karl growled in victory and then with the lighter squirmed through the opening into the tenebrous hall. The dancing flame before him would serve as a guide in the dark. He had to use it sparingly, not knowing how much fluid remained in the cylinder. Hesitantly, he moved along the corridor using an open palm against the wall as a brace, as a feeler. He switched the lighter on and off every few feet to keep himself on course. Despite working in the office every day for years, Karl still felt disoriented. It was impossible to push this creeping terror away. The darkness was unsettling; it literally swallowed him whole. He had a lunatic messing with him. Some weirdo was out-finessing him, toying with him for reasons he didn't understand. That's what rattled him more: knowing there was no answer, no quick solution as there always was in the boardroom. *How does one prepare for something when there's no defense? What if this nut gets to me? Can I burn him with this small flame I hold? Is this my only chance?*

The questions were unstoppable. Karl was so distraught that he had to shit. There was no time to find a bathroom, and it sure as hell wasn't safe to go looking for one. So he defecated in his pants, felt the excrement filling his underwear. The dreadful turn of events overshadowed what he had just done. He realized that fear alters the human condition, makes people do disgusting things.

From down the hall there were footfalls gaining on him. Uneven breathing accompanied the patter of feet. The footsteps grew louder, closer. Karl's tongue felt heavy and dry, coppery. He worried about his own discernible breathing in the empty halls. Would he become an easy target for his nemesis? He had tiptoed no more than ten feet when he lost his footing and stumbled against a door to his right. The door gave way, the hinges groaned under the pressure of his body weight, and he ended up wobbling into another room. As he struggled to regain his balance, the lighter slipped from his sweaty grip. He heard it skip across the cement floor and break apart. The one thing he had was gone, but he stayed on his feet. He found himself isolated in a stairwell. That's what it had to be, he assumed. His footsteps, his breath, and even the closing door reverberated in the alcove. He extended his hands, reaching for the walls. If he took too many steps in the wrong direction he'd fall down the steep flight of stairs and suffer serious damage—or perhaps death. So he moved cautiously, arms outstretched and fingers splayed.

Karl shuffled over the tile surface, advancing one cautious step at a time. He inched farther, the trepidation mounting rapidly. *Oh please. Don't fall. Don't make a costly mistake.* He began coaching himself through each movement. He was petrified, aware that his stalker knew the way around and was hiding somewhere out there. But where? Hidden in a corner? Waiting by the elevators? Under a desk? Armed and dangerous? He wished he could stop for a minute to compose himself. While back-stepping, his right foot struck something firm and unyielding. He teetered again, but stayed upright. He closed his eyes, inhaled deeply, and anchored his legs in place. He bent over to figure out what was impeding his path. His fingers touched flesh…a face.

"Oh Christ," Karl said. His hand twitched, recoiled. Something compelled him to feel around. Maybe he'd find a weapon or a key or a flashlight, something useful on the body. He even whispered to the motionless figure on the cold floor.

"Are you alive? Can you hear me?"

He poked the body, nudged it—no response. With his hand he continued probing. His fingertips moved along the chest and then to the neck where they made contact with something wet. Karl knew it was blood. He failed to detect a pulse in the neck. Despite his revulsion he groped lower, until his thumb was pricked by a sharp object. He fingered it, whatever it was, and from the shape he concluded it must be a guard's tag. On the back of the object he felt a pin, and the scalloped edges he fondled were reminiscent of a badge. *Damn. Is this Fairbanks?*

A hand clamped down on Karl's mouth. Then an arm clutched his torso, pulling him backwards. Karl tried to thwart the attack but the grip was too powerful to counter. He was being manhandled, outmuscled. Karl was pushed face first into the cement wall, his nose squashed on contact, causing excruciating pain. Everything was happening fast. Karl tried to be strong—a waste of time and energy. There was nothing he could do. He'd grown weak and tired and lost in tragedy. Rivulets of blood seeped into his mouth, choking him. He labored to stabilize his breathing. A second time the attacker shoved him into the cement wall, this time back first. His skull snapped back, firing a rocket of pain through his head. He felt as though he were being bludgeoned with a hammer, couldn't tell whether he'd blacked out or not. Darkness was everywhere, enveloping him like an airless, lifeless body bag. What difference did it make now anyway? He was falling apart, losing the ongoing confrontation, enduring a beating he couldn't withstand much longer. The herculean stranger raised Karl onto his shoulder, and before Karl realized what was happening, the attacker charged into the wall, using him as a battering ram, a buffer. When his backbone met the rock-hard cement he started losing consciousness, succumbing to the unrelenting reality of doom.

He sank to the cold floor in a broken heap, wheezing, grappling for air. Unfortunately there wasn't much left. Flurries of oxygen escaped him, his lungs burned like scorching flames. Karl experienced a respite from the pummeling. The intense pain served one purpose and one only: each searing jab of misery reminded him that he was not dead yet. In fact he wasn't all that sure he had much left of life, or to live for. *What would Charlene think of all this?* Part of him wished she knew he was in danger. But then again, this was not how he wanted Charlene to see him, remember him, in what he imagined was a bloody, destroyed mound of broken bones. While lying on the floor he heard a voice in his ear—the attacker's. At first, all he felt were baritone vibrations feathering his earlobe. He struggled to understand, to decipher what was being said. He heard garbled words…

"How's it feel to be on the chopping block, jerk off? Never kill the messenger, destroy the source…I'll make sure Charlene finds out what kind of man you really are."

Charlene finished up a steamy shower and dropped down onto the couch with a book. It was so late. She despised it when Karl worked later than he promised. *I thought he looked forward to our Friday nights?* She'd noticed that Karl had bought her a new dress and left it behind this morning in one of his attaché cases in the closet. She decided she'd wear it, entice him when he came home. *What a nice surprise! It's been a long time since we've done this. I'll play along.*

In the light of the lamp on the end table she read *The Rain Dance.* All week she'd been reading it and now that Karl was running late she decided to catch up on the second half, flip through a few pages. A quiet night; the house possessed by stillness, the kind when all you hear are the creaks, the house settling, the joints and wood fibers making odd sounds. Charlene turned the page, and then heard a noise outside. It filtered its way in through the kitchen. She shoved the bookmark into the novel and pried herself from the couch to investigate. She crossed the hardwood floor moving toward the kitchen, looking everywhere. Her mental gears were in motion.

Charlene made it past the refrigerator, then focused on the window above the breakfast table, which was open halfway. She stood an arm's reach away, peering outside through the undulating curtains. Her eyes widened. She took a step to the left and hit a switch, turning on the outside lights. The door to their metal shed was open. Leaves that once blocked the sliding doors had been pushed aside.

Karl?

Her body stiffened. She wrapped her arms around herself, scared and chilled. *What's going on?* The phone jingled on the wall behind her. She paused for a moment, and then picked it up.

"Hello?"

"Mrs. Stevens?"

"Y…Yes?"

"You may or may not recognize my voice. That's not important though."

"What is this? Who is this?" she asked.

"I'm sorry to have to be the bearer of bad news, Charlene. But let me tell you something."

"What the hell…? What…?" Charlene was nervous, tongue-tied.

"Humans are such a volatile species, aren't they? But they can't disregard their true composition. That's what I believe. Don't you?"

"Who are you? What do you want from me? Is this you, Karl? Is this your idea of a twisted joke?

"No, Charlene, this is not a ruse. With a little patience, my dear, your questions will be answered."

She stood immobile. Her lips trembled, her gaping eyes welled up.

The voice continued. "Do you like fruit?" He paused for a few seconds. "I know Karl didn't. And yet his existence reminded me of an apple in a sense. I like apples. They carry a deeper meaning for me than one would think. When you peel away the layers, the core is the same. Do you agree with that?"

Silence, except for the chattering of her teeth.

The voice continued. "Do you know what I see at the core of all human beings?"

Charlene remained unresponsive. The voice carried on. "I see many things I don't like. I see evil, Charlene. I see a population brimming with rotten vermin, just like your husband."

"What have you done to him?" she shouted.

"I've broken down his layers, exposed his core. He's not hard to find. He had a rough day at the office, so I dumped him in the elevator shaft. Come and see for yourself."

SPLIT SECOND

Donald ambled into the master bedroom of his home. The furnishings were ordinary and just about right for his meager salary. He was a simple man, not striving at all for life's bigger picture, never had been. He earned enough to support his kid and to send alimony checks to his ruthless wife who wanted to bleed him dry of every dime he'd earned during his less than spectacular existence. Tears poured down his face. His skin glistened as the afternoon sun tore a path through the window behind the work desk. He opened the top drawer with his key and there it sat in all its glory, shiny and mean…a Smith and Wesson.

The evil-looking pistol nose stretched a good six inches long. Without a doubt, it was the most immaculately polished weapon of any collector's arsenal. Donald stared down at the gun. His tears would not cease. The pain swelled inside him, the pressure surged. The dam was about to burst. Hands trembling, he reached down toward the gleaming revolver. Beads of sweat slid from his palm, staining the terry cloth underneath the pistol. He looked around the room and felt as though the four walls were sliding toward him to crush him. The meaning of his life had vanished without a trace, and the solution to all that destroyed his psyche was right there, sitting in the drawer, waiting for his exacting embrace. He wrapped his hand around the handle, allowing himself to feel its grittiness in his palm, his fingers urgently squeezing the thick metal grip.

Donald peered toward the window. The sunlight accented his bloodshot eyes; the tears now drizzling down his chin smeared his defeated face. To the left on the dresser was an old family photo with the three of them together: him, his ex-wife, and his fifteen-year-old son, A.J. They occupied each of his outstretched arms. That photo once meant something to him. The picture at one time in the ancient past conjured up flashes of an almost-perfect marriage. That was his favorite photo—not because they were all together but because it was the only photo where his son wore a happy face. Donald knew his kid had been used as leverage in the divorce and he wanted desperately to right the wrong. But it was easier for him to just blast a hole through his throat and not deal with the litany of failures that he'd left in his path. He wished his son was around so *he* could pull the trigger for him; do his father a well-deserved favor. He had dragged poor A.J. through enough misery for a lifetime. A.J. certainly wanted him dead (at least he believed that), and that's why his son never talked much and why their visitations came off as cold and painfully awkward.

He held the gun out in front of him, licked some of the pity-laced tear drops from his lips. His body shook violently, like that of a soldier suffering from gangrene or some fierce disease. He thought hard about how much easier it would be to be ridden with some illness and accept the suffering that was due him. The top of his desk was covered with unpaid bills, letters from debt collectors, and at least half a dozen official letters from his ex-wife's attorney. His life lay before him decimated, an assortment of continual and irreparable damage.

The sun's rays were starting to stream through the other bedroom window, slowly inching their way across the disheveled white bed sheets. This was Donald's day to see his son, and he was running late for that now too. He'd fallen apart long, long ago and it all led up to this. The shame soon manifested itself deep within his soul and now the root of it all was trying to pry its way out. He wanted to release the anguish before it bound him for life, and that's what was driving him mad. It pained him to face his own son again. Fortunately, A.J. was staying with his mother, and if he could just pull the trigger now while he had the chance, no one would have to see it. Hear it? The neighbors would hear the thunderous report from a Smith and Wesson without a doubt.

But he was wasting time now, precious time. He forced himself to take another look around the room he once shared with a loving wife, one who had a while back found happiness and comfort in the arms of another man, a better man, one she anxiously leaned on during her and Donald's episodes of disorder and chaos.

Donald inserted the barrel of the gun into his mouth, pushing it so far back that he felt it poking the farthermost lining of his throat. On the main dresser to his left, he saw the bookends were separated from the row of journals and magazines they usually kept in place. One of the magazines was gone. He was missing the *Guns and Ammo* magazine. Only that one had been removed from its permanent place. A.J. always messed with his things when he visited, and repeatedly Donald had asked the kid to request permission before taking anything. Did any of this really matter now? No…he had his path etched in stone. He understood what had to be done and why.

He pulled the trigger—no gunshot…dead air.

He pulled it again: a *click*…no smoke, no pain, nothing.

Donald was agitated by the silence, by the lack of a blast. He had shut his eyes while pulling the trigger, hoping it would all be painless and fast. But now the situation escalated. He withdrew the pistol from his mouth and popped open the barrel. The gun was empty. Every chamber in the barrel was a void staring him in the face and laughing. How could he have forgotten to load it? Had his only son been fiddling with his arsenal? Yesterday it was loaded. He did it himself when he had planned this madness. At least he thought he did. He had worked up the courage to take that next horrifying step, and yet now it all fell apart.

Then a better plan came to mind, a way to bow out of this turmoil, this debacle, on his own terms. Donald bent down and unlocked the filing cabinet door on his mahogany desk and reached inside. There sat a box of bullets that looked like mini-missiles. He tried to control his emotions, to rethink his method of suicide, and to get the task done correctly this time; no more screw ups. He grabbed a handful of shiny-points from the box and loaded the chamber on the left side of the barrel. Then, to ensure death, he filled the chamber next to that one with a bullet and pushed the barrel into place. The tears on his face had dried. He fell into a deep well of concentration. No obstacle would come between him and that bullet entering his head at the perfect angle, guaranteeing him the fate he was yearning for.

Out of the blue he changed tactics. He pressed the metal pistol nose to his right temple, then walked over to the window. Donald wanted one final glance at the fake life he lived, one last panoramic view of the thriving block, the homes of happy families. In some sick, sadistic way he was humoring himself. Suddenly he felt so alone and pathetic, submerged in his own mix of dementia and sadness. Several neighbors were out strolling on this glorious day. Not one of them had an inkling of what was about to transpire, or about the pending roar of the firearm and the horrible sound of tragedy that was about to rock the neighborhood.

At the window he stood implacable. The sun streaked across his sweaty forehead and tiny rivers of perspiration crawled down into his eyebrows. Donald was never more ready. He positioned the Smith and Wesson perfectly. He looped his finger through the ring of the trigger and poised himself. Straight ahead in the window of the house across from him sat a blooming houseplant. It captivated him, stole his attention, however briefly, stalling him. Stems were shooting out from the flowerpot in various directions, forming a cluster of cheerful colors. That's the last thing Donald wanted to see before he ended his life. It was something he had always counted on, an uplifting image he greeted every morning when the sun came up. This was the finale, though. He now could leave the world witnessing one last speck of beauty.

He pulled the trigger. Again, no explosion. The shiny-points remained undetonated. His eyes stretched open in a state of disheartened wonder. Now the anticipation of death was frightening him more than if the gun had just gone off and splashed his brains all over the walls. Behind him in the hallway above the stairs he heard a noise.

He whirled, and his son was standing there.

A.J. ran to his father, his lanky frame appearing weak, his face pale. He pulled the gun away from his father's head in disgust. Donald did not resist the interference.

"What? What are you doing here? Damn you!" Donald's voice was strained, hoarse.

"Do you know why you're still alive, Dad? Do you?" A.J. asked.

A.J. pointed at the Smith and Wesson, the weapon wobbling in his father's jittery hand. "You always load your gun to the left. Remember, Dad? Don't ya? You showed me that last year, and last month, and last week."

Now A.J's tone changed. He became frantic. . . "That's a Smith and Wesson in your hand. It's just that you're so whacked out of your mind that you failed to catch that little detail, didn't you? That barrel fires to the left, genius! Your favorite's the Colt…that one fires to the right."

Donald turned white as a ghost and dropped his gun, collapsed to his knees. A.J. crouched down and observed the cowardice staining his father's complexion. "You know, Dad, the Colt is your 'go-to' pistol as you always said. It would have killed you if I hadn't switched it last night. I thought about doing something stupid, too, hurting myself, but I wanted to do it with your favorite firearm, the one you always bragged about having, the one that does some 'serious damage,' as you once put it. But I changed my mind and stole Mom's car to come see you, to talk."

He placed the Colt on the carpeted floor and opened the barrel to show his dad the empty chambers. "I took it, replaced it with the Smith…was afraid an empty drawer would tip you off that I had it. I wrapped it in a magazine so nobody would see it."

Donald stared into empty space, baffled, scared.

A.J. shook his head. "I guess Mom's right. You are insane after all…and we both need help."

Father and son embraced. When they broke their embrace, Donald held A.J. by his shoulders and looked into his eyes. "You saved my life, son."

"No I didn't," responded A.J.

Donald glared at his son, jaw sagging in disbelief. "How can you say that? You came to me when it counted. Thank God you were there."

A.J. shook his head slowly. "I don't think you would've done it."

"What?" Donald mumbled. "How…?"

A.J. hugged his father again. "You were about to, Dad…but you *didn't* pull the trigger. Because you really want to live, even though sometimes you hurt a lot."

FRICTION

Two a.m. The traffic light at the intersection of Marsden and Dakota was blinking red. In a daze, Kevin Ryerson squeezed the steering wheel. The gentle breeze of the air conditioner cooled his face, his skin gluey from sweat. His wife, Laura, was staring out the passenger side window, her arms folded tightly in front of her. "Ya gonna go or what?"

Kevin grimaced, sensing the palpable uneasiness between them. "The light's red, can't you see that?"

Laura replied contemptuously. "It's *flashing* red—you can go." Then she turned toward him. "Need a refresher course?"

Her comment bothered him but he fought the urge to joust with her. He couldn't believe that beneath her impeccable countenance there was so much built-up anger—nor did he have any idea where it had come from or why she had been flippant all night. Kevin drove through the intersection and stayed on Dakota for about a half mile, reluctant to make eye contact with his wife. Dakota was a typical city street: cars parallel parked, a variety of shops and restaurants, and a long series of traffic lights. Unlike many bustling cities at this time of night, Bantam Township was quiet and peaceful.

Kevin watched bulging clouds pass over the moon, shifting from east to west, and tried to get lost in their fluid motion, distracting himself from the discord inside the car. Despite his calm disposition, his temper was festering. About a hundred feet ahead on his right, Kevin saw a young girl dressed in a short skirt and high heels flagging a cab. She was likely going home after a night of bar hopping. A couple of trendy clubs were within walking distance. Couples occasionally took long walks after hours; they nuzzled under the glow of streetlamps or snuggled on park benches. Kevin glanced at the girl, his stare lingered.

"You wanna fuck her too?" Laura asked. "Or did Deanna do it for you?"

Kevin stopped the car in the middle of the road. Fortunately there was no oncoming traffic and no one behind him. "Look, I told you I was sorry about the rumors circulating—but I *didn't* touch her."

"Oh, no?" Laura said, incredulous, her eyes agape. "Then why did she have her foot in your crotch at the table?"

Kevin's face reddened. He was clearly embarrassed, dumbfounded. "It's…it's not what it seems. Let me expla—"

"It most certainly is what it seems. I can't believe I didn't pick up on your little game sooner, you son of a bitch. I saw the way that trollop looked at you. That's not the first time I've spotted her little seductive gestures. But you just couldn't keep that little pecker of yours in your pants, could you?"

Kevin inhaled dramatically. "I'm gonna say it once and only once: *I. Did. Not. Fuck. Deanna.* During dinner I gave her a dirty look that you apparently didn't see. I didn't want to make a scene in front of all those people either, especially since one of them—the guy sitting to *your* left—is my boss."

Laura's eyes watered, mascara smeared her cheeks. "You expect me to believe that? You can lie all you want for business, but you sure as shit can't—"

"I don't care if you believe me or not," Kevin shouted. "That's all there is to tell." He put the car in gear and let it roll a few feet. "And I'm sick and tired of your accusations. Enough is enough." As he looked down the street he noticed an open convenience store, a red and green neon sign glowing in the window. He abruptly pulled off the road and parked in front. He got out of the car and slammed the door.

Laura rolled down the window. "What the hell are you doing now," she asked. "I'm tired and I want to go home."

"I'm getting cigarettes."

"But you don't smoke," Laura said. "And you know I don't like that crap!"

"Deal with it," he said authoritatively.

Inside the store Kevin went directly to the back counter and poured himself a cup of coffee. He didn't care for coffee, but he was too distressed to dismiss the sudden impulse to drink some. He even grabbed a pack of gum from the shelf on the way to the main counter: He didn't chew gum either but he wanted to rid himself of tension by any means. He took a sip of his coffee; it tasted like sludge. It was better, however, than getting back into the car and listening to his wife's bullshit. Laura hadn't been this irate in a long time, and now he felt himself losing his ability to remain passive. His heart was thumping his chest, his mind spinning.

He stood at the register, pointed at the rack behind the counter which held several shelves full of cigarettes. "Gimme a pack, please." The cashier, his greasy hair spilling from under his work cap, squinted. "What kind do you want, pal?"

"Surprise me, guy," Kevin said in a dispirited tone. He tried to remember what brand of cigarette his neighbor Mr. Estrada smoked, but the name escaped him now. Estrada had started smoking in his early thirties. He'd told Kevin numerous times that nicotine not only relieves anxiety and stress, but has also helped him maintain his weight (his body was chiseled). When he and Kevin had gotten together from time to time, Estrada always offered him a smoke, but he turned it down. Not this time, though.

The cashier looked down at Kevin's hands. They trembled on the counter. One hand was open, the other balled into a fist.

"Rough night, Mister?" the cashier asked with a feeble smile.

Kevin hesitated for a few seconds, rubbed his eyes. "Save the banter, man—not in the mood."

The cashier glanced out the front door and saw Kevin's wife in the car, wiping her face with a tissue, then looked back at Kevin who was rubbing his temples. The cashier's name tag read "Lester." "You should try Scotch. It works faster...and lasts longer." He handed Kevin cigarettes and change. "Take it easy, man."

In a brief awkward moment, Kevin held his jittery hand in front of his face and appraised his gold wedding band. Blue patches under his eyes marred his pallid face, his handsome features diminished by melancholy and exhaustion. He turned the ring, groped it as if he had no idea what it was. "What does this thing mean anyway?"

It was a rhetorical question but the cashier responded to it. "Don't know—not married." He removed his dingy cap, wiped his brow, and put it back on his head.

"I didn't have an affair with that girl," Kevin uttered, his voice a notch above a whisper.

The cashier put up his hands as if he was proclaiming his innocence, as if he was the one involved in the conflict. "Hey—not my biz, Mister."

"Just thinking out loud, buddy," Kevin said. He loosened his tie, nodded to the clerk, and left the store.

The rest of the ride home was painfully silent. For a split second he considered driving to Estrada's house and staying there for the night, keeping his wife at a tolerable distance. Estrada had always been a good talker but an even better listener. All those years in high-pressure sales had taught him how to tame even the most out of control situations. But now, with too many conflicted feelings whirling in his head, he dismissed the notion. Kevin felt anxiety-induced sweat dripping down his back, his polyester suit shirt hardly absorbing the moisture. He couldn't wait to get home, take a shower, and smoke a butt, perhaps try some Scotch as the cashier had suggested. He had some in the liquor cabinet at home; a few shots would take the edge off. Now wouldn't be a good time to visit his neighbor after all; he was bound to say something he'd regret, and he wouldn't want Estrada in the middle of this crap. Kevin just needed time on his own to decompress.

As the feuding couple pulled into their driveway they heard their beagle, Blazer, whimpering. Kevin got out of the car without thinking clearly and left his keys in the ignition. Laura had a set of her own and was the first inside, doing what she could to avoid further confrontation.

In the bedroom Kevin collected some clothes, grabbed a cigarette, and went to the bathroom to take a long cold shower. He desperately needed to cool off—it was a sultry night and Laura had pissed him off immensely. If nothing else helped remedy his problems, the next step would be getting a hotel room for a few days and giving each other space to sort things out—even obtaining a lawyer if they couldn't resolve the problem. He was certain that in her state of mind Laura was thinking the same thing. He was troubled by their endless bickering over the last few months. Laura's jealousy and unsubstantiated accusations only put their problems on a more disastrous level. Something would have to be done soon before matters worsened. But for now he just tried to calm himself.

The bathroom was spacious and luxuriant, brightened by spring colors with matching towels and tile. Laura's knack for decorating was exceptional. Kevin had always praised his wife's creative indulgences and spent sizable funds to highlight her creative flair. Even the ornate toilet paper holder was exquisitely designed and ornamented. And now it irritated him that he'd given them such an ideal life: money, a nice home on a wonderful expansive property, first-rate vacations, and fancy cars and clothes. Yet none of that mattered, did it? Because happiness cannot be bought, and he was learning that reality firsthand.

He slid down the dimmer switch, then put on the exhaust fan and lit a cigarette. The first drag had a celestial taste to it. And now he had even more reason to stick to the habit since Laura vehemently detested it. In some way, he believed, this sudden streak of rebellion would give him the upper hand—and teach her a lesson. As he stepped into the tub the caress of cascading water gave him instant relief. By holding his left hand outside the shower, he managed to keep the cigarette burning, and, between puffs, placed his cigarette on the edge of the marble sink. He clutched a bar of soap from the nearby ledge and began lathering himself.

Downstairs in the den Laura was leafing through pages of GQ and admiring the stellar-looking men. Movie stars, athletes, musicians, and other popular hunks graced every page, their blissful lifestyles seemingly devoid of adversity or tension. Lately, whenever she was angry or frustrated, she could find solace in trifling outlets such as magazines or television shows. And now here she was, at past three o' clock in the morning, attempting to recover from the latest of the many spats she and Kevin had had over the years—but this one was taking an emotional toll, eating away inside, and now she was on the verge of going to bed stressed and embroiled in turmoil, her marriage in jeopardy. She tilted her head back on the cushion and closed her eyes, trying to let her troubles drift away.

Kevin was still basking in the invigorating sensation of soothing cold water. He'd been in the shower for over thirty minutes. This was just what he needed. Once he was done he had decided that he was going to rent a hotel room for the night. Under the circumstances, that was the best course of action. Then he would ponder the idea of going to his office tomorrow morning and inquiring about an arbiter his boss knew, someone he could pay to sit down with him and Laura and do what needed to be done, for better or worse. That had to be the next step, he thought. It was something he could afford and Robinson, the arbiter, was one of the best around—he got results. If his and Laura's marriage could be salvaged, they would have to take extreme measures to find out if any love was left between them.

Just minutes earlier Laura had fallen asleep on the couch and was in deep repose, oblivious to what Kevin was feeling—and the change of weather outdoors. Crickets made a racket. A thunderstorm was developing. Heat lightning flashed sporadically across the sky, followed by outbreaks of thunder, though the din did not arouse Laura from her nap. In the backyard, spotlights glinted on the pool, a foam lounge chair wobbled like a buoy on the rippling surface. A shot of thunder followed another round of lightning, and rain started peppering the windows. Still Laura slept.

Next door, Mr. Estrada had just finished a late-night snack and was about to relax on the couch and read a book, then go to bed as soon as his eyes grew tired. His wife had already fallen asleep hours ago while watching television. He went to the front door to switch off the light above the front stoop and, with a quick glance through the side window panels, saw that the Ryersons' car's headlights were still on, the conical beams gleaming on their garage door. Their lights were on inside, too, and he assumed someone was awake. He decided to get his robe on and walk over to inform them of the car.

Kevin finished showering and put on his robe. He left the bathroom and glancing down into the living room, saw Laura asleep. After getting dressed he went to his office down the hall and swallowed two shots of Scotch, then loaded a duffel bag with a night's provisions.

Down in the living room Kevin shook his wife. "Wake up. I'm getting out of here."

Laura spoke a few incoherent words and slowly opened her eyes. Kevin stared impatiently at his wife as she came out of her slumber. "Come on, where are my keys?"

"In the car," she said. "Why? Where you goin'?"

"To a hotel. I don't wanna stay here tonight, not on these terms. I'll be in touch."

Laura was now fully awake, pulling hair away from her eyes and yawning. "You're just gonna leave me here alone, is that it?"

"What do you care? No matter where I go or what I do you've already decided I'm a slime. So let's just quit while we're ahead before this evening gets uglier."

They exchanged intense glances, like two people about to do battle. Laura rolled up a magazine and used it to point at him. "The situation's ugly because you made it that way. Don't push your guilt on me, Kevin."

"I'm tired of listening to your venom. You need help…and I'm outta here," he said, and started walking away.

"Good, get out of my house and stay out!" Laura growled.

Kevin pivoted toward her. "*Your* house?" he said, his voice rising in pitch.

"That's right," she said. "Go ahead and leave me!" Now she began yelling, and with her right foot, she kicked him in the shin. "I'll see to it that Robinson cleans you out financially. You think I don't know that you're going to call that shark? If you push it you'll be living in that hotel for the rest of your life—all because you forgot the meaning of fidelity."

Kevin leaned over and grabbed Laura by the shoulders and held her firmly in his grasp. Her body trembled in his grip, her eyes were wide open with shock. Kevin felt himself losing his once rock-solid composure. "You bitch! I told you I didn't touch her—and *never* hit me again, got it?"

"Why?" she snapped back. "Are you a wife beater too?"

The doorbell rang. Then rang again. Outside Mr. Estrada was waiting for someone to answer. Curious, he peered through their window and saw Kevin and Laura Ryerson arguing, Kevin towering over her with his hand raised in the air, as if about to strike her. Mr. Estrada

41

pounded on the door a few times, his attention still focused on the squabble. "Damn it, Kevin, calm down!" he bellowed from outside.

The Ryersons heard nothing. If they did they were ignoring it. Kevin pushed his wife against the wall. "Stop it, stop it, stop it!" he screamed. Laura shrank away from him, unsure what he'd do next.

"I swear on anything that I never cheated," he said, his voice so loud it frightened Laura. He turned and punched the wall behind him. A picture frame fell to the floor and shattered into pieces. "I swear on my mother's eyes," he said, louder this time, and then leaned back into the wall and sank to the floor in a heap. With trembling hands he covered his face and wept, uttering garbled words. "You're making me fucking crazy."

Laura stood appraising her husband. He had finally broken down, something he'd never done before, not this severely. She seemed uncertain of how to respond, what to say—if anything at all—or what she should be feeling for him at this time. When Kevin had raised his hand to her minutes ago she had seen an entirely different man standing above her, a man who had lost touch with his sanity—and she realized then and there that she was to blame, and, more importantly, that her husband, who was shivering and sobbing on the floor, was indeed a decent man, an honorable man, and that her jealousy—among other things—had created this long stretch of tension in their marriage. She crouched down and wrapped her arms around him. She stroked his back and felt his body jerking from the overwhelming surge of emotion churning inside him. Kevin stared for a long time at the wedding ring on his finger as tears fell upon his quavering hand. Then, surprisingly, he said, "I still love you, Laura." His voice sounded faint but loud enough for her to understand him. She didn't answer, although she remained beside him on the floor.

Kevin Ryerson grabbed his wife's hand and held it before him, at the same time struggling to compose himself. With his index finger he gently stroked her wedding band and looked into her eyes. "Does this still mean something to you? At all?"

Tears filled her eyes.

Estrada was still watching from the outside. He had a hand covering his mouth, his eyes were glazed with tears of his own, witnessing firsthand the pain that suspicion can cause. He had given up on his attempt to knock on the door—not because Kevin Ryerson didn't hit Laura, but because he knew he *wouldn't* hit her. He was also certain that Laura had finally told her husband the truth: that once she was convinced of her husband's affair, she had retaliated by initiating a one-night stand with him, her foolish and long regretful neighbor. Should his wife learn of his affair, could he convince her to stay with him? Could he deliver the ultimate sales pitch, the biggest of his life to keep his marriage on track? Could he face Kevin Ryerson, confess his despicable actions, and somehow remain his friend? All of this was highly unlikely. This much was clear: Kevin Ryerson still loved his wife, but would that be enough to overcome the new wounds that were about to be inflicted on him?

Estrada walked over to the car, opened the door, and turned off their headlights. Then he started on his way home. He wiped tears from his cheek and hoped the Ryersons' marriage would survive as long as his, or perhaps longer. One day he too would have to tell his wife the truth—or, quite possibly, the truth would find her.

YOUR TURN

(*Saturday, June 30^h 2022, 10:00 a.m.*—on the heels of a major change in the political climate. A new regime presides over the United States and a new order has infiltrated communities around the world. No more elections. Outlaws with strong and influential ties are running the country. Society as we know it has been dramatically altered. Citizens go about living in a heightened state of consciousness, yet a palpable calm has descended upon the country. It is strange and confusing at the same time.)

(Three weeks ago)

Michael Garvey had learned that Kenny McAndrews was a cunning snake. Both of them had been working at a water treatment plant. Michael had been maneuvering for a desk job as he approached forty. He wanted to admit that long nights at the factory had taken their physical and emotional toll. He arranged a meeting with management to discuss the possibility of shifting to a position at the front office.

At the time, Kenny McAndrews had been employed by the company less than half as long as Garvey, but was well liked and respected by his coworkers for his sense of humor and gregariousness, unlike Garvey who was more reserved and moody, a loner living in an old shoddy farm house out in the sticks, never reading the newspaper or watching television. Garvey had confided in Kenny about his plans and Kenny used the information against him in a carefully constructed lie.

Kenny went straight to the factory bosses and said that Garvey was conspiring to bring a health code lawsuit against them for conditions in the workplace, and that a shift to the front office was the angle Michael needed to do "undercover" work—and, more importantly, he believed Michael Garvey had been gathering evidence for years. Garvey was astonished that everyone bought into Kenny's story; insulted was a better word for it. But somehow Kenny was better at rubbing shoulders with the right people and knew how to use Garvey's weaknesses against him, convincing those in power that Garvey's demeanor was a front for his private scheme. Soon thereafter, Garvey confronted Kenny in the parking lot after the late shift and pleaded with him to come clean. Kenny refused. Garvey was fired. He lost his sole income and his pride at being a long-standing reputable worker, and was given no chance to disprove the accusations against him.

The following night, a distraught Michael Garvey withdrew from the bank what little savings he had. He was infuriated and fast losing control. After walking up and down Kenny McAndrews's street, he knocked on his door, intent on settling the score. Kenny didn't answer. Michael Garvey pounded on the door, screamed, "This isn't over, you fuck! Your time will come!" Kenny called the police but Garvey was long gone.

(Present day, Town of Hartsville, New Jersey, early summer)
(Case # 761022)

On this outstanding day of perfect weather, the parking lot at Bayberry Plaza was filling with cars. Shoppers shuffled in and out. Michael Garvey circled the lot at least twice, his short chestnut hair drenched, streams of perspiration dripping down his forehead and over his pale, pimply face, his hands trembling on the steering wheel, the motor of his old car sputtering as he repeatedly pressed the accelerator. His eyes were fixed on a pedestrian, a shopper with spiked hair. Garvey waited patiently for the perfect time. He had no inclination to park his car, preferring to stalk the shopper like a hawk, keeping him in his line of sight. Anger festering, Garvey punched the steering wheel a few times. He asked himself repeatedly: *Can I do it? Do I really care what happens to me? Do I have what it takes?*

Michael Garvey turned onto the back corner of the lot and had an unobstructed view of the shopper. Inside his muggy car he basked in the smell of his own sweat, potent within the confines of the four-door Corolla, the license plates dented and dirty, the front plate dangling from a rusty screw. Garvey watched the shopper swaggering across the lane toward his car. The man reached into his pocket and pulled out his keys. Unable to control his rage any longer, Michael Garvey brought his car to a screeching halt and, with a knife clutched in his right hand, jumped out and tackled the man before he got to his car. He stabbed him in the stomach, opening a shallow gash. The man screamed in pain. Garvey fired a punch to the man's nose, which broke with a crack. Then Garvey plunged his knife deep into the man's abdomen a few times in succession, ripping through his flesh like scissors through paper. The man howled again and again, writhed spasmodically. Shoppers froze, turned toward the assault and watched the fight. A few of the people even moved closer to the chaos. Garvey slit the man's neck and shoulder numerous times, crying shrilly, "I fuckin' hate you! I told you it wasn't over yet, motherfucker! How does it feel, Kenny?"

Kenny was in severe and hopeless pain, unable to hold off an enraged Garvey. He was losing a great deal of blood. He never had a chance from the moment he was attacked. Garvey had caught him completely off guard, throwing his two-hundred-fifty-pound frame on top of Kenny's lanky hundred and fifty pounds. Kenny remained at Garvey's mercy, pinned to the pavement under his knees, blood leaking from numerous stab wounds, the ground blotched crimson underneath their tangled bodies. A circle of witnesses watched the two men, none of them trying to stop the murderous scuffle unfolding before them.

A few in the circle shook their heads as Michael Garvey wiped a splash of blood from his eyes and rose to his feet, panting, lungs hot and overworked from the release of aggression. His pale complexion, purple lips and sweaty face glistened under the sunlight. The crowd around him was speechless. Some of them began leaving the scene nonchalantly, like spectators at a sporting event that had come to an abrupt end. No one in the vicinity showed alarm. Not one of them called for help.

Michael Garvey held the knife in his hand, staring at it while the sun reflected off the razor-sharp blade, blood dripping from the jagged edge to the heated blacktop. His thoughts floated to the past. He wanted to kill Kenny and had carried out his promise to himself. The son of a bitch deserved it. He had told everyone that he wouldn't be responsible for his actions should their paths cross—and they finally did—much to his content. A shot of panic rushed through him. He dropped the knife and ran to his car about twenty feet away, the motor idling. He got in, shifted into drive, and sped away, the squealing of rubber clawing the pavement and echoing throughout the parking lot.

Michael Garvey blazed down Interstate 70. He hadn't once glanced in his mirrors; traffic concerns did not weigh heavily on his mind. He had just wasted a man in cold blood out in the open without a second's thought of being caught or arrested. His anger had been brewing so long that he could no longer control his mind's primal urges to take action. After driving a few miles, he eased his foot from the accelerator, taking ten miles an hour from his speed. He glanced at his bloody hands and was instantly dumbstruck by his crime. When he returned his concentration to the road he lost control of the car, veering toward the shoulder. The Corolla was headed straight for a tree.

Garvey couldn't avoid a collision, so he braced himself behind the wheel. The car crashed grill first into the trunk of a sizable pine. Garvey was thrust into the windshield, tearing open the soft flesh above his eye. The impact caused ripples of buckling glass. The Corolla's hood was contorted into a tepee of steel. Smoke billowed from underneath like a dragon's breath. Stunned but conscious, Garvey opened his eyes and felt his head throbbing, the intensity increasing with each second. His vision was glazed. Stray bullets of burning pain ricocheted in his forehead. He could, however, hear the traffic behind him, horns honking, motors roaring. Within minutes a man pulled off the road and approached Garvey's car. He put his head through the broken window. Though Garvey's hearing was impaired, he heard the stranger speak. "Are you okay, man?"

Garvey nodded.

The man got a good view of Michael Garvey's forehead. "You've got one hell of a cut, buddy. I'll call an ambulance."

Garvey wiped a smearing of blood away from his eyes and shook his head.

Puzzled, the stranger squinted. "What're you trying to say, fella? You're banged up pretty bad. You'll need a few stitches."

Garvey kept shaking his head. He coughed hard a few times—the last cough brought up blood—then he turned and stared at the man at the window. "I'm going down for this."

Listening to his voice, the man realized that Garvey's awareness was slowly returning. The pitch of the words was a little higher and clearer than before. The man assured him everything was going to be all right. "I know what you did and you'll be fine. *Trust me*."

Garvey began crying. He held his blood-caked hands to his face and stared at them. "How can you say that? I killed a man." He dropped his face in his palms and wept.

The man heard Garvey say "It's...over...for me." About ten seconds of silence followed. Garvey shouted: "Over!"

"Take it easy," the man said. Garvey leaned back and closed his eyes, tears sliding down his cheeks. The man leaned forward, placed his hand on Garvey's shoulder. "Hey, man, help is on the way, so listen up. You're not going to jail so get that nonsense out of your head. Don't you remember the revolution, man?"

Garvey's eyes opened slightly but he didn't respond. The stranger held up his index finger. "Once a month, that's right, once a month you can kill someone without penalty. A group of crazy anarchists stormed the fuckin' Whitehouse and took charge 'bout a few months ago. Where the hell *you* been? It's like total frigging anarchy in this country. No shit, I tell ya. Don't piss anybody off or you'll be looking over your shoulder every minute. Keep your nose clean."

Garvey hung on every word the man was saying, though he had difficulty accepting what he heard. For a moment Michael Garvey imagined life in a cement cell, bars blocking him from the free world. He wondered about the things he'd miss out on if he was forced to spend a lifetime in a penitentiary or was sentenced to death. A chorus of sirens closed in on Michael Garvey's car. Paramedics rushed to him with a gurney. One of the personnel, a tall man with a pony tail and glasses, spoke. "This is the third accident today in a matter of hours. Damn, this is crazy!"

The emergency team worked diligently to extract Michael from the car and then laid him on the flatbed. They covered him with a blanket and strapped him down, then applied an oxygen mask to his face, forcing a few bursts into his lungs. The stranger watched Garvey being loaded in the ambulance. "Take care of him," he said and started walking to his car. They locked the gurney in position and raced from the scene.

Inside, Garvey was breathing normally again. They pulled the mask from his face. He homed in on the hypnotic sound of sirens and the groaning engine. His eyes were wide open now. The medic on his left, a pretty brunette, wrapped a blood pressure monitor around his arm and pumped for a reading. She looked down at him, her eyes pools of intensity and professionalism. "How are you feeling, Mr...?"

He coughed gently. "Garvey, Michael Garvey." Then a subtle smile formed. "I'm feeling better already."

(In the emergency room, a television newscast explained that all crimes (murder, robbery, rape, assault, etc.) must be justified by those who commit them. If explanation is approved, a citizen's actions will be excused without punishment. However, if a crime goes unjustified, participants automatically

become slaves to the outlaws and can never return to civilization again. Furthermore, since the inception of the new governing body, the entire world has undergone drastic yet promising transformations. Despite a variety of brutal killings on a monthly basis and a series of misdemeanors, the masses have become a more tolerable, polite, and more caring species. Gangs are virtually non-existent, as the stronger outlaws have taken over and wiped them out, and the police are cooperating with the regime and helping with a new "rebuilding process" developed by the world order. Other major changes are in store. People are both frightened and intrigued. Other countries are now asking to be involved.

Michael Garvey received proper medical attention and was released. He spoke before a jury, discussing honestly, and in detail, why he attacked Kenny McAndrews. The leader of the outlaws accepted his excuse. Michael Garvey has returned to his normal life and rarely attempts contact with the outside world. He works at a local grocery store. To many, he is considered a model citizen. His story has been permanently logged into the government's database for future reference as Case # 761022.)

OPEN WOUND

All through high school I had many friends. I knew the jocks, the geeks, the popular people, the rich folk; I knew them all. One Friday I met a boy I've always called Ricky Sundance. That's not his name, but I refer to him that way because when I think of him and I look up I believe the sun dances across the sky. He is a special person.

When we met he was a shy guy. When I said my first words to him his face blushed redder than a fire hydrant he was so nervous. I had dated a few cute boys during my high school years, more than most. It used to be flattering when the best looking guys in class would flirt with me, but I'd watch Ricky staring at me without the slightest glimmer of jealously on his face.

But as time went on I spent more and more time with Ricky Sundance. He was a gentleman. Not only that, but he actually had no trouble making me laugh, which was a blessing compared to most of the "macho men" I had spent time with. Anyway, following the holidays, a big gang of us had gone to the beach to party like crazy. My best friend at the time, Connie, had managed to convince her parents to let us use their shore house for the weekend as long as we didn't break anything. There must have been ten, fifteen kids at the party. The place was pretty wild. Most of my friends were typical teens, always looking for a better time, a rowdier party.

Ricky asked me to take a walk with him. I accepted. His approach was harmless. I didn't take his invitation as an opportunity to flirt with me, not at all. We stood outside in the street that night and drank our beers, talked with the jocks about sports things. A couple of them took some jabs at Ricky, mocking his physique, his lack of sports knowledge. If it bothered him he didn't show it at all.

One factor always planted itself in my brain. Despite Ricky's frail appearance, his wiry frame, and his nervousness in a crowd, he was the perfect gentleman and walked around with his head up. We had maintained our friendship for many years. And no one cares to believe me when I say this, but Ricky and I never shared any intimacy. Not so much as a kiss linked us together. He never tried a thing, and to be honest I never felt that way about him. He was simply a great guy. However, after that conversation in the street we went for a walk on the beach. It was dark. Ricky clutched my hand, guided me through the night. He had his chance to make a move on me, certainly. In fact, for much of our walk, when he held my hand, it was done in a peculiar way, a non-threatening way, a way that didn't suggest a thing. He was merely guiding me along, tenderly. We strolled through the sands that night. We prowled about the dunes, ran barefoot through the water's edge right where the rush of frothy currents splashed the shoreline. The waves rolling toward shore created a hypnotizing sound that gave freedom and wonder to the night. The temperature was balmy for the winter, pushing the fifties. The air was crisp and clean.

After a solid half hour of walking and treading through the thick sand bed beneath us, we turned back. We had covered so much ground that it was nearly impossible to see the lights from the house in the distance. We just kept walking, continued chatting like kids do. There was no tension. No suggestive behavior. No preconceived notion about how our friendly little walk should end. We were just boy and girl sharing good company. All of my girlfriends always asked, "What do you see in him?" I felt obligated to keep telling them he was a genuine friend—that they were making too much out of things. They were always looking for the gossip or the scandal in every situation, I guess. Their lives were full of it.

Fifteen minutes later we encountered a bench behind one of the sand dunes and sat for a few minutes. Then we talked, delved into many topics: family, friends, dreams, high school memories, goofy teachers. Our conversation ran the gamut for a good ten minutes until we decided to carry on with our late-night journey.

As I've said, we walked pretty far and at this time of night it was generally quiet. A few lights were lit in a couple of the homes, but that was all. The shore was quiet. Most of the crowds had gone north for the winter. We just kept on walking until a cold breeze drifted in from the shoreline and chilled me a bit. Even with a sweater and jacket my body was cold. Ricky had on less than me. He was always the warm one anyway. He kindly offered me his jacket and I accepted. That's what I mean about him. He was kind and gentle—not just making a sweet gesture with the hopes of getting me into bed. Guys like that are hard to find.

We strolled on another fifty feet or so when suddenly we were startled by a sound. It was the ruffling of the nearby currents. The noise stopped us in our tracks. We blindly traced the sound and for reasons unknown, inched in that direction—curiosity, perhaps. By this time our eyes had adjusted to the dark and we stared in front of us. What we thought we saw was a man. He was wading through the shallow water, making his way toward Ricky and me. I don't think he had seen us just yet, so we broke into a jog to avoid being seen. I was in front of Ricky. He guided me forward with his hand.

We walked away from the scene. I recall Ricky stepping on a sea shell. It scraped the arch of his foot, forcing him to groan in pain. But he covered his mouth and motioned to me to keep silent. He came close to me, nuzzled. He whispered in my ear. The words tickled my skin. He spoke with caution in his voice. "Coming out of the water this late at night? We've got to be careful. Let's get out of here." The man left the water and moved toward us. There was no urgency to his stride. He just pushed himself along in the sand. We kept moving away, looking for a place to hide, hoping not to be detected.

We didn't trust the moment, the hour of the night, or a man who could emerge from the waters the way he did. He didn't look at all like a surfer. He had no business being there—that's what Ricky said. I just followed his instincts, his lead. He suspected something. Something was out of place and he was reacting. Certain flashes in life can, and sometimes do, change your life forever. This was one of them.

Ricky and I found refuge behind one of those stilts that raise the bayside homes from high tides when the ocean's anger is stirred up. We angled ourselves behind the pillar, concealing our figures until the stranger passed. We stood out of his range, in a place where we could keep an eye on him. If we moved from there he was going to hear us. We stood still, quiet. The man approached the home where we were hiding and went for the front door on the other side of the foundation. That was his home. Damn it, I thought. I felt nervous. My heart was speeding up. Ricky was calm and controlled. If he was alarmed he didn't show it in the least. I stared at him from the side, realizing for a second how lucky I was. Sure, I had half the jocks back at the party waiting for me, to treat me good enough to get me in the sack. They were all smooth talkers, easy on the eyes, and every girl wanted them. Hell, I wanted a shot at every one of them too or had at some point when they first became friends of mine.

But here I was in the middle of some mysterious situation with a guy who soaking wet couldn't weigh more than a hundred-thirty pounds—and yet I felt safe. The man entered the house. Ricky whispered in my ear again, rolling off instructions. He informed me about a fast escape route. "Look, we have to make it over to that garage then hang a left. We'll stay straight for a block or two. When we reach the general store we're just about home free. Then we hustle home from there. Are you ready?" he asked.

I nodded. We ran from under the house and jogged toward the garage. We did finally make it back to the party in one piece that night. But much to our surprise our friends had left. They went to another party with Connie. They had left a note telling us about their change of plans. I couldn't believe they had abandoned us like that.

Ricky and I went inside. He made a fire. We sat in front of the fireplace, toasted marshmallows and sipped instant coffee. That's all we had in the cupboards, so we made the best of it. He sat across from me, keeping polite distance, careful not to come across as presumptuous. Part of me felt something in that moment, some chemistry at work. I remember trying to fight the unusual feeling. After settling down we talked for a while longer about life, joked about that weirdo we saw in the ocean. I asked Ricky, "Why did you react like that, what'd you see?" Ricky was watching the fire. But he turned toward me, looked me in the eye. The flames cast a trail of light across his face; shadows stroked the walls of the living room. "I don't know. Sometimes being a guy gives me the ability to sense stuff. I didn't trust the situation, that's all. I'm glad you listened. That's all in the past." I reached over and gave Ricky a big hug, thanked him for being so kind. He humbly smiled and said, "Thanks." That was it.

We chatted for an hour or so and then went to bed. Ricky crashed on the couch. I fell asleep on a recliner across from him. I remember when the fire died and how the room got cold. Then I remember opening my eyes later on for a second. Ricky had found a blanket of some kind, draped it over me. I nodded off again. It was around three o'clock in the morning when I opened my eyes and heard a noise. Ricky was still snoozing in the chair. Behind him was a row of windows. You could look out and get a great view of the beach on a clear day. But now something was different. It was pitch black except for the motion lights. They went off and on at intervals, depending on the wind or an animal scurrying past. Something was moving outside. A blurred shape of a human form moved across the exterior. I sensed trouble. Suddenly the knob on the front door started shaking, then stopped…started again…stopped again. I barely got out of my chair to wake up Ricky when I saw the figure move past the windows again. Boy, did I almost crap my pants. I ran to Ricky and woke him. I pulled him right out of a deep sleep. The first thing out of his mouth was, "Are you all right?" He was unlike most men, that's for sure.

I told him exactly what I saw and he sprung into action. We knew all the doors were locked so we ran upstairs and hid in one of the bedrooms. Of course we found out the hard way that the telephone lines were disconnected for the season. We heard a pounding, felt a sudden vibration. Ricky peered out the window from a safe angle, recognized the man we saw earlier on the beach. He was swinging a sledge hammer against one of the supports that braced the house. We were both shook. I know I was frightened. The man pounded the foundation at least a dozen times. Then he started whacking another section a few times.

Minutes later, all hell broke loose. The man spoke, sending chills up my spine. His voice was a disturbing blend of smoker's voice and drunkenness. "You spy on me, I come after you!"

He spoke again. His voice climbed a notch. "Sooner or later you're gonna have to face me! I'll come back here with my truck and yank these goddamn posts right out from under your young juicy ass. Try me, you stupid teenage prick!"

Ricky grabbed me firmly by the shoulders. "If he wants to get in, he'll get in. Get a weapon."

I ran downstairs to the kitchen, grabbed a knife from the cutlery holder, a nice serrated steak knife. The man had stopped his hammering and was staring up at the window. Ricky stood looking down at him, then spoke to me without moving his lips, like a ventriloquist. "I don't think he knows you're here." I can't describe the expression he had on his face when he told me that. Part of me wanted to feel comforted by what he'd said, but I didn't. I wanted us both to get out of this alive. So I asked him if we should both go hide.

Once again we heard the man attacking the post with the sledgehammer. Ricky laid out the horrifying details for me. "With that sledge he can get in here whenever he wants. He's playing a game with me, and I'm certain he hasn't seen you. You know what you have to do, right?"

I was beside myself. "Ricky, what are you trying to say, I am not—"

"Yes. You are. Find some help. We are only a quarter-mile from the main strip. There has to be someone that can help. You have to go on foot, though. Those friends of ours took the only car we had."

"But please, Ricky. Don't make me—"

"It'll be fine. I can distract him long enough for you to get out. Go out the back, closer to the beach side. He'll never see you. Run along the beach and up to the center. Head right for the police station eight blocks down."

I remember slipping out that night. Indeed Ricky was right; with the man slamming the hammer into the post and Ricky staying at the window where he could be seen, I had the chance to get away. He had called it right once more. His gut reaction paid off. I ran a considerable distance from the house then my emotions got the best of me. I started to cry thinking about leaving him behind. Suddenly, I heard glass shattering. I knew what it meant. That man got into the house. I looked around as if somehow there were answers on a cue card waiting for me—to guide me—but there was nothing. The answer all along was staring me in the face. I should have never left the house.

We were in this together. At that moment, as I began walking back toward the house, I saw the lights go on inside the living room. Through the ocean-front windows I spotted Ricky running away from the charging man. I was closer, only thirty feet from the door, when I watched the most horrible thing in the world transpire. The man pulled a knife out. It was big, sharp. He grabbed Ricky by the hair, snapped his head back, and sliced him from ear to ear. I watched Ricky's body crash to the floor. I shrieked in desperation. Then I ran for my life. I followed the instructions Ricky had given me and only stopped to catch my breath a couple of times. When

I turned the corner on the main strip I saw a police station.

My face was wet with tears. I wanted to just get out of that town and away from the shore, never to return again. Maybe the on-duty cop would shoot the bastard and take me home. That's what I really wanted. I entered the station, screamed as loud as I could. My throat was aching, my lungs were burning. It felt like I had swallowed a pack of lit matches. As I approached the front desk I saw that the officer on duty had sprung from his chair and was running to me.

"I need help," I told him. "Someone murdered my friend and he's after me; it's 212 Scenic Lane right by the beach!" The officer took me into his arms like a safety net. I would live to see another day.

So—that's my story. I sit here in my bedroom with a recorder in my hand. There is plenty of tape left to roll but that is all you need to know. It was such a grisly experience—something most never would want to live through. But it happened to me and that's the deal. I was committed to a special center for a couple of months afterwards when I'd sunk into a bad place that I couldn't get out of. I soon realized there were no drugs that could cleanse my soul of the anguish I had lived with since that fateful day, when a young man never gave a second's thought to letting me escape from a dangerous situation, while he stood strong.

This wasn't like the movies to me, where the tough man on screen comes and saves the day for the woman in peril. This was always about a regular guy that had the guts to put me first even when he didn't have any idea of how things would turn out—fatally in this case. My life wasn't the same for a long time. I wasn't able to get close to other men in the days that followed. Maybe it was because they paled in comparison to the inner strength and poise that Ricky had but which nobody but me experienced. I was doing my best to cope. I really was.

But all I had thought about every day since his death was how big his heart was, and how the world wasn't big enough to hold it. The way I had acted since the funeral one would think we were in love or had been married a long time. It tore me apart inside. I can't lie. I just wasn't the same girl. I couldn't help it. Drugs did little to remedy the pain—and besides, that's no way to live.

So I was placed in a mental health center until my condition cleared up; fortunately it was only a couple of months. At the time my parents couldn't handle me so they shoved me off on this temporary summer program. All they ever asked me there was why I couldn't get over the trauma and find a way to come to grips with a weekend that shook the foundation of my life. When I told them they could not understand because they didn't know Ricky Sundance, they just rolled their eyes and came at me with another needle, or another empty piece of advice, or another dribble of fancy talk. Or called in another shrink whose palms were greased thanks to what they call "unique cases" like mine. My emotional wounds were not healing as fast as they'd hoped for. My body aches when I think about those sixty days. Sometimes I feel as though I'm reliving that terrible night at the shore over and over again. I remember that the doctors used to

Abandoned in the Dark

ask me to repeat the story while they took pages and pages of notes and I went on feeling like complete shit. Then they all went out to ritzy lunches and discussed how they wished there was something more they could do.

Overeducated doctors and fancy medicine did nothing at all to help. What it did do, however, was force me to step outside of the ugliness I'd lived through—all of that love and loss—and find renewed breath. You wanna know the truth? Sometimes I wish I had died with Ricky. I miss him tremendously. I loved him in a way I can't really explain to anyone. He was a special kind of person who didn't for one second grasp his own courage, and I will forever carry his memory until I fall off the face of this earth. I had to say that.

After my discharge I went out with a few nice boys, all of them were fun to pass the time with, but not delightful to share the days with. Strange contrast, huh? I did go out on a date with a guy named Max Freedman. After a couple of dates he'd tried to feel me up and I almost gouged his eyes out—literally. I remember shouting at him from the top of my lungs in the middle of Bristle Street behind the lake. "Don't you ever come near me again! Do you hear me?" That little bastard got out of the car and draped his arm on the hood, said the wrong thing. "I bet Ricky got a good feel, huh? Bet ya he felt you up real good."

Well, I lost my head, ran up to him and slapped him across the face. Following that night I began writing diligently in my journal and socializing more. I had to make a change in my life—counteract the emotional toxins. In fact, I even went out with a couple of decent guys, one of whom was Darryl Lufkin. He was so charming and sweet and he also knew Ricky somewhat from running in similar circles. We dated for a long time. He respected my feelings and where my head was (or wasn't) sometimes.

I'll never forget what he did when our first month together came around. It was the dead of winter and pretty freezing outside—bitter actually. Darryl sensed my mood was sort of in the dumps—not as bad as before, but still tough and he knew why. He was well aware of my unpredictable streaks. He went to my closet and pulled out my winter coat. I looked at him like he had ten heads. "Put this on," he said with an intense look on his face. I was not feeling inclined to leave the house and I knew where this was going. It had to be a practical joke of some kind—he was no stranger to those. Normally I liked his sense of humor, but not that day.

"Darryl please…What're you up to? I just want to relax and stay inside."

"Trust me," he said. "Just this one time."

I reluctantly went along with his request, bundled up and took his hand. We ended up getting in his car and he asked me to keep my eyes closed. I agreed—but I was losing my patience. Well, the car finally stopped and before I knew what had happened I felt the cold air overwhelming me, whipping the exposed areas of my skin with some pretty fierce lashings. The frigid wind nibbled painfully on my ears. I felt so uncomfortable and stiff. *I just want to go home!*

Finally, Darryl asked me to open my eyes. When I did I swear my heart skipped a beat and then came to a screaming halt in my chest. A blend of blustery cold conditions and sheer surprise worked me over. Right before my eyes stood the tombstone of Ricky Sundance. I felt a tear sliding from the corner of my eye and I wasn't sure how I felt about this moment but my thoughts drifted away. I lost myself in the flash of time. I brought my gloved hand to my mouth and choked on my rising emotions. Darryl put his arm around me and spoke. "It has been a month for us. I wanted to give you something that would make you happy. I wanted to pay my respects to someone who meant so much to you. We can come here as often as you'd like. I'd be honored, actually. I understand what he meant to you. He left behind a legacy."

I hugged him and cried. He stroked my hair as I spilled tears. They stuck to my skin due to the icy air mass that surrounded us. It was like a winter jungle out there but miraculously the discomfort faded away during the fleeting seconds that Darryl and I embraced.

"Let's celebrate his life, not mourn his death. He would've wanted that," he said.

Well, my story has come to an end. I must go now. Darryl's picking me up soon. Tonight will be special. It's our one-year anniversary. Goodbye.

THE LESSON

(Friday - 4:30 p.m.)

Content, Drake Masters sat smiling at his desk. This was going to be a stupendous day. A surprising promotion had lined his pockets with hundreds more a week. He was anxious to cash his check and live it up. He would spend his surplus income on his two favorite things in the world—the two vices that destroyed his marriage— liquor and women. Drake couldn't wait until quitting time.

(Friday - 4:40 p.m.)

Over an hour before the work day was over, Drake's boss came to his cubicle and leaned against the wall, took off his glasses and observed Drake, who was typing. Copy machines and other office equipment groaned in the background. A group of employees were huddled at the water cooler nearby chatting about the day's events, eavesdropping on conversations, especially the one taking place between Drake and the manager.

"Why don't you head out early today, my main man?" Drake's boss said. "Enjoy one of the perks of climbing the corporate ladder."

A few of the workers heard the boss dismissing Drake for the day. None of them were pleased.

"Oh?" Drake said. He glanced at his wristwatch. "All...all right. Sounds like a good plan to me."

He put on his jacket, grabbed his briefcase from the shelf behind his chair and left in a hurry, forgetting to shut down his computer. His jealous coworkers, watching him leave the building, glowered behind his back. The manager had always been a stringent pain in the ass, pushing the staff until at least six or seven. But not today—not with Drake.

(Friday - 10:00 p.m.)

Drake had been sitting in the booth for hours. Alexia, accustomed to Drake's generous tipping, grinded on his lap. The club was dark, despite lights flashing on the ceiling, the walls, the floor. The stench of cigarettes and booze overpowered the room. Drake was enjoying a nice buzz; the Tequila shots were abnormally strong. He hadn't felt this fuzzy and relaxed from just a few shots before. What the heck did the bartender put in his drinks? It didn't matter anyway. The sensation he was experiencing was ecstasy, a feeling that had eluded him for a long time. This dancer was a raving beauty, beyond what he had seen in magazines or in movies. Long blonde hair cascaded down her back and grazed her tight buttocks. Her lips were soft and perky. As she slithered them down Drake's neck he got hot and horny.

(Friday - 10:30 p.m.)

The party continued in the parking lot under a broken street light. A massive oak tree prevented moonbeams from shining in Drake's car. Snow flurries dusted the night. Three beautiful women were now taking special care of him, treating him like the reliable customer he was. Each of the girls took turns groping Drake's muscular body, making him feel as if he were the only man in the world, a real stud, a local celebrity of sorts. He was more turned on now than ever before in his life. His ex-wife, Sally, could never perform as these girls did. She didn't know the tricks of the trade, the magic touches. He had completely forgotten how many drinks he had or what they were spiked with to make them so strong. All he cared about now was relishing the rewards of fortune and pleasure and success—and the weekend was still young. One of the girls shoved her finger into his mouth and massaged his tongue. Drake did the same to her. This was a night he'd never forget. Because their meetings had never gone this far or been so sensuous. There he was, Drake Masters, nude in the passenger seat of his Hummer with three women who were taking him to sexual heights he thought only existed in wild fantasies. Without warning he passed out.

(Saturday - 12:30 a.m.)

Drake opened his eyes. The world surrounding him was staggeringly black and frightening. A frosty wind and plummeting temperatures had him shuddering. His penis was throbbing too, burning in fact. To make matters worse, he had been stripped of his clothes. He also was lost. He must have been pushed out of his car and dumped on a random street; he felt crumbs of pavement poking his flesh like needles.

Although his body rebelled against his every move, he managed to get to his feet. He attempted to walk but seething pain brought him to his knees. A stabbing sensation surged in his rectum. He placed his hand near the injured area to figure out what the problem was. He slid his fingers closer to his cheeks, feeling slime of some kind. At that moment he became light-headed. Discovering that the substance was blood, he panicked. No more than a minute later he blacked out again.

(Saturday - 8:00 a.m.)

When Drake awakened for the second time, he still had no idea what had happened to him or where he was. The hazy glow of a lamp on a wooden shelf across from him gave him the chance to see the room he was in. He was alone. A musty odor assailed him. His equilibrium was out of balance. The room appeared to be floating. He felt as if he were under water. By way of a cracked mirror at floor level he was able to get a look at himself. He was distraught by what he saw. His entire body was bruised and covered with welts. Leeches had spread over his skin. All of them were feeding on him, bloating. Drake lacked the strength and desire to get up and escape. He shivered uncontrollably. His stomach was sour. Trying to move around only caused him searing threads of pain. Drake was clueless. He dry heaved and coughed. The uneven floor was damp, cold, and clammy. The room spun more intensely and he closed his eyes and lost consciousness again.

(Sunday - 6:00 a.m.)

Drake's eyes opened to witness another day. Delirious with a headache, he was unprepared to face the next reality. He blinked cobwebs from his eyes and everything within the four walls started to take shape. This time he was strapped to a chair, his hands tied to the arms with nylon rope, his ankles bound to the legs. A sock, sodden with grime, was stuffed in his mouth, the smell hindering his ability to draw breath. This room was just like the others: unfit for life. On a metal desk in front of him he saw cigarettes, pills, and a couple of pairs of brass knuckles.

Where am I? Am I dreaming? Behind him…a sound…a door opening. Rusty hinges groaned, announcing the entry of someone—something. Drake craned his head to see who had imprisoned him. Turning left, he saw nothing. He pivoted right and before his eyes could focus on the presence standing before him, he was punched in the jaw. Spots shimmered behind his eye lids. Again he was plunged into abysmal darkness.

(Sunday - 10:00 a.m.)

A sunny day greeted Drake. Miraculously, he was in his own bed, where the yellow sheets accented his horrid pallor. The sheets were crumpled up under his chin. He could see everything around him. He was home at last—but how did he get there?

He ripped the covers off and examined the wounds that had been inflicted upon him. All of it—every pain and fear he felt—was real. He hated to imagine what had been inserted into his anus. What kind of toxin had made him so sick and dizzy and lethargic? What kind of assault had left him bleeding? Blood stains were all over his mattress. Drake was ashamed and humiliated. This was something he would not speak of ever again. He took a shower and scrubbed every inch of his body, practically breaking the skin. He had no choice. Drake considered going to the doctor for a thorough exam, but how could he possibly explain all of this? And again, the shame of being violated made him not want to go anywhere, let alone to a doctor's.

After his shower he looked out the window. His Hummer was parked along the curb in the same condition as he left it. *How is that possible?* He hoped all this was nothing more than a repulsive nightmare. But the reality of his circumstances could not be denied. He had survived a traumatic experience. Drake sat in bed against the backboard, his arms hugging his knees. All he could do was stare at the walls and think about why this had happened and, more importantly, who could have done it. He fell asleep again, sitting upright.

(Monday- 8:45 a.m.)

    Drake eased into Monday cautiously. He parked his car and went inside to his office. On a shelf above his desk he had a bottle of aspirin. He took three and swallowed them dry. He placed his hand on the computer's mouse and the desktop appeared. The message: "Hey, Masters, look in your top drawer."

    Drake cleared his throat, scratched his temple. *Was this somebody's idea of a game?* Could the message be a note from his boss? Besides, what could possibly happen to him here at the office, right? Slowly, hesitantly, he opened the top drawer, where he found a picture but nothing else. He held it up in front of him and analyzed it, recognizing the man in the photo: Norman Thayer. Drake had replaced him six months ago. Even though he'd been warned about his outbursts, Norman had threatened a coworker and was fired shortly thereafter. When asked to explain his actions, Norman said this to the Department Managers: "I couldn't stop myself. My behavior is not without reason. Some people's ignorance brings out the worst in me and sets me off." He paused. "As you know, my wife was taken from me. We had it all. Some piece of garbage was speeding home after a night of debauchery with his mistress and ran her over. She was crossing the street from the grocery store. I live with the pain and the loss and the loneliness every single day. When I look at Drake Masters, all I see is a man who ruined the marital bliss he once had because he's a selfish, overindulgent prick. It wasn't enough to be married to a beautiful, loyal, enchanting woman. All he ever talked about was drinking and women, partying and sexy dancers, all the while having a wife to go home to, a priceless sanctuary. And the thought of him being so well liked and respected and admired for his work in this company makes me sick; it's downright despicable and unjustified. Everyone in this damn place buys into him and thinks he's righteous and cool. Not me. I see right through him and his cocky ways. He's nothing but a phony and a miscreant. And one day I'm...."

VISIONS

Dwayne was working on a new serum. He'd spent years alone in his apartment toiling in a makeshift laboratory putting the finishing touches on a chemical that he strongly believed would transport a human being into the future, for a short time at least.

His family had always wondered what had gotten into him—a twenty-five year-old man cramming the years of his youth into one small room in his apartment. He cared little about sports and parties. Girls weren't attracted to a man with greasy hair and buckteeth, and most people his age considered him weird and eccentric. He grew up in a decent family: two working parents and a sibling, a sister, Natasha, who had been avoiding him lately. When Dwayne moved out in his early twenties the whole family was surprised.

He pulled it off rather easily, though, holding a steady job and earning a respectable living. Fortunately he didn't live an extravagant life, a particular that made the transition from living with his parents to life on his own a little smoother. Most of his earnings were spent on the secret drug he was developing, and when the time was right, perhaps he would share his discovery if it proved functional. Dwayne knew the human brain was the most powerful organism in the world, more powerful than any computer known to mankind. To him it was a vast wonderland of unexplored hidden caverns, so he labored tirelessly in his lab at home playing with chemical compounds that he believed—when put to the test—would alter the mind's perception of reality, depending on the strength of the serum's properties. The person, the specimen who would take the injection, would be able to peer ahead in time. But there was a risk that he was trying to tweak: the aftermath. How would the nervous system respond to such a radical test? How about the body? Would there be a metamorphosis?

He had studied the government's once popular theory of freezing the human body. Some speculated it might one day become a worthy experiment, but Dwayne wanted more. He couldn't wait any longer to explore the possibilities. He hungered for alternatives: hard proof that a time warp was possible. The time he'd spent at the library and locked in his room was astounding. He had read countless magazines and books on the human brain, and journals on medicine and chemical compounds. Burying himself in research, Dwayne would go to work all day and then come home to his experiment and tune out the world around him. By this time, his family was not an important part of his existence. Who was for that matter? His parents communicated with him occasionally, but possessed no knowledge of his latest project. Natasha had given up on him a long time ago and never stopped by his place anymore. She hung out with her friends and did girly things, weaved in and out of a triangle of boyfriends. She was in her own little world, much like her brother. She'd considered visiting him a few times but then changed her mind. She and Dwayne had grown apart over the years and neither was in a rush to mend the bridge.

Dwayne had become friends with some of his work mates at Bio Labs Corporation. They were guys who didn't hang out with the popular folks, guys who were private people. Each of them, however, had demonstrated that he could be confided in. Dwayne found it to his advantage keeping company with them, and on one glorious afternoon he took the next step.

The lunch hour sun hung low in the sky, throwing excess heat down on the July day. As always, lunch time was hectic. The crowds were thick, going to and from the parking lots. Bio Labs was a glass fortress that stood twelve floors high, a building surrounded by beautiful landscaping and lush fields of grass. Dwayne found a picnic table sequestered under the cool umbrella of a shade tree. The scenery was spectacular, the flowerbeds around the site bursting with color, all the perennials in full bloom. He sat alone reading one of his chemical journals, picked at his burger and fries. Raising his head for a moment and looking across the courtyard, he noticed two of his friends on their way to another bench to eat. He waved at them, shouted. "Hey guys, over here."

Other people raised their heads. Dwayne made eye-contact with the men and waved them over. When they sat down one of the guys, Ricky, motioned with his head at the book.

"Every time I see you your head's in that book... interesting stuff?"

Dwayne smiled confidently. "Fascinating, actually," he exclaimed.

Ricky took a bite of his sandwich, chewed his food. "Fill us in."

Dwayne looked around discreetly. "I think I'm on to something huge. But if you want to know..." He scratched his chin in contemplation.

Ricky put down his sandwich, arched his brow. "Well, we're waiting."

Dwayne took a deep breath and stared intensely at the people around him, the look on his face that of a colonel planning a war strategy. "If you really want to know...?" Another dramatic pause. "You have to come to my place and find out."

Ricky's friend Brian squinted. "What is it, top secret?"

Another look of determination came to Dwayne's face. "Yes."

One of the guys rang Dwayne's doorbell. His friend looked around him as darkness began supplanting daylight. The light of the moon deepened shadows; the clouds' formations became easier to distinguish. Dwayne answered quickly, ushered them in and closed the door. "There's not much of a grand tour so I'll get to the point."

The guys joked. "What, no beer?"

"Forgive my manners," Dwayne said. "Help yourselves and we'll move on."

Brian went to the fridge and opened the door. "Holy..."

"What is it, man?" Ricky asked.

Brian glanced at Dwayne. "What's with all the

beakers? They're filled with some weird colored stuff."

Dwayne grinned. "Just grab your beers and follow me. I'll explain."

The three men entered a large closet. A slab of wood partitioned the far right side. Dwayne moved it out of the way, revealing a tiny nook, enough for a person or two to sit in. Above a small work surface hung a reading light. The windowless closet contained a few clothes but not much else. The slab of plywood concealed his miniature lab from visitors. Dwayne pointed to the floor. "Please, sit down." They sat. Each took a big swig of beer.

Dwayne started explaining his secret. "Look guys. I'm not crazy, so get that idea out of your heads. I'm going to tell you something that you may think is downright bizarre. If you feel you can't handle it, or you are going to rat me out, speak now."

Brian spoke on their behalf. "It's cool, okay?"

Dwayne pointed over his shoulder at a small chalkboard overrun with complex equations. Perplexed, the guys stared at the jumble of marks on the board, none of which made any sense to them.

"This behind me is an extensive experiment," Dwayne said. "It has taken years of my time and devotion. I firmly believe by injecting the mixture of drugs you saw in the refrigerator, at just the right dosage, I can see into the future." He pressed his fingers to his temples. "With *stunning* clarity."

Brian blinked quickly a few times. Ricky shook his head, sniveled in disbelief.

Dwayne had expected that reaction. "Well, I figured you'd doubt me so I'm willing to prove my theory, ready to take the plunge myself."

Ricky assumed he was bluffing. "All right, you're on."

Dwayne accepted their challenge and was prepared to legitimize his theory. "Here's the deal. I'm going to carefully measure what I need for my experiment. All you have to do is be my eyes. Watch everything I do, everything I say, and record it. Any data you collect is valuable to me. No matter what happens—no matter what you see me do—you cannot wake me until the drug runs its course. It may take hours—or even longer. There's no way of knowing how my nervous system will respond."

The guys looked at each other apprehensively. Ricky asked. "But, what if—"

"Don't worry. I've perfected it," Dwayne said.

The two men sat still and watched Dwayne meticulously measuring liquids into numerous beakers, sipping their drinks without talking. They seemed a bit uneasy, perhaps a bit skeptical too, but were compelled to bear witness to what they believed was a monumental failure in the making. Dwayne worked diligently for an hour preparing the exact amount of serum. He held it up to his face, observing the transparent yellow liquid. He watched as the particles floated in the test tube. This procedure was larger than life to him. This was the triumph he had craved for so long, the product of his hard work. In his mind he had found a means to manipulate sections of the brain, massaging them, so to speak. His analysis led him to imagine that when the fluid channeled throughout his bloodstream, it would stimulate nerves in the brain, bridging anew the left side of the brain and the right. It would create a reality never before experienced. To him this was a breakthrough that could possibly open doors to all types of extensive research.

Dwayne opened a cabinet, pulled out a large box. He put it on the table and opened the lid. The men watched every move he made. He pulled out a large syringe, larger than either of them had ever seen before: about two inches in diameter with a needle about five inches long it was intimidating. The injector at the top rose from a plastic sphere, ending with a loop for the thumb. Dwayne carefully poured the serum into the needle, filling the cylinder to the top.

Dwayne entered his closet, his pals followed him. He got down on the floor and wrapped a tourniquet around his bicep. He peered up at the men. "No matter what, leave me as I am. Got it?"

Brian raised his hands. "You're the maestro."

Dwayne held the needle in his hand and took one last look at the murky fluid he was about to have inside him. "I have one last request. Don't leave me alone."

Brian nodded, then Ricky.

With the needle Dwayne pierced his vein. The men cringed. About half of the fluid had left the tube. Dwayne looked woozy, withdrawn. His eyes rolled back in his head, fatigue overtook him. Seconds later the tube emptied…and Dwayne passed out. The needle remained in his arm, the tourniquet strapped to his flesh. The experiment had begun…

Dwayne's eyes opened to a new world, a mysterious world: a musty-smelling underground chamber of sorts crammed with boxes and debris, a branch of light cutting through a small window and widening on the cement floor where he lay. Dust particles floated inside the beam of polychromatic light. Confused and disoriented, Dwayne surveyed the ominous room: a basement, he guessed. Dead bodies were stacked on the opposite side of the room—blindfolded, limbless, rotting, foul-smelling.

What the hell? Who...?

Although he felt as if he'd just come out of a coma, Dwayne got to his feet and reclaimed his balance. A set of double doors atop a flight of narrow stairs leading to the street awaited him. He grabbed the handles, pushed outward, and emerged into the light of day on a city street, a street occupied by sparse pockets of pedestrians. A man passed him, almost grazing him. He seemed to be an ordinary man, a businessman. He glowered at Dwayne, his face inflamed with rage. Dwayne was unnerved but turned away from him and moved on.

The sun, bright and burning strong, warmed his face. He kept walking on the sidewalk, its surface marred by small depressions and indelible stains. A block or two farther brought him to a newspaper stand where he saw a middle-aged couple looking at him disdainfully, their eyes piercing him like ice-cold daggers.

Vexed, he continued. After covering a few more blocks he came to a traffic light and waited for it to change. The heat of the day had weakened him but he was not inclined to retreat. When the light turned green he made his way to the other side of the road. As soon as he got there he smelled something. The odor of meat cooking nearby was unmistakable. Diagonal from him was a busy café. A large colorful canopy distended from the building's façade. He glanced in the oversized window and his eyes fell upon a man and woman eating. It chilled him the way the man was carving his meat, rather methodically, intently. The man wore close-cut greasy hair...and he had a glass eye. The woman dining with him sipped a glass of wine and chatted with a waiter. Suddenly and unexpectedly, the strange man locked eyes with Dwayne. Grinning, the man continued cutting his steak, putting forkfuls into his mouth, yet never taking his eyes off Dwayne. Dwayne didn't like the looks of this guy, so he made haste.

He still had no idea where he was or the best direction to go in. This city in many ways reminded him of New York City. The buildings were towering pointed structures reaching aggressively for the sky. Billboards covered with cigarette ads and sexy celebrities hung from storefronts. Monstrous marquees were flashing advertisements intermittently, selling products Dwayne had never even seen or heard of before.

Time passed swiftly. He had gone far but only felt more lost, scared, and alone. Nobody would talk to him. He was feeling the lassitude of his aimless trek, his empty search for understanding and purpose. He desperately needed to find help, someone who could make sense of the madness that hindered his every move. He took a left down an alley and found a few people huddled around a metal garbage drum. Crackling tongues of flame were leaping over the rim. Dense plumes of smoke squirmed above their heads and brushed the dilapidated brick building behind them.

Dwayne walked forward and stopped about fifteen feet from the gang. He couldn't get any closer; the stench coming from the drum was rancid. He tried talking to the gang. "Excuse me, I need help."

They didn't answer. But they turned toward him, their faces gnarled.

"Can you tell me where I am?" Dwayne asked in a shaky voice.

Failing to answer him, the people fled toward the back alley. What were they hiding? Would they find Dwayne later in another alley? Hurt him? Their stare, when it met his, penetrated deeply—cruel, menacing eyes with malice behind them.

Dwayne ventured into a different alley, staying close to the buildings, repeatedly looking over his shoulder, making sure no one suspicious was stalking him. Not far down the alley he found an open door that led to a flight of stairs, stairs dividing two apartments. He heard a noise coming from inside the open door at the crown of the staircase. He went through the door and ascended the steps, only to find a television tuned to a news channel and a reporter speaking fervently.

"Yet another three are dead this week. And STILL the authorities are without clues! More news on our ten o'clock coverage."

The reporter dropped his papers on his desk and shook his head.

"What the hell is going on?" Dwayne said.

He searched the shabby apartment. It was vacant for the most part. On a corner shelf a digital clock was flashing: *Sunday, April 8th 2022, 6:02 pm*, but he hadn't noticed as he walked past it. A short hall led to another open door. He entered and flicked on the light. Substantial light filled the room, a bathroom, and shone on a dead body in the tub. The tub, sink, and shower curtain were smeared with blood, the whole room doused with it. Dwayne was in shock. The corpse was a middle-aged man, his ash-gray hair caked with blood from a stab wound. Deep gashes disfigured his head. His scalp was peeled back, his cranium exposed.

Dwayne gazed in the mirror and for the first time since he'd awakened in the basement saw his own reflection. He looked much older and haggard. He had longer hair and an overgrown, slovenly beard. A scar ran from the corner of his eye to the bottom of his ear. Standing in front of the mirror, he carefully traced the scar with his index finger. *Why am I so hideous? My god, are these the side-effects of the drugs? How far have I traveled? What have I become?*

He left the bathroom, deciding to check out the apartment a bit more. Next was the bedroom. After crossing through the small kitchen he made a left, entered the quarters and put on the light. As he hit the switch one of the bulbs flickered and fizzled. The bed was in proper order, blankets pulled taut, pillows arranged neatly against the headboard. Nothing about the room struck him as odd until...

On the dresser Dwayne found a few family photos. He analyzed them briefly. The first photo was of the dead man in the shower. He was standing arm in arm with his wife. Behind them a huge banner was hanging from the wall. It said:

"Happy 20th Anniversary! Mark & Debbie, April 1, 2022."

Where was this man's wife now? One picture in particular demanded more of his attention. A young lady was mounted on a horse. Dwayne recognized her as the girl from the restaurant. She was the one talking with the waiter when the man with the glass eye gave him that weird look. What on earth had he walked into? He got out of there in a hurry.

A chilly night clung to the city. It was very late. Dwayne was exhausted and still roaming aimlessly for a place to hide, to regroup—to figure things out. The city had undergone a drastic change. Few people milled about now; the streets were no longer as active as before. In the center of the street smoke drifted up through apertures in the manhole covers giving the city block a feeling of grimness. He continued through the maze of the sleeping city, wandering like a lost child left in the dark. Just ahead Dwayne spotted a wino pushing a grocery cart across the street at the intersection, not at all concerned with traffic because there was none now. His cart was filled with old dirty clothes, liquor bottles, and food from the garbage. Dwayne stood pondering his next move—or anything that came to mind at this point.

A sudden detonation—gunshots in the distance startled him. Then another blast shook the night—and another. He felt the report of the guns under his feet and all around him. Dwayne soon arrived at the center of a long narrow alley, a street populated by riffraff that he dreaded going down. No signs of police anywhere. Based on what he'd seen in the bathtub earlier, no one was patrolling this horrid city. In his vicinity broken bottles, papers and other rubbish defaced the grounds. The filthy street was only one of the many armpits of this arcane land. Windows at various heights were smashed—in some places all that remained were gaping holes and splintered wood, chasms of dark, dreary decay. Graffiti disgraced storefronts and alley walls. Dwayne was shaken by the ruins before him.

Farther up the alley he stumbled upon a few pedestrians, nobody he felt secure about asking for help. They, too, avoided him. At the next block, across from a shattered marquee, he arrived at a store before crossing Newberry Street. A huge sign in the window blinked, *Name Your Price!* The store was stockpiled with stereos, televisions, DVD players; all kinds of electronic appliances, most of them damaged, were arranged disorderly. The unsavory images were troubling Dwayne more and more; he had never felt so alone, so uncertain, so confused, so petrified.

The temperature had plummeted. Dwayne shook feverishly. The insufficient clothes he had on were loose, threadbare; but he had to get by on what little he had. Five blocks later he finally found a glimmer of hope: lights glowing behind the open curtains of a well-maintained building, a hotel. The vandalized sign read, "...Hotel." The other letters had been removed and shoddy rivets were left behind on the frame. Inside, a security guard was sleeping at the reception desk with a set of headphones over his ears.

Dwayne went inside and snuck past the guard. A corridor separated two banks of elevators. Straight out in front of him, at the end of the hall, was a revolving door that led to the back lot. Couches lined the opposite walls of the lobby. Magazines were strewn on a glass table in front of the couches. He made his way past the elevators and came to a short hall. Hanging above him was a small wooden sign: *Lounge, Restrooms.* An arrow pointed down the corridor. He followed the sign to a water fountain and a vending machine. He sought nourishment and was relieved to have found something. But he would have to break into the machine because he had no money, and he was afraid of drawing the guard's attention. He entered the lounge to his left. On a round table was an assortment of magazines and a few crumpled up newspapers. Another table on the other side of the room held a plastic bag filled with pretzels. He wolfed them down and scouted the room for something else.

Small recessed lights burned down on him. But he wanted to turn them off. He walked over to the wall panel where there were three different switches. He pushed down the first two. The room darkened. Dwayne hid in the corner and ate the rest of his snack. He stretched his legs. He could feel the cold tiles through his thin khaki pants. He closed his eyes.

Outside and down the hall at the security booth the guard had snapped out of his slumber. He peeked at the monitor: 2:00 a.m. He'd been asleep for hours and had forgotten to perform his point checks. He stood up and smoothed out the wrinkles in his shirt, circled the desk and walked past the lobby toward the elevators, yawning, stretching his back. Everything was in good standing there. The guard stood in front of the glass by the elevator and combed his hair. His name tag shined in the glare of the elevator light: "Lorenzo." After securing the lobby he strolled to the back room and opened the lounge door. When the handle jerked open it startled Dwayne. The guard walked into the room and turned on the lights. Dwayne slowly rose to his feet, his heart racing. The guard was equally alarmed. He had jumped back when he noticed Dwayne in the corner. "What the hell! Who are you?"

Dwayne was nervous. This was the first time since he'd arrived in this strange city that he was forced to confront someone. The guard came toward him, his hand lowering toward his weapons belt. Lorenzo stood six feet and was a meaty two hundred pounds, every bit of it muscle.

"Look man, just back off...okay?" Dwayne said. "I don't want any trouble."

The guard unzipped his jacket. "Well, you just found some. You have no business being here and I'm calling this in."

The security guard reached to his belt, pulled out a radio, and hit the button to speak. He extended his arm, palm up, signaling to Dwayne... *Stay put.*

"Control Room, it's me Lorenzo. We have a situation here in the—"

Dwayne lost his composure and lunged at the guard throwing all his weight onto him. During their tussle they tumbled backward and fell over the round table, splitting it in half. The radio loosened from the guard's grip and slid a few feet away. The men wrestled on the floor and for a few moments each fought for the upper hand. Dwayne was out-powered as they rolled back and forth on the floor, each jockeying for the advantage. The guard dug his fingers into Dwayne's face. Dwayne somehow was able to free his right hand and reach for the radio, the device only five inches away. With his left hand he tried to pry Lorenzo's hand from his face, reaching for the radio at the same time. The guard's sweaty grip slipped, giving Dwayne a chance to grab the radio, but not before taking a quick fist to his jaw. He was stunned but hanging tough. With the radio securely in his grip he nailed the guard square in the corner of the eye. The security guard howled in pain and rolled off him.

Dwayne got to his feet, balanced himself, and began hammering the guard in loops with the radio, firing uppercuts and slashing him with side swipes, opening gashes on his face. Dwayne swung at least six times, sending the man to the floor like a sack of beaten meat. Dwayne stood above him, crouched and bracing himself with his hands on his knees. He was panting heavily, trying to get his wind back, when something caught his eye: a newspaper on the floor. He picked up the newspaper and holding it in his trembling hands read it. On the front page was a photo of him, exactly as he'd looked in the mirror earlier when he discovered the dead body. At the top of the page the headline was written in bold letters:

"***Serial Killers At Large!***"

Below the headline, two faces: one of Dwayne and the other equally familiar. In fact a dead-ringer: the man in the restaurant with the glass eye. Dwayne was beside himself. A chain of questions entangled themselves in his mind. *Where am I? How many did I kill? When did this all start? Why? How can this be?* The voices in his head wouldn't quit.

He left the building and limped through the streets. After a few minutes he encountered a gang throwing pieces of cement at a lamp post. Dwayne ducked into a doorway and waited until they finished their mischief. From out of nowhere he heard glass shattering and when he peered around the corner he saw the gang had smashed the street lamp and run into an alley. Dwayne came out from hiding and walked the street cautiously, watching his back at all times. He walked faster, shifting in and out of the shadows. The sudden appearance of a lady, some twenty-odd feet ahead, froze Dwayne in his tracks. She wore a long ragged coat and had the saddest look on her face. She stood like a statue in the glow of a neon sign. An old tattered hat masked her features. Dwayne couldn't take his eyes off her. He was immobile. Her head turned toward the building adjacent to him. A light about ten floors up flickered behind a mesh curtain. The other rooms were dark. The lady reached up and removed her hat. A mass of hair fell over her shoulders. She started toward him. Dwayne swallowed. His pulse soared. The lady stopped ten feet away from him and he obtained a better look at her features. An ice-cold sensation fluttered inside him when he realized who it was behind the grungy coat and underneath the weather-beaten hat. It was his sister, Natasha. She opened her jacket. There was a knife protruding from her heart. Dwayne recoiled. More questions dominated him. *Was she real? A ghost? Was this really happening to him? Did he somehow kill his own sister? If not him, who?*

A window exploded in the high-rise next to him. When he looked up, a wide swath of shards were raining down on him. He used his hand as a shield but then, even more horrifying, a body was tossed from the window and plummeted at him like a missile. He turned to avoid being flattened. His sister had vanished into thin air. The diving body struck his back, knocking him to the pavement. Dwayne's legs were pinned underneath the corpse, which had blood oozing from the mouth and head. Dwayne was unconscious.

Minutes later, a man came out of the building and stood above Dwayne and the corpse, laughing sadistically. With his glass eye, the stranger studied Dwayne's body and knelt down beside him. He plucked out Dwayne's eye. The sound of the viscera separating was awful. Dwayne didn't respond. Once the eye was removed the man slipped a new eye directly into Dwayne's empty socket—a glass eye. The man lowered his head and whispered into Dwayne's ear. "I'll see you one day soon. And with your help, the stranglehold on this city will continue. It's what you always wanted, isn't it? To be one of us? I saw that look in your face at the restaurant. You can't deny your fate."

Dwayne woke from his drug-induced state. He was still in the closet. Everything was dark. His head was throbbing mercilessly. His entire body was sore and weak. When he sat up the needle dislodged itself and rolled away. He rose to his feet, sought purchase with his hands against the walls. He left the closet and lumbered into the kitchen where a nightlight burned on the wall. Nobody was there. He was all alone. His friends had left him. They had written nothing of his experiments as he'd requested. He sat down at the table and stared into space. He felt sick to his stomach and hot with fever.

The phone rang on the end table by the couch. He wobbled over, picked it up on the sixth ring.

"Hello?" he said, his voice barely audible.

"Dwayne? It's me...sis...Natasha. What's wrong with you?"

"What? What do you mean?"

"I've been calling you for three days. You don't return my calls. What's wrong, damn it?"

"I haven't felt well, been sleeping a lot, Tasha. What do you care anyway?"

"Of course, I care. I sent Ricky and Brian over to check on you the other day but you didn't answer the door."

"You did what?" Dwayne asked annoyed.

"Look, I'll be over later," she said. "We need to talk. I have some stuff to get off my chest with you. I need to air some things out."

Dwayne ignored her and hung up the phone. He became dizzier and nauseous but decided to sit at the table and scribble notes about his visions. The pen couldn't keep up with his mind. He had seen more than he wanted to, each image terribly frightening, disturbing and inexplicable. How would he divulge his findings to his family? To the world? Would they listen? Would they believe him? Maybe he would do it all again and double the dosage, perhaps find a deeper understanding.

His hand shook and he lost his grip on the pen. The disgusting memories haunted him. In that other world in the future he was a *killer*. He remembered the man with the glass eye and felt as though a chain had tightened around his stomach. He got up on his feet. The room was twirling around him with lightning speed. His legs buckled. He collapsed. His head snapped back from the impact. His left eye became engorged with blood.

The door to his apartment opened. Natasha entered. She saw him on the floor and ran to his side. "Dwayne what happened?"

Blood was leaking from his mouth and onto the white tiles. He lifted his head from the ground and looked at his sister. "I saw things."

"What are you talking about? What did you see, Dwayne?"

'The...the paper...check the paper...it's all there." His eyes closed, his body stiffened.

CLOSE CALL

The phone rang.

She put the call through, pressing the crimson button. "Hello, *Helping Hands Hotline,* may I be your friend?"

A young male voice on the verge of tears said, "It hurts...it hurts too much...it never goes away...I want to—"

The operator took a deep breath, pulled back her frizzy golden hair, curling it behind her ear. She was nervous about the caller's state of mind. It was her first week of work. None of the victims had been this distressed at the outset. She sensed the pain in his voice buried deep in each breath.

"Look. Let's just calm down, what's your name?"

"Ar...Ar...Arnold."

"What hurts, my friend Arnold? I want to help you. Let me help you. That's why I'm here. Thanks for leaning on me, Arnold. I'm Jaime."

"There's just too much...too, too much to deal with." Suddenly a stitch of irritation altered his tone. "What the hell do you know about trauma anyway? Who the hell are you?"

Jaime unzipped her *Burger World* smock and wiped sweat from her forehead. She was rattled. Her hands shook over the keyboard as she typed his name and condition into the computer. The office was quiet. She was the only one working. The howling wind whipped against the building.

Nobody wanted to work the New Year's Eve shift, so she did it, missing out on attending a gathering with her friends. "Well...I'm an expert in these things, Arnold. You must believe me. You know what? I have an Uncle Arnold on my mom's side. He lives on the west coast. He's a nice man, just like I bet you are."

The tone of his voice became lower. "Do you really have an uncle with my name?"

"Sure do. So let...let's talk about your pain. How can we fix it...so you can have a happy New Year and hang with your friends and family? The ball's going to drop soon."

"I don't know. Just make it go away. Can you do that?" Arnold asked.

"Yes. I can...with your help."

"What do you want from me? I'm the one who called you...what the heck am I—"

She tried to put out the fire. "Take it easy, Arnold. All I meant was for you to tell me the source of your pain. Nothing's worth doing what you *think* you want to do to yourself, right?"

Silence on the other end.

"Right, Arnold? Right?"

She listened to him breathing. It was heavy, sporadic.

He broke the silence. "Depends."

"It doesn't depend, Arnold. It's never worth it. Not to me. Hey, now that we're talking...I consider you my friend. Do you consider me yours?"

Silence again. Longer this time, ten seconds passed.

"Well...do you?" she asked.

"I...I guess so...I don't even know you."

"Sure you do. You just shared something personal with me. That's all I need to call us friends."

"All...all right then, Jaime. You're my friend."

"Good, Arnold. Now, what's ailing you? Why are you so sad and upset?"

"I have no fam...family. No...no friends. I'm all alone. Nobody cares about me...nobody!"

"Wait a second, Arnold. I care. Always remember that."

A short pause.

"Jaime."

"Yes?"

"I'm gay."

Jaime swallowed. Her throat felt parched.

"There's nothing wrong with that, Arnold. Many people are gay. One of my best friends is gay and I've known him for five years."

"Did his family and friends desert him, Jaime?"

"Well...no...not really."

"What do you mean, 'not really'?"

"At first his parents—his whole family—went into shock. But one day he fought back. He was courageous. He brought his boyfriend home and shoved his lifestyle right in their face, you know, made them accept it."

"What happened after that, Jaime? It backfired, didn't it?"

"They were ashamed of him, Arnold, yes, especially his dad. But, they had to deal with it Arnold. They had no choice. He risked it all and...and it took some time...but, but it all worked out. He is better off for letting go of what troubled him so deeply."

"Jaime."

"Yes Arnold?"

"I'm...I'm slipping."

"You just hold on now...don't talk like that. Tell me more. I want to help you."

"Jaime, I opened up to my family...and they told me never come home again. My friends are really, really mad and won't even look at me or talk to me. I skipped town and, and found someone to room with. The pain lingers, Jaime, like a long dreadful disease without a cure."

"Arnold?"

"What?"

"As much as you're hurting, you need to understand. You did the right thing. It takes guts to reveal who you really are."

"But Jaime...do you see where it got me? Don't you sense my emptiness...my longing to be treated like a normal human being, like everyone else? I'll never have that now. It was taken away from me."

"But, Arnold—"

"Jaime. You don't know shit, do you? I feel worse just talking to you. How did you even get that job, huh? What do you know about isolation?"

Silence again on her end. Jaime's eyes swelled with tears, streams slid down her face. Arnold listened to her crying through the phone. "Since when does the counselor cry to the suicidal?"

"Arnold?"

Jaime tried pulling herself together.

Arnold snapped at her. "How much more bullshit are you going to hand me? I mean—"

"Arnold!"

"What?"

"I'm an overeater...I'm obese and...and sick."

"So what?"

"You asked me how I got this job, right?"

"Yeah."

"Well, a month ago I was in your shoes." Jaime controlled her crying.

Arnold was getting agitated. "Oh, will you stop already."

"Arnold, listen to me, okay? I listened to you."

"Go ahead."

"About a month ago I tried to kill myself. I overdosed on everything I could find in the medicine cabinet."

"Are you making this up just to—"

"No! Arnold...When the doctors saved me and I felt better I decided I wanted to live after all. So now I work at Burger World until ten and then I volunteer my time here at the hotline. It makes me feel good to help people who suffer and are thinking about ending their life. You see, we all have to find our purpose instead of complaining and blaming others. You know, it's better to deal with your demons. I work at a place that would normally make me eat more, but I don't. I won't. I will overcome my obstacles and so will you."

"Well...it's almost midnight. Let me go do what I have to do, Jaime."

"Arnold?"

"Don't try and stall me anymore, Jaime."

"I just want to ask you a simple question, can I do that?"

"*What?*"

"What would it take to make you feel better inside, to make you ring in the New Year, happily?"

"That's an easy question. I would rather you have asked me that first instead of all the mindless chit-chat. If I was looking for someone to push me over the edge, you did a stellar job."

"Tell me then, Arnold. What would make you feel better?"

"I want them all to pay for the anguish I feel, each and every one of those assholes that call themselves human."

"Who?"

"The ones that turned their backs on me—that made me feel worthless, unloved, unwanted, ugly inside. That's who."

"Is that really going to solve anything, Arnold?"

"For me...yes...*it will!*"

"It will only make matters worse, Arnold."

"Listen to you, Ms. Turn My Life Around. Let me ask you an honest question."

"Come on now, Arnold, let's not g—"

"Listen for Christ's sake! Just listen to my fuckin' question. You mean to tell me you never thought about revenge? All those people that mocked your eating habits, that called you every fat name in the book, laughed at you in public, looked you up and down with judging eyes. You can sit there and tell me you rose above that internal urge so you could sit where you are and listen to a bunch of god damn strangers teetering on the edge? I don't buy it."

"No...I do this to feel better about myself... in the hopes that one day something good might come of it...like good karma."

"Nothing *good* will come of it, trust me."

"How can you say that, Arnold? That's a horrible outlook!"

"Because...Well...I'm sorry to spoil the mood, but all of your heartfelt compassion hasn't done a damn bit of good. I am going to kill myself when the clock strikes midnight. That's a promise."

Jaime spoke with urgency. She felt the situation falling apart. "Arnold, don't talk that way! You're not going to do anything like that. You're a fighter. Just hold on now. I'm here for you. Don't give up. Don't go through this alone."

"I'm not, Jaime. I thought about this long enough. This is all making sense to me now, finally. I know a way I can begin healing if only for a moment, before I leave this shitty world. I know of a way I can find peace."

"Good. Don't be alone tonight. Go anywhere, somewhere, interact with people; get your mind out of the dumps."

"I'm already taking the next step. I'm in my car on my way to Brumwell."

"Oh?"

"Jaime, do you really think I would kill myself

without taking someone with me? What fun would that be?"

"But...But what? Why are you coming to...?"

"I'm on my way to the Brumwell County Suicide Prevention Center, where you're sitting right now, talking to me. I am going to kill you first...then me...I'm going to put us both out of our misery. I'm almost *theeeere*."

"Please, Arnold— "

He hung up.

Jaime decided to call the police. She trusted her instincts. Mysterious callers had said weird things to her before, yelled at her, condescended to her; but never threatened her life. The police station was not far away. Having that in the back of her mind eased the mounting tension pressing between her temples. *They'd better get here fast.* Fingers twitching, she pressed the buttons 911. She spoke to the operator, explained what Arnold had said, and tried to catch her breath. She informed the operator that it was a typical call for a suicidal, up until the end. "He told me he'd...that he'd...he was coming to kill me first," she said, her voice shaking, her eyes scanning the room.

"As we speak, Jaime, there is an officer en route to the center. Just stay on the line with me until Officer McHale arrives on the scene."

"Thank you so much. I'm...I'm so scared," Jaime said. She crossed her arms nervously, rubbed them.

"No need to be. Just calm down," the operator urged. "Usually this ends up being somebody just playing a gag on a friend, or...or even someone desperate for attention. Hang tight, Jaime."

Jaime got up from her desk and walked as far as

the phone cord allowed, extending her arm and turning off the lights. This way he couldn't see her from the outside. The room was dark except for the computer screen. She hit the button, powering it down. She sat on the floor next to her desk, curled into a ball. Her skin was covered with gooseflesh. The operator kept Jaime alert. "Are you still with me? Are you okay? Officer McHale should be there any minute."

The dispatcher listened to Jaime's heavy breathing. "Did you make sure to lock the doors after the suspect threatened you?"

"No. There are automatic locks after 10:00p.m. Only I can release them with my key. I'll let the officer in when he gets here."

"Officer McHale just notified me that he's pulling into the parking lot as we speak, Jaime."

"Thank you so much," Jaime said, her voice cracking with relief.

"You're welcome...sit tight, wait until he knocks on the door and let him in. You can hear from where you are, right Jaime?"

"Yes."

Jaime sat up straight. She peered over the row of desks in front of her. Through the window she saw the police lights flickering, bouncing off the screen of pine trees along the parking lot entrance. Help was only feet away. A wave of relief fluttered in her stomach, breaking up the knots. Jaime became restless. "What the hell is taking so long?" The seconds felt endless.

The operator eased her fears. "The officer is securing the outside, Jaime. He'll be at the front door in a few seconds. Stay with me, a veteran officer is outside. You're in good hands."

She looked at the lights once more. They shimmered throughout the parking lot—red and white colors jumping from one part of the landscape to the next—giving hope to a dreadful night. A pounding sound on the glass came from down the long hallway, the hallway leading to the main door.

"He's here! It's him! I'm going to let him in." Jaime ripped the headset off and dropped it on the desk. She walked carefully to the hallway, a dark hallway. She approached a switch, flipped it. The overhead incandescent lights came to life one by one (although a few of them failed to kindle) and she stood unmoving until the corridor was adequately lit. Jaime looked at the front door, stopped in her tracks. She noticed a roaming flashlight beam on the other side of the door. She walked slowly toward what she prayed was the waiting officer. She closed to within twenty feet of the entrance.

A voice broke the silence. "Jaime? Jaime, is that you? It's all right. I'm Officer McHale. The outside is secure. I'm going to get you out of here. Open the door now, Jaime." She saw the silhouette of a man, nothing more, no certain evidence he was a policeman. She remembered her father always saying, "You don't have to let them in, unless you see proof they are the real thing."

The man pounded harder on the glass, jiggling the bar. "C'mon," he shouted. "Open up! I want to get you out of here!"

Confused, she turned away from him. She studied the other side of the hallway for a few moments and then refocused her attention on the officer, who shined the flashlight on himself, highlighting his polished badge, a large oval badge that gleamed under the splash of light. The insignias on his collar glistened like jewels. As Jaime moved cautiously toward the door, a misty rain began falling.

"Jaime!" the officer yelled again, frustrated by her unresponsiveness. "Didn't the dispatcher tell you I was coming? Let's go!"

She went to the wall, to a round protrusion—a primary master lock—and inserted her key. There was a clicking sound. The lock released and the officer gained access. "What were you waiting for?" he asked. "We have to move!"

McHale was struck on the head with a branch and collapsed onto a cluster of bushes. A man jumped from the roof, grabbing the nightstick from the officer's holster. The man, tall and gaunt and balding, gave Jaime a sinister smile. Jaime, eyes wide with abject fear, retreated toward the other door. The man came at her, his long wiry legs propelling him slowly but steadily. Jaime had somehow built a sizable lead. At the other end of the hall she inserted a key into the housing of the secondary lock and turned it back and forth. When she glanced back she found the stranger getting closer...

The door opened. Jaime ran outside screaming. She now treaded a desolate road. Nobody was around to hear her, save her. The factory across the street, a massive brick building surrounded by a chain-link fence, was closed and dark, but she noticed a light burning in one of the houses in the distance, a house screened by a row of hedges. Jaime hobbled toward it, out of breath, her heart pounding like an unruly piston. She glanced back and saw that Arnold remained in pursuit. Jaime saw the house at the end of an expanse, tried to run faster, as her hefty, sweat-drenched body overexerted itself. Arnold stumbled, dropping his club on the pavement with a thud; then it started rolling away from him toward the edge of the road. He prevented it from falling into a ditch by stepping on it. Grunting and wheezing, he picked it up.

Jaime wasn't far from the house now, but she felt as though she had cement blocks tied to her legs, every stride had become an exhausting effort. She finally crossed the grassy property and entered the screened porch, pounded on the front door with her fist, then kicked the bottom of the door twice, rocking the entire frame. Nobody answered. "C'mon god damn it! I need help!" She knocked again—still no response. Jaime looked behind her… Arnold was gone.

Panting heavily still, she ran around the side of the house and found another entrance, an unsecured door; overgrown, neglected weeds crowded the threshold. She wiggled the knob, opened the door, and entered a small room with a work bench against the wall. An incandescent lamp flickered above a shelf full of tools, a cord dangled from the lamp's housing. Jaime yanked the cord, turning off the light. She peeked outside through the lone window but couldn't see Arnold, not a trace of him. The rain intensified, stippling the stained glass. A car was parked across the street—a shoddy relic in front of the factory, and two others on West River Highway. The tires were deflated. *Where did he go?*

A voice cracked the silence. "Jaime! Jaime!" It was Officer McHale calling to her from his radio car. The patrolman was rounding the corner approaching the house. The colorful lights drew her out of hiding. She bolted from the house and ran to the car. Officer McHale assisted her into the cruiser while maintaining a close watch on his surroundings. He squeezed the trigger on his radio. "Car 45 to dispatch, I have the girl with me. I was assaulted from behind before, the suspect is gone. I couldn't see his face to make a positive I.D. I'll try and get something from the girl later. All is secure. Do you copy?"

"Ten four," dispatch replied.

They pulled away from the scene. Jaime looked back, watching as the building disappeared behind the trees. The patrol car drove into the night.

"Look, Jaime, hopefully there's not a next time, but if there is, answer the door a little faster, okay? A split second can be the difference between life and death."

Jaime was wiping tears away with her shirt sleeve, staring out the window. "I know. I'm sorry. I just froze for some reason. It's...It's been a long night."

Jaime sat alone in the kitchen in her pajamas, staring at the wall clock. She sipped a cup of tea and tried to unwind. Her parents were on their way home. They had been only a couple hours away visiting a business acquaintance. The police had contacted them earlier once Jaime was safe. Everything still taunted her. All she could think of now was that voice on the other line, how it had changed on a dime. Jaime had walked out on her shift, abandoning others in need who may have called in. She felt a little guilty, but knew in time she'd overcome her misgivings—just like the other obstacles in her life—just as she had tried to teach Arnold.

She had escaped with her life. That was all that mattered. In the morning she was prepared to call the manager of the hotline and resign from her position as a *helping hand*. She walked upstairs to her bedroom and locked the door. She dimmed the lights and, from her desk, pulled out her diary (which she wrote in every day) and began writing.

Tonight was frightening. It will take time to get that voice out of my head. I wish someone else could have heard it and understood the effect it had on me. Hearing someone say they are going to kill you is unlike anything else a human could ever experience. I don't know what to liken it to. When the doctors told me I could die if I kept eating and taking pills it terrified me. It put life in perspective. But someone threatening to kill you is an entirely different animal. I hope that Arnold was just trying to scare me. That's what the police think is possible but they are investigating. Fortunately I'm alive and unharmed. I was lucky. I'm glad I called the cops instead of taking it as a joke. One thing will haunt me for a while. Who was he? Why did he want to hurt me? Where did he go? Will he find me again? Somehow I don't feel this is over yet. I feel bad about barging into that house. But I was scared and alone. I had no choice. The police are going to call the owners and explain what happened. Officer McHale told me the call was made from a cell phone and when they tracked its owner it was registered to a woman who lives hundreds of miles from here. She said she had lost the phone a few days ago. The lady told the police she owns two phones—one for work and one for personal use—and then explained that she uses the work phone most of the time. She told Officer McHale that her queer son probably stole it. The police said her personality was rough around the edges. She hasn't seen her son for a while. He had stormed out on her in the middle of an argument. Now I can understand Arnold's pain, although I am still scared of him. The officer spent some time here with me earlier. The coast was clear and then he was called to duty elsewhere. I hope someone can find Arnold before he does something stupid, unless he already has. Anyway, I had to get this off my chest. I'm still shaken. My parents are on the way home. The officer gave me his direct line in case of an emergency. He is only a few blocks away.

There is a knock at the door.

PIG

A rock struck the back of Oliver Rumson's head and the world around him went black. His body toppled over the iron railing and landed on the coarse cement at the Grover Street bus stop. Oliver never saw the attack coming. At this hour, 6:00 a.m. on Sunday, there were no witnesses, no other commuters waiting for the bus.

Darleston was a sleepy town, a dry dusty speck on the map just twenty miles inside the Arizona border, a place where the heat index frequently exceeded a hundred. Beyond the bus stop terrain undulated from road to horizon and the sun had already spread savage heat across the windswept plains.

Lucky for Oliver, though, he didn't feel the impact when his torso struck the unyielding ground—he was unconscious and unaware of the pebbles and shards of broken cement that had torn the flesh of his arms and neck and forehead. A car door slammed and Oliver was hauled away, tires squealing on the pavement.

Sandy Rumson woke up and peered at the clock: 7:15 a.m. She sat up in bed and squirmed from the feeling of sweat underneath her nightgown. Her rickety air conditioner did not cool the room the way it used to. She and her

111

husband would have to buy a replacement soon. When her eyes had adjusted to the sunlight coming through the drapeless windows, she noticed that Oliver hadn't returned home from the factory. Normally he would come in and turn off the air conditioner, depending on how comfortable the room was. At the very least he would kiss her on the cheek to announce his arrival, sometimes even get something going in the sack. Sandy got out of bed and went to the kitchen for some iced tea; no coffee this time of year. Not until autumn. Then she would be back to her five cup-a-day habit. Her husband has his vices—and she has a few of her own.

She stood staring out the window, watching a bird dart across the back yard to the crotch of a sickly fruit tree, where it huddled with another bird. *Why didn't Oliver call and tell me he was going to be late?* It only takes a minute to pick up a phone, she always told him. She never asked much of him. She was an easy-going wife, undemanding and flexible. Sure, sometimes when he forgot to take out the garbage or turn off the television before bed or change the dog's water, she'd get frustrated. But she would rather overlook his mistakes than dwell on them. In this case, if the boss was going to keep him late, for any reason at all, he still should have called her; and she couldn't deny the twinge of disappointment that she felt as she watched the birds traverse the yard and settle into another tree. She finished her iced tea, placed the glass in the sink, and got dressed.

An old greenhouse sat in an open field, a deserted flatland of withering trees and shrubbery, a place where nothing thrived, except a few cacti. Willard rarely used this section of his property, a sequestered area overgrown with weeds, thistle, and scrub brush. For over twenty years Willard had worked in construction; he managed a company with two helpers, and had begun to put in extra hours after his wife died the year before from heat stroke, a freak accident for a middle-aged woman who had overexerted herself in the yard one summer afternoon while trying to plant some bushes. The tragedy had devastated Willard, so he sold what little they owned and found another place isolated in the Arizona flatlands. He made enough money to lead a good life, a quiet life filled with a moderate workload and ample reading time. He let the greenhouse remain on his property when he purchased the land. It was in poor condition but that didn't matter because he wasn't a gardener; he had no use for it then, except to store some tools and various work supplies. But now the decrepit structure had a special purpose, a reason for existing, one that Willard would finally take advantage of.

Oliver Rumson opened his eyes and felt as if he were locked in a sauna. His face and neck were crusted with dried blood, discomfort from the attack ebbing and flowing. Through the smirched panes of glass surrounding him in the confined space, the sun was ruthlessly beating down on his body, the stress on his eyes forcing him to flinch, to cower under the oppressive heat. His sweaty body felt suffocated, strangled. Encased by four thick plastic walls about an inch thick, he could only find fresh air via holes drilled in each panel: one at the top, one in back, and one in each side; their circumference sufficient for an index finger to pass through and nothing more.

Oliver's clothes were saturated. Groggy and disoriented and using his head to nudge the panel, he pushed on the wall above him, a wall only inches above his head. A chain and padlock rattled outside the compartment—he was being held in some kind of plastic trap, similar to a large pet cage but sturdier, like a magician's box, without water and deprived of oxygen. The trap of sorts was situated in the center of the greenhouse directly underneath the sun's burning path. Sweat stung his eyes, blurred his vision. He also felt a film of brine on the surface of his corneas. He started mumbling to himself. "I thin...think I'm gonna be sick...room's spinning." At the moment he was unable to ascertain where he was or who had put him there.

"That's exactly how it feels," a voice nearby said. "And you will remain as you are until you realize *why* you're here."

Oliver lay face down on the warm compartment floor, blood seeping from a rictus of broken teeth, his dry cracked lips pressing against the dirty, wet surface. "Ya...gon...kill me?" he said, his garbled words hardly distinguishable.

"Am I going to *kill* you?" the man said. "No. I don't want to end your misery—I want to prolong it. I want to find your endurance threshold." He pulled up a chair beside the container and sat, then leaned forward. "Hey...you listening to me, man? Actually, I'm not sure I should be wasting the word 'man' on you."

Oliver tried to lift his head the slightest bit, but pain splintered his neck and temple. While he fought to stay conscious, his eyes danced in their sockets, exposing the white. His assailant took out a pad and started jotting notes about his captive. He stared at the wall clock and then back at Oliver, over and over again, and scribbled little details. "Name's Willard. Stay with me," he said to Oliver. "That hot sun is mighty fierce today. This has been the most sweltering day of the year, 105 degrees. Record June high in Arizona is 122. Now...back to business. Everything I've brainstormed is going according to plan. If you want to get out of this mess you're gonna have to withstand a lot more than this."

Oliver moaned. Gagged. Coughed. His throat was painfully dry. Willard smirked. He saw Oliver's eyes closing, fatigue setting in, and he forcefully kicked the box. "*Oh. No. You. Don't.* Sleeping is not allowed. If you need to breathe you're going to have to put your lips to one of those holes. That'll keep you awake. The problem here is quite obvious: heat exhaustion has drained the life from you. Lack of oxygen is harmful to your brain and it's starting to take its toll. That's a terrible thing, isn't it? It's scary, right? And just think about that saying we all hear around the world about the 'dry heat' in Arizona. They say it's not so bad. I bet you can prove them wrong. Right, Oliver?"

Oliver groaned, louder this time, like a kid experiencing a severe stomach ache, and attempted to get up.

"That's good," Willard said. "Movement is vital to survival. It'll keep you alert, in tune with your state of mind and body and on your toes, so to speak. But if you're not careful it will consume your energy. As it stands now, you've lost *a lot* of water."

The heat in the compartment was quickly intensifying, the sun boring down on him with insufferable force. Now Oliver felt like one of the many withering plants crumbling under the sun's hot breath, losing strength, slowly succumbing to inadaptability, desperate for rations of water. With what little strength he had, he made an effort to sit up straight, but each move only made him dizzier and ratcheted up the pain; he felt as though the end were closing in.

Sandy Rumson had called Oliver's coworkers, trying to find out where her husband was. His closest friend at work, Hal, said that Oliver had left at the usual time and that his own wife, Lucy, had seen him waiting for the bus when she passed through town at 5:45 a.m. Sandy spent day and night calling friends and neighbors, Oliver's coworkers and his boss, but no new information had turned up. After twenty-plus hours of interminable phone calls, she became frustrated and called the police. It's possible that he had stopped in Holcom County for some groceries or at the tackle shop for fishing gear, she thought. He had a trip planned with his friends next week. But still something didn't seem right to her—she sensed trouble.

The policeman, tall and lanky and wearing a shirt with a badge that read "Sheriff McCall," had questioned Sandy for ten minutes. He made notes on his pad as he slowly paced the kitchen floor. He was polite yet direct. "You said he always comes home on-time, correct?"

"Yes," Sandy answered. "He works the skeleton shift on Saturday night and crashes as soon as he gets in. His work record is spotless."

"I see. You two been getting along okay lately?"

"Well, of course. Been married ten years, sheriff. We've had our ups and downs, just like everybody else, you know, but we're still standing."

"Gotcha." He flipped the page. "Does Oliver drink? Do drugs? Have any admirers? Enemies?"

Sandy shifted in her chair. With disheveled hair and without makeup, Sandy Rumson was still a stunning woman. "No," she responded, the vowel getting stuck on her tongue.

The officer sensed her discomfort but proceeded with his interrogation. He scratched his head. "No to all, Missus Rumson?"

"I beg your pardon," she shot back.

"You understand... I have to ask."

"I guess," she answered with a sigh. "Sorry, it's a touchy situation. He *used to* drink... but he quit six months ago. I told him if he couldn't straighten up on his own, I'd get him help or check him into one of those places." She crossed her legs, folded her arms in front of her. "We lead a quiet life here. Always have. Don't think he's got any enemies. It's a small town, Darleston. Everybody talks." She made a dramatic circle in the air with her finger. "If he did the whole town would know."

"And admirers?" the sheriff asked.

"Is that your way of asking if he's had affairs?"

Sheriff McCall arched his eyebrows. With her hand, Sandy Rumson wiped her face. "No way. I keep him..." A pause. "Happy."

"Thanks for your honesty, ma'am. Answering tough questions is nothing to be embarrassed about—or ashamed of. Everybody has darkness they have to face. I could write a book on that one. That's probably why I became a cop." He chuckled playfully. "I still haven't shaken all my demons. Part of my life is a fine mess. Like this for example: I'm pretty tight with my brother... but my sister keeps her distance. Don't know why. Parents think I'm too passive to be in a position of authority...yet here I am."

Sandy's eyes started to water. She failed to respond to the sheriff's comments, she had gotten lost in a daze. "I...I don't know what those fishing trips do to men...or what they're for anyway. We don't even eat fish. Oliver drank plenty on those trips; he never caught much of anything, really. Don't think he cared about that as much as he did the drinking part. Despite his getting off track sometimes," she glanced at her wedding band and nervously turned it on her finger, then looked up at their wedding picture on the dining room wall, "he's a good husband. We do all right for ourselves."

The officer managed a feeble smile, nodded. He too peeked at the photo for a moment. Oliver Rumson was a subpar looking man, not nearly as attractive as his wife. The sheriff scribbled a brief description of him on the pad. "Is it possible he went fishing today without calling? Maybe...maybe he tried calling but you didn't hear the phone?"

Sandy shook her head vehemently. "No, no. He has a trip planned for next weekend. And he *never* fishes after a late shift. Besides, his tackle box and rod are in the hall closet."

"Okay. Thank you for your cooperation." The officer scanned the room and made a few mental notes about the Rumsons' home: nothing seemed out of the ordinary, a typical middle-class house. Through a kitchen window McCall noticed a car parked in their gravel driveway, the hood open and tools scattered underneath, then spotted an open paint can next to the living room doorway, a soiled brush on top of the can. Sandy saw him looking at the items on the floor.

"That's the one thing my Oliver could be better at: finishing what he starts. He gets sidetracked sometimes. I'm trying to turn him around, but he can be... stubborn, you know? Get bored or distracted."

"How's that going for you, ma'am?"

She grinned. "'Stubborn' didn't tip you off?" A few moments of uncomfortable silence passed. The sheriff glanced at the clock on the wall and squinted. The time was not even close to accurate. Sandy had her hands in her lap; she was rubbing them together, ill at ease. "Please find him, Officer. I love him, and I want him home safely. He's my Oliver."

"I'll do my best," McCall said. "I'm sure he'll turn up soon. He probably just had a rough day and needed to be alone for a while." Sheriff McCall tipped his cap. "Good day, Missus Rumson. Stay by the phone in case we need more from you."

"Will do," she responded.

Willard got up and went to the crate, a glass of cold water clutched in his hand. He towered over his weak, helpless prisoner. "The next phase of your punishment," he said as he tilted the glass and let a stream of water trickle through the air hole above Oliver and splash the floor, "is to slurp that up before it gets horrendously warm."

Oliver looked up at Willard, his face pale and withdrawn. Willard glowered at him. "You better lick that water off the floor." He shook the empty glass in his hand. "Because you don't have the luxury of this. Be grateful you're getting a chance to drink—a chance someone else didn't get."

Desperate to stay hydrated, Oliver started licking the floor, lapping up whatever water he could get. It wasn't much of a relief but the taste of it—after being without fluids for so long—slowly began to give him torrents of energy. The tepid water was better than nothing. I'm being treated like an animal, he thought. *If I get out of here I'm going to kill Willard.*

Willard glanced at the wall clock again, then wrote something on his notebook. He wiped beads of sweat from his forehead. "Whew. It's stifling in here. A long time has passed, Mr. Rumson. If I leave you in there too long you may die... that's not the result I seek."

Oliver gave Willard a scornful look. He was going mad and trying not to faint, fearing what would happen if he lost consciousness again. If that should happen, would he ever wake up? With murky vision, Oliver watched Willard walk the perimeter of the compartment, hands folded behind his back, the body language of a curious window shopper. "Well," he said, "I think it's safe to say that you're too weakened to escape." He pulled out a key and inserted it into the padlock, turned it and released the lock: the box was open.

Oliver sat up with his back against the rear panel, his head hanging, his hair saturated, and felt a surge of fresh air. Fortunately he hadn't suffered heat stroke. Not yet. Willard walked back and forth in front of the cage, pensively stroking his chin with his index finger. "You've shown resilience and fortitude in dire circumstances. But more importantly, when this is over you'll find that I've instilled in you values you've lacked for so long: kindness and respect for humanity."

Puzzled, Oliver stared at his enemy. "Wha...what're you talking about?"

Willard sat and glared at Oliver. "You are suffering because you deserve to. And...well...your wife is going to appreciate the new Oliver Rumson." A dramatic pause. "The *wiser* Oliver Rumson."

Anger festering, Oliver responded, his voice imbued with fear. "Leave her out of this."

"Actually, Mr. Rumson. Your wife inspired me to take action. Her passiveness ignited my motivation." He pointed toward one of the windows, the clean, gleaming glass drawing in rays of intense sunlight that engulfed the cage. An antique rifle leaned against the glass beside it, polished and with bullets in the chamber. "Consider yourself lucky that I don't drag you all the way to the edge of that cliff and push you over—or do something worse."

Oliver scowled. Willard noticed the rage on Oliver's face, and smiled. "Careful now. If you get too upset you'll raise your blood pressure, and then you're in deep shit. That kind of stupidity is ill-advised." Willard reached to a nearby shelf, grabbed a bulky manila envelope, and removed the contents: photos. He pulled a pair of eyeglasses from his shirt pocket, put them on, and then appraised the first photo carefully. "Hmmm," he mumbled. "We'll start with this one." He threw a copy of the photo into the cage. "Here, follow along... if you can. We'll call that pic 'exhibit one'. I'll play judge, you play jury. Okay?"

Oliver did not respond. Apprehensively, he picked up the photo and stared at it for a long time. "Big deal." He coughed hoarsely a few times. "A picture of a meter reader. You're a voyeur. You kill her?" He rubbed his dry throat. "Rape her?"

Willard laughed heartily. "Some imagination you have, Oliver, trying to paint *me* as the bad guy, huh?" He removed his glasses and wiped them off with his shirt, then put them back on. "I see you're still disoriented, probably from dehydration." He snatched a can of warm soda from the table and rolled it into the cage. "Drink it. Maybe the photo will make more sense." He picked his nose and looked at the substance on his finger, then wiped it on his shirt. "To answer your question: no... I didn't hurt her—or kill her. I'm not a psychopath... or a murderer. Nice try, though."

Oliver picked up the can, opened it and began drinking. The warm, brackish liquid made him cringe. Willard was amused. "That rush of sugar and caffeine should take effect right away. Now examine the picture again."

Oliver tried to get comfortable in the cage, but it was impossible. To his right he saw a table on the other side of the cage panel. Atop the table lay a small pistol; he did not have the energy or the opportunity to seize it. He knew he was at Willard's mercy. "You're mad," Oliver said.

"Don't be evasive, Oliver. Just look at the fucking picture." Willard uttered these words without the slightest change in voice.

Oliver obeyed. He glanced at the picture and then looked away. "What is this all about? It's just a parked car."

Willard whipped picture number two at him. "What do you see here, Oliver? That's a better shot, don't ya think? More care was taken here. I didn't feel as rushed. The angle is more precise, the focus sharply defined."

Oliver concentrated on the photo for a few moments, his eyes moved up to meet Willard's. "You've been stalking my family?"

"No," Willard answered matter-of-factly. "What gives you that idea? I admire your keen perceptive eye, but you're off the mark."

Oliver's gaze remained fixed on Willard's. His eyes were bloodshot, his skin a grave shade of white, veins pronounced. "You're sick."

Willard grinned, exposing a few teeth. "Perhaps. But it'd be better if you thought of me simply as a concerned citizen."

"Is my wife okay?"

"Oh yes, Mr. Rumson. She's fine. This little dilemma of yours will not bring harm to your wife. But rest assured, when I'm done with you you're going to have lots of explaining to do. All that charm and charisma you use on your bar buddies is going to come in handy when you try proving your worth to Sandy. I wish I could be there for that, to see you stumble over your own words, trying to hold onto your manhood."

Oliver was fighting to stay alert. He was doing everything he could to keep his sanity yet he was too weak to lunge at his attacker or escape. "What're you going to do to me? You gonna let me out?"

"Oh yes of course," answered Willard. "But first you must face the consequences of your actions."

"You don't make sense," Oliver said. "I've done nothing wrong."

Willard pulled out another picture and scratched his temple. "Don't be so sure about that. As I see it...you're flawed, dishonest, and manipulative. And I'm going to change all of that."

Oliver was perplexed. Willard tossed another photo at his captive. Oliver did not hesitate this time; he picked up the photo and studied it thoroughly. A minute passed in utter silence then Oliver shook his head. "You're deranged. How long have you been following us?"

"I haven't been following you. Don't you listen? On the day that picture was taken, I was across the street firing off shots for a personal project of mine, a tribute to my wife—I'm a photography buff, you see. But the precious silence of the day was interrupted by a dog's barking. I turned to see where the racket was coming from. It wasn't the barking itself that stole my attention; it was the urgent sound of the bark that aroused my curiosity."

Oliver licked his cracked bleeding lips, his eyes roamed the room. Anxiety was taking hold of him with a vengeance. Droplets of sweat fell from his forehead, his neck, his nose, his chin. Willard pointed at the wall clock. "According to my calculations, you left your dog locked in your car for over two and a half hours while you got liquored up with your bar buddies at some strip joint. You didn't touch the girls, I know—but what you did do was get all worked up and then go home to your wife. You think not actually touching the dancers relieves you of wrong doing? It's disingenuous, Oliver. And how about that poor defenseless animal, huh?" Willard cleared his throat and spit on the floor. "How do ya think it felt being locked up and forgotten?"

Oliver clenched his jaw and began taking deep, exaggerated breaths, but didn't respond, didn't challenge Willard's statements—nor could he.

"You see, Oliver, the moment I saw this disgusting mistreatment of your pet my objective became quite clear: to make you experience exactly what that innocent dog did while constricted in the excruciating heat of a parked car—without air, without water, without care. Willard had used his fingers to illustrate each point, as if he were counting with his hand. Do you not know that a dog trapped in a hot car for too long can suffer permanent brain damage? The temperature in your car was well over 120 degrees. I could hardly get my finger through the opening you left in the window...you thoughtless shit. The windows were heavily smudged with sweat and saliva and traces of blood, the bodily fluids of a dog fighting tirelessly for air—for life. This kind of atrocity happens frequently nowadays, and often goes unpunished. It's the nineteen-seventies, and we haven't yet evolved as a species, have we? We haven't learned what it means to be decent. You certainly haven't, Oliver. At that time, when I saw your dog suffering, I couldn't ignore your blatant ignorance. So I followed *you*— not your wife... unlike you she's kind and compassionate. My brother told me all about her. He said she's a real class act, and I believe him. A bit gullible at times but classy nonetheless."

Oliver shook his head. Willard took out a handkerchief and wiped sweat from his forehead and neck. "Over the course of 48 hours I found out many things about you, most of which sour me. You're sort of an anomaly. You're not a rotten person, Oliver, but you *are* a careless, forgetful, and chronically neglectful son of a bitch, who needs to be put in line and understand what it means to be a good husband, a decent man. I'm willing to bet that, once you leave here, you'll be a more upstanding person who doesn't make unintelligent decisions, a man who respects and nurtures *all* living things, a man who will focus on his darling wife at home and less on booze and wasteful fishing trips with your degenerate work buddies and getting his rocks off by looking at other women. Just remember something, Oliver. Your drinkin' pals aren't the ones making your meals. Having sex with you. Cleaning the shit stains out of your underwear. Making your home a better one. Putting *you* on a pedestal. Putting *you* first. Are they? Well. Now you're going to reestablish your priorities: that lady at home—that precious dog. The reasons you said 'I do' at the altar ten years ago."

Willard stood and walked to the table at the other side of the cage. "You have endured, Oliver Rumson, and you're free to go. And when you get home and find that you're a changed man—for the better—thank your wife for tolerating you despite your faults. Be thankful that, in the wake of your terrible choices, that German shepherd of yours lived to see another day...because my wife didn't, god dammit."

Oliver mustered the strength to start making his way out of the box. Willard picked up the pistol from the table and wiped it with his handkerchief. "Depression gnaws endlessly at the human mind. It can fuck up a life, knock your thoughts and actions out of alignment. Make you do irrational things. But...but now I feel a sense of relief—of closure—and I can take the next step toward healing... fix my problems." With the pistol in his hand, Willard walked to the window and looked outside at the vast desert, the distant cliff, and kept his back to his captive. "Oh, and one more thing: Don't attempt anything stupid. Forget about retaliation. I've got eyes in the back of my head." He cocked his head to the side. "And my brother's the sheriff of Darleston." Then he pulled back the firing pin. "And if I use this, nobody will hear it out here. Now get the hell out of my sight, and consider yourself damn lucky to be alive."

GOOD INTENTIONS

Riggs' Supermarket and Wine Cellar, located in the center of Willow Square Plaza, was surrounded by a variety of businesses: laundromat, deli, craft and hardware stores. At this time of night, a quarter past ten, Riggs' was the only store still open—closing time drawing near. Few cars remained in the quiet lot. Vehicles were parked in remote corners (the staff often used the spaces closest to the building). Long-term permit users occupied the far end. The wind, moderate and steady, fluttered the flag dangling above the canopy of Riggs' entrance. The cloth snapped in the wind.

Inside the supermarket, Jason Aikman stood at the customer service counter waiting to collect his paycheck. Kelly, a tall vapid brunette, was taking her time logging the check in the supervisor's payroll journal—a requirement on payday. Jason appeared antsy, he was eager to go on a date with his girlfriend. He motioned with his hands, trying to speed up the process. . "Come on, come on, will you? I have to go, Kelly."

Kelly finished logging the check in the book and handed it to him. Jason huffed. "It's about time. I told you I had to be out of here by ten. I'm running late."

Check in hand, he left the store. Twenty-one years old, Jason had been working at Riggs' for six months and attending classes at the local community college, which had a decent and affordable automotive program; he had aspirations of becoming a mechanic. Between his small student loan and the hours he worked at the store, he could pay his bills and pursue a career. He and his girlfriend Miranda had been seeing each other for over a year. They met at a mutual friend's party, their chemistry instant. The only obstacle to overcome was their fluctuating schedules: Jason went to school during the day and worked nights. Miranda worked all day at the bank and volunteered at the animal shelter four evenings a week. Still, they made time for each other.

Jason crossed the parking lot toward his old pickup truck. A yellow car was parked three spaces behind his Chevy. He noticed a couple of stray shopping carts about eight feet from his vehicle, not at all in his way. He shook his head. "Damn it, Woody," he said. (Woody's job was to check the lot at the end of the night for loose carriages. This wasn't the first time he'd gone home without finishing his work). Jason was in a rush but, being a considerate, dependable worker, he took the initiative to push the carts into their proper storage area across from him. In the morning he would talk to Woody.

He secured the first carriage in place and just as he turned to go for the other one, it began rolling toward the yellow car. Jason tried to stop the cart from colliding with the car but it slammed into the driver's side door. Frustrated, Jason grabbed the handle and shoved the cart away from him. "Crap," he grunted. He kneeled to inspect the damage: the door was dented, the metal scratched.

From across the lot, through the darkness, Jason heard someone shout. "What the *fuck* is your problem?"

Jason turned toward the hostile voice. A tall man was coming toward him, his strides elongated and quick. "You dick, that's my car!"

Jason stood and studied the man: fortyish, ripped jeans, button shirt, and cowboy boots, his hair blond and thinning. Jason took a step back. "It's not what you think, sir. I—"

The man's hands were jittery with anger. "Don't even try to deny it, asshole. I'll pummel your ass right here."

Jason retreated a few more steps. "Hey man, this is a simple misunderstanding, an accident. The wind took the cart and—"

The man kept coming toward him. "'Accident,' my ass." He pushed Jason, knocking him to the ground. Jason's paycheck slipped out of his hand. The coarse pavement scratched his fingers.

The man towered over him. "Get up. Let's do this. Come on, pussy."

"Take it easy, all right," Jason pleaded. "I don't want a problem. I just want to fix this. I'm good with cars. I'll take care of it."

"Get up, you stupid fuck. You dent my car, I dent your face."

Jason got up and the man pushed him again. He kept his balance this time, his eyes now rounded with fear. The man rubbed his fists together, ready and eager to throw a punch. He swung and hit Jason in the face. Jason dropped to a knee then held up his arms, protecting himself in case he was struck again. "All right, prick," the enraged man said. "Now we're talking. I'm gonna—"

Jason found an opening and punched the man in the crotch, sending him to the ground howling in pain. With only a small window of time to make his next move, Jason jumped in his car and sped away. His anger and adrenaline surged inside him. As he pulled out of the lot he yelled back at the man, "Fuck you!"

Jason pulled up to the curb in front of Miranda's apartment, where she was waiting outside for him. He leaned over, pushed open the door for her, and noticed immediately that she had glanced at her watch. She got in his truck. "I'm sorry, Miranda," he said.

"What happened, Jason? You've never been this late. You had me worried."

"I know, I know," he answered, frazzled. "Believe it or not I just got into a tussle with some wacko."

"Are you hurt?" she asked, placing a hand on his shoulder.

"No, I'm fine. He only hit me once. I'll live."

Jason looked out the window, shaking his head. He didn't want to talk much more about what had transpired back at Riggs'. Miranda rubbed his neck affectionately. "I'm so glad you're all right."

He turned to her, a weak smile on his face. "Me too. Let's just get past it. We get so little time together."

They had plans to go to the scenic overlook across town and party atop Mount Caster. They stopped at a convenience store and went inside. "So, what do you have a taste for tonight, Miranda? I've got a craving for Ruffles. They're good with beer."

"I'm easy," she said. "I'll share those with you. We'll get an extra bag."

Miranda also grabbed a small packet of napkins. Jason made a funny face. "Good call. I know you can be quite the slob." Miranda playfully gave him the finger.

They placed a few small items on the counter. Jason reached into his pocket while the man behind the desk rang them up. The cashier drummed on the counter with his fingers and then glared at Miranda's breasts. She saw him admiring her chest but ignored him. "That'll be $13.75 there, sport."

Bewildered, Jason patted down his pockets. "Oh shit, Miranda. My check isn't on me. It's back at…"

The cashier gave him a weird look, as if he thought Jason were pulling a stunt to avoid paying him.

Miranda handed the clerk her own money. "Don't worry about it, Jas, I can handle this. It won't break me. At least you're a cheap date."

Jason grabbed the bag of groceries, his face flushed red with embarrassment. When they got in the car he gripped the wheel with both hands and stared ahead. He wrung his hands back and forth on the steering wheel. "My check is back in that lot. I know it! I dropped it during my run-in with that creep."

Miranda leaned toward him. "I want to know exactly what happened. We don't leave this lot until you tell me *everything*."

Jason shut off the engine and took a deep breath. His eyes scanned the interior of the car, he shifted in his seat. "I was on my way to my truck."

He hesitated, wiped his face. Miranda goaded him with her eyes. "Come on, Jason, let it out. It's okay if you're shaken up. I've never been in a fist fight before but I can certainly understand how upsetting it must be. Please, you can tell me anything. Take your time."

Jason looked outside. A man who had just finished smoking a cigarette was staring at him peculiarly on the way to his car. "Ignore him," Miranda said. "Look at me…just look at me, okay."

Tense, his fists tightened around the wheel. "I…I was putting a stupid carriage away when another one rolled into a parked car. Some idiot comes from out of nowhere all pissed off, thinking I did it."

Jason paused again and then looked up at a ripped piece of fabric dangling from the interior ceiling. Miranda placed her hand on his neck and began massaging it. "Just tell me, Jason."

He slapped the wheel, incredulous. "The asshole thinks I'm at fault so he threw a punch and knocked me on my ass. I was scared out of my mind. I feel like such a wimp. And…and…"

"Don't ever feel like less of a man. We all react in the moment, Jason. We trust our instincts. Anyway, what did you do then?"

"I got one chance, so…so I punched him in the balls. Then I got in the car and picked you up. My fuckin' paycheck got lost at some point. It's either in the lot or he has the frigging thing."

Miranda placed her hand under his jaw, turned his face gently toward hers. "It's okay. It's all over."

"No it isn't," Jason said. "I need to go back and see if my check is still there. If it's not I have to report this to my boss. I don't feel comfortable knowing that maniac could have my check, my name and address too. The thought alone makes me crazy."

"So how do you want to handle it?" Miranda asked. "Whatever you want to do, I'll help. I'm with you on this."

Jason gave her a serious look. "We have to go back and search for it."

"Are you sure, Jason? What if he's there? Then what?"

"I'll cross that bridge when I come to it."

"Can't you call your boss, tell him what happened?"

Jason glanced at the clock radio. "It's too late now. Besides, I only have the office number, not his home number."

For a few awkward seconds they stared at each other.

Jason put the car in reverse and rolled out of the space. "I'm going back."

Miranda did not respond. They pulled away from the convenience store and made their way back to Riggs' Grocery.

Jason approached the parking lot at Willow Square Plaza. He drove slowly along the shoulder, studying the area. He did not see the lunatic or his car. He turned into the parking lot. Miranda looked around too. "Where did it happen, Jason?"

He pointed toward the opposite end of a grass island. "Over there, beyond the carriage storage area."

They cruised past the storefronts, all of them dark except for one: a neon sign blinked in the window of Jake's Hardware: *Wrench Fest 1990: Ask inside for details.* After driving past two long rows of spaces, Jason made a right into the aisle where the fight had taken place; the incident was still fresh in his mind; it wouldn't dissolve anytime soon. Miranda saw the concentration on his face as anxiety took hold of him. Shocked, his eyes widened. "It's still here, Miranda…my check."

Headlamps illuminated a piece of paper on the ground in front of them, just to the left of a cement parking stop. A wind must have blown the check across the pavement. Miranda sensed his relief. He disconnected his seat belt and got out of the car. She crossed her arms and rubbed them with her hands. "Hurry," she said.

As Jason bent down to pick up his check, a car came from around the far corner. He rose to his feet and quickly got back in his car. Looking through the rearview mirror, he watched the strange car drive slowly past the stores at the front lot and then exit. He didn't recognize it.

"Who the hell was that, Jason?" Miranda asked, "especially at this hour."

Jason left right away. "I don't know and I don't want to find out. Let's just go home and call it a night."

Flex World was a popular gym just outside of Hallow County, only ten miles from Willow Square Plaza.

Working with lively animals forced Miranda to stay in shape. Sometimes she had to chase the dogs around or take them on long walks when they were acting hyper. Being physically fit had become a necessity. Miranda paced herself on the treadmill. Her friend Amy exercised beside her. She was wiping her face and neck with a towel. "Miranda, before I get going, I meant to ask you…how are you holding up?"

Miranda continued walking on the machine. "I'm doing fine. I appreciate your asking. A few weeks have changed everything, you know. Jason and I hardly talk about that night anymore."

"Sorry if I brought it up at a bad time. I'm just concerned about you guys, that's all. You've been quiet lately and I figured there must be something on your mind."

"You're sweet, Amy, thanks. But we're doing okay."

Amy put her Walkman and towel in her duffel bag and was set to leave. "See you in a few days, Miranda."

"Oh, just a second, Amy."

Amy stopped walking, turned and looked at Miranda. "Yes?"

"How about lunch Saturday afternoon?"

"Sounds like a plan. What did you have in mind?"

"We'll talk about it then, is that cool?"

"Of course. Great, I'll see you over the weekend."

"Later."

Miranda walked faster on the treadmill. A pretty blonde stepped onto the unoccupied machine on her left, and a man stepped on one to her right. The girl, wearing headphones, smiled at her. Miranda smiled back. The girl pulled one of her ear pieces away from her head and spoke. "Too many sweets yesterday," she said as she increased the speed on her treadmill.

Miranda laughed then glanced over at the guy on her right who was walking on his treadmill at a much slower pace, whereas the guy next to him was walking briskly, breathing heavily. She made eye contact with the gentleman next to her. "I know," he said, making conversation. "How much slower can one go, huh? I'm not much for cardio but I thought I'd give it a try. Think I might reconsider and tell the wife to accept me as is. Been coming here for so long, trying to lose a few and recapture the old me."

"We're both in the same club," she said. She extended her hand. "I'm Miranda."

He accepted her greeting. "I'm Brian. Brian 'Doesn't Care Anymore' McDonough."

Miranda laughed and turned the dial on her machine, increasing the intensity of her workout. "Ah, don't sweat it. You look fit to me."

"You're very kind, Miranda, and you have a nice smile, if you don't mind my saying so."

Miranda blushed. "Thank you. My boyfriend always tells me that. Now I have two members in my fan club."

Brian chuckled and draped a towel around his neck. "Anyway, I'm a salesman. I sell everything leather: pocketbooks, wallets, suitcases, bags, you name it. What do you do, Miranda?"

"Nothing that interesting," she said. "I work at a

bank all day… and volunteer at the local animal shelter in my spare time."

"Wow, that's mighty generous of you. Hey, you know what? How about I send you a free purse for helping those innocent animals?"

"Oh no, I couldn't," she said. "But thank you for the gesture." She pointed her head at her duffel bag. "I practically live out of that thing. That's all I really need."

"Gotcha. My offer would have been with no strings attached. I always have extra samples on hand, for surprise visits to clients and such."

"Oh, I know it was an innocent offer, Brian. I'm just not much of a leather person, but thanks."

His grin turned into a smirk. He dismounted the machine. "Well…I'm out of breath already," he said. "I'm getting out of this sweat pen." He pointed to the guy next to him, who was still going strong, his pace just short of a jog. The man turned toward them with sweat pouring down his intense face. Brian shook his head. "This guy's got stamina, man, and he's probably got ten years on me. Anyway, it was nice talking with you, Miranda. Take care now."

"Yeah, you too."

Miranda's apartment was on the second floor of her building. A few senior citizens lived below her. A young couple about her age lived a few doors down. She put her laundry away and took a shower. It had been a long day and, with some luck, she hoped Jason would call her tonight to get together. She glanced at the clock: 9:00 p.m.

She knew that he worked late, but in the past he had called before his shift was over if he planned to stop by. After a tiresome shift at the animal shelter, all Miranda wanted to do was relax and watch some television. Wrapped in a bathrobe, she got in bed under the covers and flipped through the channels.

For Jason, the night was coming to an end at Riggs'. The crew still had plenty of work to do in the back. He was helping his coworkers sweep the floors, cutting up cardboard boxes, and putting bags of trash in the dumpster. Over the loudspeaker Jason heard his name being called to report to the customer service desk. He handed his broom to a coworker and kindly asked him to finish where he'd left off, and then proceeded to the front of the store. As he approached the counter he saw only the clerk Kelly standing there, no one else was in the vicinity. Annoyed, Jason put his hands in the air. "Kelly, will you stop playing around with that loudspeaker, I'm trying to finish so I can go home."

Kelly huffed. "I'm not playing, Jason. You always think I'm up to something."

"You usually are," he said.

"Look, Jason, I'm telling you. There was a guy here a minute ago looking for you. He just left, didn't say too much."

Jason's face reddened. "What was his name, Kelly?"

"He mumbled something but I didn't catch it. Everything happened so fast."

"Maybe if you stopped reading those damn magazines and started paying more attention, you'd actually remember things."

Kelly got snippy. "Maybe if you didn't take so long getting here—"

"Oh, come on, Kelly, I came right away. Don't make excuses for your screw ups."

She rolled her eyes. "Whatever."

"That's your answer to everything: 'whatever'. How about saying something more intelligent?"

Kelly gave him a dirty look.

"Did you at least get a good look at him, Kelly?"

"Again, negative. I'm not your personal secretary. I was reading *Star*. This issue's full of scandals."

The oddity of the moment made Jason feel nervous again. He had an idea who had come. *Is that guy still mad over the car? If so, why would he wait weeks to confront me again?* Since the incident, security had been hired to patrol the lot every night. Right away he called Miranda, who was glad to hear his voice. "I was just thinking about you. Can you come over later?"

"Maybe. Look, there's something important I have to ask you?"

"What is it?"

"Did you have somebody ask for me at work? A friend... anybody?"

"No. Of course not, babe. Why? Are you okay?"

"Yeah, I'm fine. Or how about your friend from the shelter, little Stevie, the kid who wanted me to fix his car two weeks ago, the guy I said I'd help when I had some spare time. How about him?"

"No, Jason. What's going on?"

"Some guy came looking for me at work, and when I came out to see who it was he was gone. That idiot Kelly doesn't remember shit. No name, no face, nothing. To be honest, I didn't get a clear look at him that night. I don't think I'd recognize him if I saw him again. His image is a bit fuzzy in my mind."

"Do you think it's…?"

"I'm not sure. Everything's been calm lately but you never know."

"What're you going to do?"

"As soon as I finish up here, I'll shoot over to your place. We can sort this out together."

"Great idea, Jason."

"I love you, Miranda." Jason kissed the phone.

"I love you too, Jason. I can't wait to see you."

They hung up. Miranda looked at the clock. He'd be over soon so she decided to change clothes, put some soup on the stove for him (he was always hungry after work), and wait patiently. She walked over and checked her door, made sure it was locked, just to feel safer.

In the kitchen, she opened the cabinet and pulled out a can of chicken soup (one of Jason's favorite meals) and placed a saucepan on the stove—he would arrive to a nice warm dinner. She couldn't help wondering who had come to see him at work. The world wasn't short on practical jokers either (most of Riggs' staff were wise-asses). She also knew that her friend Stevie had a tendency to be a pain in the ass, especially when it came to his car. He also had a big mouth but wouldn't have left the store without talking Jason's ear off had he stopped in.

These thoughts were revolving in her mind.

Miranda walked over to the stove and stirred the simmering soup. Afterwards, she made her way to the bed, removed the towel from around her head and dried her hair. She wanted to get dressed: a pair of jeans and a shirt would do just fine. She walked across the floor and opened her closet door. Someone socked her in the face and she collapsed.

When Miranda opened her eyes she had no way of knowing how much time had passed. The reality was beyond nightmarish: she was sitting on the floor tied with a cable to a bed post. The intruder was standing above her with a tire iron, and, worst of all, where was Jason? His soup had boiled over on the stove and soiled the counter, splashed onto the floor. Miranda's left eye was swollen. Pain hammered her head. Her vision was hazy at best. To her right was an open bottle with strange pills inside. The voice she heard above her sounded familiar. "That's right, look at them, honey, because you're going to be swallowing them…*all* of them."

Miranda looked up at him through her good eye. She recognized his face: the man from the gym—Brian— towered over her. Suddenly she was having trouble focusing, and felt on the cusp of fainting. Her attention drifted back to the bottle. Out of the blue, a cold steel rod was thrust underneath her chin, the sharp end poking her throat. "There's no way around it, you sexy thing. Swallow them all." The smoothness of his voice haunted her.

Tears streaked Miranda's face. Her swollen eye pulsed more intensely now. Her heartbeat became wilder and more erratic. Words rushed through her mind: *Hurry up, Jason. Where the hell are you? I can't hold on much longer.*

Approximately a mile and a half away, Jason was on his way, ready to put that troublesome night behind him. Eager to see Miranda, he was heavy on the pedal, driving fifty-five in a forty mile-per-hour zone. Needing more time to think, he decided not to listen to the radio. Coming toward him, in the opposite lane, was a large truck, its lights bright and overpowering, blinding. Jason lowered his visor to shield his eyes, but, as it passed him, his focus on the road diminished, forcing his car to skitter. Something exploded under his car: glass splintered under his tire. Shards of a broken bottle sprayed everywhere. A blowout forced him to the shoulder. "What the hell!" he shouted. He pulled off the road and began changing the tire.

All the lights had been turned off in her apartment except for a lamp. The intruder bent down to Miranda's level on the floor and looked her in the eyes. "What're you waiting for? Swallow… and I leave."

She reached out and wrapped her shaking fingers around the bottle of pills. "Al…most… there," he said, taunting her.

Miranda glanced up at him again, her lips quivering, her throbbing eye almost completely swollen shut. She realized she was running out of choices. Brian jabbed her other eye with the iron bar and she yelped in pain. He pointed sternly at the pills. "Don't stall me. You're prolonging this, not me…unless?" He rubbed his crotch and smiled. "You get some of this. That can be arranged."

Miranda's focus was dwindling rapidly, her will to hang on fleeting. She looked down at the numerous pills in the bottle and hated to imagine how her life would end, which method of suffering would feel worse: taking mysterious pills, or having this lunatic inside her. In a moment of sheer, unrelenting terror, Miranda came to terms with the only way out and did what she had to do.

Jason finished changing the tire, got back in his car, and glanced at his watch. "Shit, I'm so late." He blazed down the highway, pissed that, once again, he'd gotten side-tracked. He pulled up in front of her house, hurried to the front door and entered. The lights in the lobby, usually on a timer, had been turned off. He carefully climbed the steps leading to the second floor. The odor of dog feces pervaded the lobby (probably Mrs. Lambert's poodle). He proceeded quietly as possible, being careful not to wake the whole apartment complex.

Jason knocked gingerly on Miranda's door, cautious once again not to tap too hard and disturb anyone. There was no answer. He tapped again. "Miranda?" he whispered. "Come on, open up, it's me," he said, his tone muffled. Still nothing.

Impatient, he jiggled the knob and the door squeaked open. Miranda's lamp was on and, without having to take another step, he found her unconscious on the floor. She was face down, her robe still covering her body, her arms twisted: the left one pulled backward, the right contorted in the cable. Blood-streaked foam was seeping from her mouth. To her left, on the carpet, was the empty pill bottle. Jason picked it up and examined the label: He couldn't understand the description. He couldn't even pronounce the name on the bottle—smudges concealed the letters. He shook Miranda but she was unresponsive. He ran to the phone and called 911. An ambulance was on the way.

He ran to the bathroom and got a wet rag and began cleaning her face, removing the froth from her mouth. With a kitchen knife he cut the cables from her wrist and tried to get her comfortable until the paramedics arrived. Behind him he heard a noise, and turned. The stove was still on, the flame still hissing. Jason immediately shut it off. Finally, he heard sirens wailing, help now just moments away.

On a night stand beside the window he noticed Miranda's answering machine message light blinking. He went over to the table and pushed the button. An electronic voice began speaking. *Saturday, 11:03 p.m., you have a new message*: A man's voice, even-toned and smooth: "I'd say we're even now, Aikman. You dent my pride and joy, and I dent yours. Miranda won't die. She's young and healthy. You should've seen her at the gym. Very impressive. A real sweetie, a *loyal* one too. Most ladies can't resist my charms but you got yourself a real keeper. No worries, by the way. She's sleeping off an overdose of animal sedatives. They'll wear off in an hour or two, or the medics can work their magic and speed things up. I

145

had to get everything off my chest.   You'll never hear from me—or find me—again, unless you dare to."

DEVOURED

When Scott opened his eyes, total darkness seized him, enveloped him. His skin crawled with a rash from the frigid air of ferocious and persistent gales. *Where am I? What's wrong with me? What the hell is this?*

Another blast of wind slapped his face, forcing him to turn his head away from the beating it was taking. He cleared the haze from his eyes and looking up, saw a sky splashed with a blur of stars and a chilling, skulking, crescent-shaped moon. Scott felt indefinable fear and a twisting, wrenching pain in his gut; it was as though he'd swallowed a ball of needles. Clutching his abdomen, Scott braced himself, certain the affliction would worsen. Both sweaty palms had rubber underneath them, soft and smooth to touch. His fingers probed for a place to secure a hold, but found no such handle, no grip. Something struck his hand with tremendous pressure, wedged his fingers against the rubber and tore open the skin. As the left side of whatever it was rose high and crashed down, he panicked. The collision diverted his attention, however briefly, from the stabbing sensation in his belly, overwhelming him with a new set of problems. The danger escalated. He was bouncing on rough waves, spinning out of control on a raft, abandoned in the dark ocean. This was too much to fathom at once. He had no chance to think about what was going on or who was to blame for these deadly circumstances.

This had been his and Brianna's first cruise together, their honeymoon getaway. They boarded the vessel *The Queen of the Seas* in the Port of New York and were en route to the Grand Cayman Islands. That had been his wife's island of dreams to visit. They had been putting aside extra vacation money for a long time. Brianna's sister Maggie offered to defer some of the costs—her wedding gift to them, a substantial amount, more than she could likely afford. They accepted her offer and off they went.

Just a week before they left, they had enjoyed the fun gatherings their friends had organized for them— bachelor and bachelorette parties. They received additional gifts—money which they planned to use as pocket cash on their vacation.

Scott tried to ignore the pain and think of Brianna. He hoped she was okay, that whoever plotted all of this didn't hurt her too. Just the thought of harm coming to his precious Brianna increased the pain spiking inside him. Scott sat helplessly as his position in the vast ocean shifted dramatically. The moon distanced itself. The constant swells of the turbulent seas formed a barricade he couldn't breach. His raft rocked violently. His body lurched back and forth. Bugs started nibbling on his flesh. At first he was assailed by intermittent pinches then within a matter of seconds their feasting grew more intense. He heard a swarm closing in to attack, more and more of them kept coming with insatiable appetites for warm blood. He heard their wings whirring around him, a maddening sound. He couldn't escape. Though his limbs were alive with a venomous burn, Scott could hardly endure the sting of the bites. Within minutes a fiery itching began spreading all over his flesh.

Nowhere could he see the lights of the cruise ship. They had left him behind like a worthless piece of bait. *The Queen of the Seas* was long gone, had disappeared, never to return. By this time, he had surrendered to the malevolent bugs. Cold, salty water splashed over the rim of the raft, saturating his body. The sediment stung his eyes. He feared the raft would soon become deluged with water and tip over. What if it did? What if he was washed over and could not find his raft in the blackness? It would be impossible for him to swim for long. Without a vest he would soon be submerged in a dark abyss of death.

Scott attempted to steer himself through the choppy waters but was repeatedly forced in a different direction; the wind and waves stymied his every move. He failed to find even a simple groove, a momentum of any kind. He had no defense against the ruthless sway of the hostile currents. He had no idea how far he'd gone or exactly where he was, but what little strength and determination he had were fading swiftly.

The bugs had stopped snacking on his flesh. For how long, though, he didn't know. Scott refused to stop paddling, hoping that land awaited him somewhere. He dunked his hands into the cold water, stroked away at the percolating sea with bursts of raw energy. He was laboring on sheer adrenaline—it was all he had left to do battle with. He dredged back palmfuls of water, one after another for what seemed like hours, although only minutes had passed. His meager progress was not enough to save him. What was the alternative? Floating in the dark depths of the ocean, relying on someone to rescue him? These thoughts were insufferable.

Scott's arms started to feel the pain from his war against the mad ocean. His joints were cramping. He leaned back and tried to relax in the tiny space he had. Drained of energy, his muscles had surrendered to a paralysis of sorts, quivering from being unconditioned, and now overworked. His eyes felt heavy. He remembered Brianna nagging him about his ability to nod off anywhere. She never let that one go. But he knew she was right. He could sleep in the middle of a Nascar race with engines blazing hundreds of miles an hour. Scott missed her teasing now. *Will I ever see her again? What is she doing now? Thinking of me?*

The bugs returned for another meal. Maybe their appetites were heightened by Scott's pungent body odor, the perspiration brought on by clawing to stay afloat. One of the bugs landed on his neck and sank its pinchers into his wet flesh. He grumbled in pain. The sons of bitches were relentless. He realized the more he swatted them away the more the tube wobbled like a top—so he gave in. It's only bugs and some rough waves, he thought. Not a shark. The thought of confronting one of those razor-toothed man-eaters only added a new level to his fear.

His uncontrollable thoughts took him back to places he dreaded thinking about—most recently aboard the cruise ship. He would've preferred to reflect on the glorious time they were having and where they were headed, across the seas under a glimmering sun, on their way to the Grand Cayman Islands, where they could savor the rewards away from life's monotonies.

Scathing images entered his mind; he couldn't chase them away. He saw Brianna in a form-fitting flowery dress (supposed to be for his pleasure only) leaning against the railing on the top deck of the ship, twirling her beautiful golden curly hair while speaking cheerfully to one of the Spanish deck hands next to a lifeboat. He ignored it then—thought not a damn thing about it. She had the right to talk with other men. It was harmless enough at the time, but recalling it now completely destroyed his state of mind. What were they talking about? Why was she so giddy? He knew the signs she exhibited when she found a man attractive, remembered them from when they had first met, and they were all on display then. Why were these damn flashbacks tormenting him now?

Scott was infuriated. He recalled the first day of the cruise when they had run into the Latino fellow at the main gate. He charmed the pants off Brianna. She giggled like a little girl with each word he said and remarked how much she adored his accent. At the end of the conversation they had spoken a few words in Spanish, which Scott did not know. He wanted to pretend these were innocuous visions.

Sorting through the cluster of undesirable images was not something he could deal with rationally now. His head snapped up. Awake, he heard the bugs fluttering around his skull in a dizzying dance, preparing to feed again until they drained his body of life. Something smacked into the raft and tossed him over and into the cold water. His arms cycled furiously to keep him from drowning; and in the struggle he lost contact with the raft. Scott kicked his legs frantically. But soon he would tire, and reality would force him to confront a horror like no other.

Something brushed up against his feet underwater. He jerked his leg, shook it off. It pecked at him again and again. Each painful bite felt as though he'd stepped on a pile of broken glass. The waves sloshed into him, rolled over him, submerged him.

A short distance away he heard splashing, followed by a *crunch*. It sounded like a piece of plywood snapping in half. Was that a shark shredding a seal to pieces? Was there something out there that became chum for the creatures below the surface of the undulating water? He started blubbering like a defeated soul; eventually his cries became shrill and infused with pure terror. He lurched ahead, feeling for the raft—nothing. He lunged in a different direction—nothing. No tube, no driftwood—zilch. His strength was shrinking quickly. He tried to catch his breath—inhaled, exhaled—inhaled, exhaled—gasping for air however he could get it. His legs and arms had become limp and useless. This was not how he wanted to die. He didn't want to die at all, but death was ready to ruthlessly snatch him away. He cupped his hands, stroked the water, and fought against the mighty rolling sea. Everything was failing, faster and faster. There was nobody to stop it—certainly not Brianna. He wondered if she was devastated, missing him?

The water level rose; surges of it crept into his mouth. Swallowing too much too fast caused him to gag. His lungs were overworked and rebelling. He was sinking and he knew it. The unstable ocean was sucking him in, yanking him down with merciless, indefensible pressure. He kicked his legs one last time, giving himself one last chance to live, to breathe, to see his wife again, if it were at all possible. But his legs and his body were downright useless now, worn and atrophied. The mischievous sea was opening its jaws, swallowing him whole like quicksand. An image of Brianna flashed in his mind and then disappeared in a nanosecond. As Scott began sinking like a human anchor, the last thing he saw was the fading light of the devious moon.

The early sun poured through the windows of *The Queen of the Seas* with a bright, majestic splendor. Cabin #864 had the curtains half drawn but a stream of light still found its way through the balcony sliders and glinted off a pair of high heels and women's underwear. The occupants were tangled together in bed, moaning and groaning. Salsa music played at a low volume. A pair of white coveralls hung wrinkled over the top of the closet door. Black work-boots sat on the floor underneath.

"Oh Pablo," the lady gasped in the heat of pleasure. "Oh my God. Don't stop. Don't ever tell anyone."

Pablo worked harder, caressing her body, feeling her curves. He pulled her hair and kissed her neck sensuously; each move aroused her more. A rough wave hit the ship and rattled the dresser drawers. The coveralls slid to the floor. The two of them continued making love despite the unsteady ship.

On deck #2 the ship's crew searched for Pablo, who had vanished the night before, neglecting his duty. His co-worker had called him numerous times on the walkie-talkie. The calls went unanswered. A few of the crew spread out and searched for him, careful not to draw attention from passengers. Mario, one of Pablo's workmates, did a thorough walkthrough of the bottom deck, where only authorized employees had access with a key card. Pablo had one of them. He had been there a few times during the night. They found his duffel bag filled with a change of clothes and other assorted belongings in one of the recreation rooms. When they opened the door to Storage Room B, Mario discovered a few missing items. Someone had taken a spare access key from the lock-box and one of the black safety rafts used on ocean drills. Mario walked the vessel, looking for his missing employee.

The radio attached to Mario's shirt pocket buzzed. He hit the button and listened. "Boss, it's me, Pablo. I fall asleep, make problem for you. I sorry. I come to work now."

Brianna put on her robe and walked into the ray of sunlight, pulling open the curtains all the way. The beaming morning sun greeted her. She approached Pablo as he put on his coveralls, wrapped her arms around him and kissed him, inserted her tongue deeply into his mouth for the last time, saying goodbye in a way he'd never forget.

Pablo whispered in her ear. "I hope good life for you, my love. You start new, get good man. I never say nothing to nobody. I promise."

Pablo returned to work. Brianna sat on the edge of

the bed. The smile of elation she wore so proudly minutes ago had faded. Tears began to flow. She pulled up a wad of bed sheets and wiped her face. Then she glanced at the closet across the cabin where her bags were stored. Face red and wet, Brianna rose from the bed and ambled over to the closet, dragging a trail of sheets behind her. No matter how hard she tried, she couldn't stop crying; the sun coming through the glass sliders on the balcony highlighted her tear-stained face.

The sky was a painting, an enchanting shade of blue. Each airy cloud seemed cleverly placed. From inside the room she heard footsteps shuffling down the hall. Vacationers were scurrying around to start the day. The breakfast crowd was making their way to the main deck to crowd the buffet lines. But room # 864 harbored a different scene. Curled up in a ball, Brianna sat in front of the open closet door with an overnight bag in her lap. She cried harder, harder than she had ever cried before. Tear drops flecked her hand bag. Her open mouth had threads of saliva joining the lips together. She was a horrible mess.

She began unzipping the bag. Her hands shook. She was aware of what she was going to find inside but opened it anyway. She needed justification for her rendezvous with the Latin deckhand. She had the urge to find reasoning in the horrible thing they had done in the wee hours of the morning when the ship was quiet and the other passengers were nestled in their beds. Brianna believed her actions were warranted. She thought of herself as a battered woman of sorts. Maybe others wouldn't believe her, but she was prepared to prove herself in any way she could.

Brianna pulled out the photos from the slot in her purse and held them in front of her face. The contents revealed a harsh truth. That was definitely Scott in the photos, days before their wedding. He couldn't go to the bachelor party and be a man, could he? Instead he had become a shameful little boy who had no idea that she was watching closely—and taking pictures—and would one day bare her vengeful face, the one Scott had never seen before.

How dare he fuck that stripper! All my years of staying pretty for him and it still wasn't enough. That evil prick! Less than two days on the ship and he couldn't stop flirting. He had no idea what I was capable of, that deceptive, no good, cheating asshole. I showed him. Maybe he shouldn't have gotten drunk and taken a raft when he knew he couldn't swim well. That's what I'll tell his gullible family back home. Stupid asses could never unravel this mystery—or any other for that matter. I won't tell them the rest. Pablo really came through.

When she appraised the final picture, she covered her mouth trying to hold back last night's liquor, a result of the vodka tonics she and the deckhand had shared. The next photo was even more painful to look at. She would never have forgiven this one, not in any lifetime. The humiliation ate through her like acid: that sleazy stripper going down on Scott in the bathroom—the window fogging up from his heavy breathing, the ecstasy in his eyes. *He never had that look with me. How much of our money did he pay that slime? How could he?*

Brianna ripped up the photos, sank to the floor, and wept. She had done what she had set out to do. The initial shock would soon wear off—and her life would be hers again.

LACUNA

Gazing out at his sprawling backyard and sipping his tea as the sun beamed through the sliding windows, Barton Williams analyzed the unevenness of the privet hedges lining the fence at the outermost end. The gardener had done maintenance only two weeks ago, but until now Barton hadn't seen for himself the imperfections, the untrimmed spikes standing crookedly atop his precious shrubbery. Why hadn't he noticed this before today?

"Morning, Bart," his wife said as she came into the kitchen, her blonde hair tied in a bun, her robe dragging the floor. "You're running late, aren't you? And don't forget about your pills on the table when you leave. Doc Weinstein said to take five a day. That'll keep your condition in check."

Barton heard his wife's comments, and responded by laughing under his breath. He finished his tea, rinsed the glass, and dried it with a towel, then put it back in the cabinet. His wife watched him rather scrupulously. Barton took one last look at the unfinished work on the bushes. "Gloria, call the gardener and have him shape the hedges the way he's supposed to—the way I like them."

Gloria was removing a frying pan from the cabinet, and as she turned around to face Barton, she arched her brow. "I thought you were happy with Raymond's work." She folded her arms in front of her and grinned, bringing a quizzical look to her face. "You tipped him a hundred dollars, Barty…a hundred dollars," she reiterated, putting emphasis on the word *hundred*.

Barton removed his wallet from his trousers, pulled out two hundred-dollar bills, and placed them on the counter. "Tell him I'll double his money if he gets it done today. Any problems, call me at the office." He put his wallet in his jacket, which lay on the kitchen chair. "We've always been good to Ray. I'm sure he'll take care of this right away."

"Whatever you want," Gloria said, "whatever makes life easier." She resumed cooking.

Barton pulled back his shirt cuff. "No watch? Darn it!" After a fleeting glance at the kitchen clock, he grabbed his jacket and walked toward the front door. "Gotta go. Be home early today."

Setting a plate on the table for herself, Gloria faced Barton and took a bite of a piece of bacon. "Great news, what's the occasion?"

Barton opened the door. Before stepping onto the porch, he paused in the doorway, allowing himself a few seconds to savor the sight of the azure sky, the vibrant sun—signs of a promising new day. "I'm the boss, aren't I? I can take liberties. As long as my workload is caught up, I can spend some time with my wife, right?"

As Barton left the house, he winked at Gloria. She returned his smile and mouthed, "I love you."

Barton was crossing the driveway to get in his car. He draped his tweed jacket over his shoulder and without his realizing it, his wallet slipped out of the pocket and fell on the lawn. Eager to get his work done so he could leave the office early, he got into his car and drove away.

In the Williamses' kitchen, Gloria's breakfast had become a mess; grease splattered her and the stove, her eggs had overcooked and clung to the pan. She pushed the pan off the flame, then hurriedly went to the table by the front door and picked up the bottle containing Barton's pills, which she had told him not to forget. By the time she got outside to give them to him, Barton was long gone. She immediately called his office and left a message, reminding him. *What's gotten into him?*

Barton adored the community of Woodsworth. Everything and everyone in it infused him with a small-town feeling, even though Woodsworth itself was rather large and citylike. Parks, ranch-houses, small mom-and-pop markets, quaint cafés—these were the highlights of Woodsworth, the common landmarks that warmed his heart and soul. Once his real estate firm had become successful years ago, he and Gloria had moved to Woodsworth to live a peaceful, normal life, a life far away from the hectic suburbs of Los Angeles, where they had been unable to get comfortable, no matter how much time and energy they invested. The Williamses were financially secure, but preferred living modestly. Their neighbors thought of them as kind and unpretentious, an upstanding couple. A man who understood money and how to spend it carefully, Barton provided most handsomely for his family. He had a daughter, Allison, who lived on campus at a prestigious college on the west coast. Allison had always been his little girl, his only child. When she had gone off to college to begin life on her own, she made friends on campus rather quickly, called home less often and sent fewer letters, leaving Barton no choice but to wonder if her newly-found independence would eventually diminish the loving bond they'd shared over the years—a possibility that pained him.

To keep his mind off this inevitable change, he participated in more constructive affairs, maintained a busy schedule. A philanthropist, Barton donated generously to local charities, a few of which his wife had been overseeing and drawing awareness to: The Literacy Foundation, The War Veterans' Fund, and the Obsessive Compulsive Disorder Foundation—OCD was Barton's affliction.

Not long ago his life had changed; he discovered troubling evidence that something was psychologically amiss. Occurrences that were subtle and easy to control at first later became accumulative and dominant. His life was hindered by what seemed to be more than just ordinary idiosyncrasies: repeatedly removing lint from his clothes, constantly straightening his tie, brushing his teeth six times a day (his dentist had told him that constant brushing was overkill but Barton ignored the advice), over and over again checking the contents of his wallet, and counting his money and reviewing his credit cards for fading. He never thought of his actions as life-ruining oddities. He did, however, want to curtail these ongoing quirks.

The pills he had at home—the bottle he had forgotten to take with him—was a prescription his wife's doctor had written for him without having conducted an extensive examination. The medication, a generic drug which relieves anxiety and compulsion, is often administered to patients with similar impairments. With Barton's connections and reputation, he could generally get what he wanted without resistance, without a fuss, without anyone knowing. While on vacation a few months back, Barton sought something to get him though a rough bout of acute, debilitating anxiety. With his doctor out of town on business, he decided to ask Gloria's doctor for a prescription; the physician wrote him one. For a week or so Barton had been battling the side-effects of the drugs: periodic nausea and drowsiness among other ailments. Sometimes the drugs themselves made him sickly, but being medicated was the tradeoff to his edginess and compulsive behavior. Despite the setbacks, he was determined to persevere, to find the perfect balance.

As Barton drove through the business district he passed a convenience store and pulled over, needing something to drink. Although he had no drugs in his bloodstream, his body had already acclimated itself to the medicine and he was reeling. The effects taunted him. His mouth felt cottony and grainy, his tongue sandpapery. When he got out of the car he forgot to lock the door (he had never forgotten to double-check the locks) and went inside. If Gloria were with him she would have been shocked by his series of mistakes, his inability to focus.

Inside the store he wrestled with pangs of guilt and despondency. Not only had he chosen not to take his pills, but he was irked that he had driven to the store by speeding excessively, an act of carelessness and irresponsibility; his conscience gnawed at him. What was his problem? Why was his mind faltering? Was all this nothing more than a disjointed dream? But it was much too real to be imagined or dreamt, he thought.

Barton stared at his polished shoes and felt his heart palpitating. Should I take the medicine as advised? Would a quick fix put an end to this emotional overload? Questions without answers assaulted him. Sure, he had been trying to get off the pills, but how far could he go? How much mental hardship could he endure? This strange day had become a test he had unwittingly accepted.

As he stood in the aisle searching the shelves of soft drinks, he began to perspire profusely. Using his hand, Barton groped his neck and forehead, his skin felt warm and tacky. The store had adequate air-conditioning, yet he felt feverish and withdrawn. Why out of the blue was he experiencing a heightened state of anxiety exceeding anything he'd grappled with before?

Suddenly, timing impeccable, he remembered stashing pills (two or three) in a plastic sandwich bag in the watch-pocket of his pants, just in case he found himself getting overly tense. Buoyed by a gust of relief, he cracked a smile, baring his healthy white teeth. The mere thought of having an option lifted his spirits. The doctor had recommended a dosage of two capsules, even though one alone would suffice. Just a single pill—so small yet so potent—would extricate him from another crisis. His heartbeat would return to normal, his sweating would cease, and his whirlwind thoughts would be extinguished. Anxious to feel good again, he reached into his pocket to get the bag—No pills. "Oh, damn," he mumbled.

Barton's hands started twitching. Blood swarmed to his head. And as he looked around the store, unbridled gloom seizing him, he detected something perturbing: the store manager had a keen eye on him, as if he were about to shoplift—or do something worse. Barton's smile faded. His pulse soared. His thirst became damn near unbearable. He opened the refrigerator and pulled out a bottle of water, unscrewed the cap and took a sip. Unbeknownst to him, the cooler had only recently been replenished, and the water tasted tepid. Barton grimaced. "This is absurd," he grunted.

Standing in line, he stared menacingly at the cashier, although she had nothing to do with his dissatisfaction. In Barton's state of mind such logic did not matter. He was not in a reasoning mood. Three customers were ahead of him; a long line had formed behind him too. Uneasy and jittery, he loosened his tie. The line hadn't budged. He could feel the overhead lights beating down on him, intensifying his sweating. At the main entrance he saw a young lady coming in with her small child sleeping on her shoulder, its thumb in its mouth. Something in Barton triggered a smile, though the stiffness of his mouth could hardly be called such. And even though the image of the sleeping baby conjured up positive thoughts, it did nothing to alter his disposition.

Barton stood only second in line. The customer in front of him had required a price check, a delay that quickly compounded his misery. Feeling overheated and constricted, he undid the top button of his shirt, exposing his wet, glistening skin; his neatly-combed brown hair had fallen out of place and looked untidy. If Barton had been able to see his messy hair, he would have immediately combed it. He would have stood in front of a mirror and meticulously finessed every strand until his hair was exactly as he wanted it, but more pressing matters negated the urge.

The store manager *had* been watching him from a distance. Little did he know that the real Barton Williams couldn't—or wouldn't—do anything unethical, didn't possess the makings of a troublemaker or a criminal.

Barton's turn in line had finally come. He approached the register and slammed the half-empty bottle of water on the counter. The cashier saw the beads of sweat on Barton's forehead, her face reddened with trepidation. She swallowed, nervously licked her lips, and greeted Barton. "Can I help you, sir?"

Handkerchiefs were displayed on the rack next to the register. Barton removed one from the counter and wiped his face. "I want my money back."

The teenage cashier scratched her forehead. This wasn't the first time she'd had tough customers or complaints. She fidgeted with a ring on her middle finger, one of many on her manicured hand. "But you didn't buy anything yet...and you did drink that water without paying first. That'll be a dollar-five, sir—and ninety-nine cents for the handkerchief."

Barton blinked thrice. His foot tapped the floor with rapidity. He bent his neck to loosen a kink. "I was terribly thirsty. Had no choice. I had every intention of paying—until I swallowed a mouthful of *bathwater*."

"Sir, that happens from time to time," the girl said. "The refrigerator is set to the correct temperature, I assure you...sometimes the stock is not rotated properly, but that's beyond our control."

Barton bit his lip, clenched his jaw. "Beyond your control, huh? I beg to differ."

The cashier adjusted her glasses. "Please pay me for the items. I've got a long line." Her eyes darted toward the far side of the counter, and then refocused on Barton. "And my boss is watching me."

Barton laid the bottle on the counter, label facing up. "Read the fine print here, will you? You can read, can't you?" Barton's tone had risen just enough to rattle her; she sighed. Customers behind Barton had huffed numerous times but he ignored them. The manager, sensing trouble, came to the counter. "Is everything okay here, Kimberly?"

As the girl started explaining what was happening, Barton interrupted her. "She's denying me a refund...so I asked her to read the label on the bottle, and she completely disregarded my request."

The manager tried to solve the problem. He nodded at the cashier, urging her to read the label, to placate the customer.

Barton wiped the label with the handkerchief. "Follow along with me now," he said. "The fine print clearly states: 'if for any reason you are unsatisfied with this product, simply return the bottle to your nearest retailer.'" Barton pointed condescendingly at the store manager—"that would be you"— 'for a full refund.'"

The cashier glanced at her boss, who seemed baffled, at a loss for words.

Barton was chewing his tongue. "Now," he asked, "can we settle this?"

The manager removed his glasses, wiped his face. "Look...uh...you're absolutely right, sir. This is my fault." He scanned his corporate card in the machine and the water rang up gratis. He knew that Barton had also taken the handkerchief without paying but he didn't question him, nor did he want to prolong the confrontation. "Have a good day, sir," he said and walked away.

Barton was unresponsive. He made his way toward the exit. On both sides of the door stood large trash barrels and magazine stands. As he passed the barrels on his way to the parking lot, he tossed his bottle of water and the handkerchief into one of them. He shoved open the exit door but didn't hold it open for the customer behind him. "This damn place," he mumbled. "Never coming back here again."

Barton's secretary, Sheila, answered the phone at his office. "He has not arrived yet, Mrs. Williams. He may have stopped for groceries for the break room. He restocks the cupboards at least twice a week. His first meeting's not until 9:30. The last thing scheduled for today is an eleven o' clock with John Hall, his lawyer."

While talking, Gloria fingered the phone cord and straightened a picture on the wall in the main hallway. "Could you please have him call me as soon as he gets in, Sheila? He forgot something at home, and I want to know if he'd like to come get it or have me bring it to him."

The secretary giggled. "Barton forgot something, Mrs. Williams? That would be a first."

Gloria laughed as well. "Well, Sheila, that day has finally come."

"Mrs. Williams, I'll have him contact you as soon as he sets foot in the office, okay?"

"Thank you, Sheila. Have a nice day, now."

Hanging up the phone, Gloria went to the bedroom. As she opened the door she saw a pair of Barton's shoes sitting on the bed. He had never left his clothes on the furniture. His belongings, especially his clothes, had always been stored neatly in their spacious closet. She picked up his shoes and put them on a shelf in the closet, where she saw a wad of cash inside a sneaker. Examining the wad more closely, she realized it was Barton's money-clip holding together a roll of bills. Her discovery engendered a series of thoughts. What has gone wrong? This forgetfulness is completely out of character. And now he's gone to work without money? What'll I find next? The one thing she was certain about she said aloud: "He better get back on those pills."

About a mile or two from the office, Barton pulled off the road and tried to compose himself; his mind was whirling. Drenched in sweat and shaking was no way to start the day. He hoped his condition would not deteriorate further, but he had little reason to be encouraged; his body for some time now had been rebelling in myriad ways.

After leaving the store earlier, he had taken the

same roads he had traveled in the past to get to work. However, after following his usual route, he found himself riddled with uncertainty. He wasn't entirely sure if he had read the street signs correctly; he was positive, however, that they looked different. Had his vision blurred or deceived him? Or had his judgment been clouded?

Barton wiped sweat from his face and neck, and tried to level his breathing. He peered across the shoulder into the woods about fifty feet away, an expanse shrouded by thriving evergreens and miscellaneous shrubbery. Rich color was in full display. The vigorous sun shining through the apertures in the crowns of the trees had carved paths through ground-level foliage. In a moment of reflection, Barton lost himself in the scenery, nature's dazzling show. About fifty feet beyond wood's edge he saw the eyes of a deer (Allison's favorite animal) peering at him through the crotch of a felled tree. The sight rewarded him with a modicum of relief, precious seconds he wished he could have frozen. He had made a donation in Allison's name to the Wildlife Foundation before she left home for school. Why hadn't he thought to tell her about it before now?

A knock on the driver's side window snapped his concentration. He turned. An officer was standing by his door, his shiny metal badge staring him in the face. Barton lowered the window. A shaft of sunlight strained his eyes; he used his hand to shield them. "Yes, officer?"

"Everything all right, sir?"

"Yes, of course," Barton said. "I...I didn't feel very well, something came over me, so I pulled to the shoulder. I got lost in a trance, I suppose."

"Are you sick, sir, because...Oh wait! Is that you, Mr. Williams? I'm sorry I didn't recognize you. Your face is very pale, sir. Guess I didn't notice you right away. Sorry about that."

Cars sped past them. Vehicles in the slow lane were rubbernecking, gawking at Barton and the officer. The drivers' nosiness, their slowing down to stare, upset Barton but he did his best to shake it off.

"No need to be sorry. We all lose our train of thought from time to time."

"Sure you're going to be okay? Do you need a ride home? Or to a doctor, Mr. Williams?"

"I'll be fine. I just needed a moment to unwind. I haven't been sleeping well lately. I'm feeling better now, though. That little breather helped."

"Well, then, have a good day," the policeman said, and returned to his patrol car.

Barton eased his car onto the highway and drove to his last stop of the morning, The Bank of Prosperity, where he would withdraw petty cash for the office. He observed his reflection in the rearview mirror, cringed at the purple blotches under his eyes, his pale complexion—a total metamorphosis from this morning. And this sense of defeat, of being dominated by his mind and body, had him teetering on the precipice of tears, on the fringe of breakdown. Why was a man who had done so many noble things struggling and delirious? Could this chain of experiences be the effects of not taking his medicine? Was that scenario possible? Though he was trying not to become dependent on pills, he wished he had one now to assuage the pressure, to unravel the madness.

The Bank of Prosperity had just opened—a bank with clerks on one side, tellers on the other. One customer was standing at the front of the line, no one behind him. Another customer was filling out forms at a table next to the main lobby. Barton was relieved that the bank was not as crowded as the convenience store he had gone to earlier. At least one thing had worked in his favor today.

He reached into his jacket and pulled out a withdrawal slip he'd filled out last night, then meandered toward the counter and waited to be served. Above him a vent circulated cool, fresh air; he tilted his head back and appreciated the draft. Though he still felt lost in a murky daze, he tried to settle down.

"Next in line," a voice said.

Barton went to the window, the only one open, and greeted the teller. "Hello, Dana. How are you today?"

Dana smiled in response to his salutation. "I'm fine, thank you, Mr. Williams. What is your transaction?"

He handed her his document. "I'd like to take out that amount, please. That'll be all."

"Okay. Can I see your driver's license, please?"

Barton scowled. "Okay...fine." He reached into his jacket; his wallet wasn't where he thought it should be. Confused, he searched all his pockets. With his fingers he felt inside each one.

"It's okay, Mr. Williams," Dana said. "Take your time."

Barton patted down his entire body twice. The searches proved unsuccessful. A third inspection turned up a pack of gum and a lock-box key for the office—but no wallet. "I have it somewhere, Dana, I know I do." Suddenly, that singular feeling of immense mental strain had returned—and intensified. Out of the blue he felt the world bearing down on him like a monstrous boulder. His skin tingled, his pores oozed fear of a new kind. The dread he had experienced in the store had manifested itself again, only now the setting and the characters and the situation were different. "I can't believe this. I don't have the fuckin' thing."

His vulgarity made Dana uncomfortable. In all the years she had known him he had never said anything stronger than "darn." His remarks even aroused the attention of Dana's coworkers, whose gazes now shifted in their direction.

"Look, Mr. Williams, why don't you have a seat in the lobby, and check your pockets again too. When you're ready, I'll be here to assist you."

Barton's eyes gaped. "Let's make this a little easier, *Dana*. Give me my money and I'll get on with my day. Save us both some trouble, all right?"

"I'm sorry but I can't do that, Mr. Williams. I must see—"

"Call me Barton, for crying out loud. Drop the ridiculous formality." He shook his head, bewildered. "How long have I been coming here?"

Dana's heart battered her chest, her bottom lip started to tremble as if she were about to cry. She gathered breath, spoke sententiously. "Years, sir."

"That's right," Barton replied. "Years. Many years." Perspiration irritated his eye. He wiped his face with his shirt sleeve. "So why the drastic change? Why address me differently than you normally do? Why the hell are you asking *me* for my license? I could buy this damn bank if I wanted to."

"I know you could, but—"

"But nothing, Dana. Cut me some slack...show me some respect. I was here just a week ago, and now you act as though we've never met before. This inconsistency is uncalled for."

While thinking of a response, Dana nervously ran her fingers through her hair. Tension was emblazoned on her face. "Well, I—"

Barton cut in again. "You used to look me up in this," he said tapping the top of the computer on the counter, "and verify my account. These new procedures are unwarranted, in my opinion, especially for someone (he pointed his thumb at himself) who puts copious funds in this bank."

Dana scanned the perimeter and made eye contact with her coworkers, none of whom were about to intervene. None of them said a word; none of them could ignore the drama either. Everyone's attention was fixed. Dana returned her focus to the customer. "Barton, I'm sorry you feel the way you do. You're a loyal customer and I for one appreciate your using The Bank of Prosperity—we are grateful for your business. But our staff has been reduced and policy has changed...you're not the only one who's having issues with—"

Barton roughly scratched the back of his head, then hollered, "This is not an issue; this is a *real* problem. Don't try to distort the truth with fancy talk."

Dana twirled a pen in her sweaty hand. "Sir, it's

the truth. Protocol suggests that we—"

"One more fluffed-up business term out of your mouth and I will go insane. The Dana I know never talked that way. She was polite, and gracious, and never questioned me as you are now." Through the glass of the drive-thru, Barton saw the manager, a thirty-something male with a patch of hair on his chin and wearing glasses, coming up behind him. As the man ceremoniously removed his glasses he addressed Barton in an authoritative, controlled tone. "Sir, please conduct your business… and then leave." The young man pointed over his shoulder. "If Debbie (the clerk) pushes the button the cops will be here in a flash (he lied: the button was on Dana's side of the store). Come on now, let's just get on with our day, okay? We've known you a long time. Let's not argue."

Barton replied in a husky voice, a voice with little vigor. "Don't you get it? My whole day has already turned to shit. Why are you making life even more difficult for me? You're changing the course of my daily routine. This deviation—this complete altering of the rules—is unacceptable and without justification."

The man swallowed. The room was smothered in silence.

Barton sniveled, as if he had a nasty cold then rubbed his temple. "I was on meds for this thing, whatever the hell it is. The pills are a trap… they mess with my head. I end up sleeping… or feeling grumpy…or lost—that's no way to live, is it?"

"Your life is none of my business, Mr. Williams. Can we just move on with—"

"You see," Barton said. "Nobody wants to listen. I mean *genuinely* listen. They just want to put a band-aid on the wound…to stand in derision…to pretend I'm unstable or unbalanced. Is the world they've put me in better than this one, this spectacle?"

The manager hadn't moved, or spoken. He did, however, stroke the hair on his chin, as if buying time for rebuttal, for a sure-fire escape plan.

With his fingertips Barton removed moisture from his eyes. "We have to deal with our problems, right, Mr. Manager? Isn't that the new-age philosophy? Somebody made me believe I have a problem, that I need help. But you…yes, you…you changed the rules here, for no reason whatsoever. You tried to fix what wasn't broken. And now I have somehow become a malcontent?"

More customers were about to enter the bank. The clatter of shoes on the lobby floor echoed as, in a rush, several business types cramped the space before the swinging double-doors, the ones with the bank's name engraved in the shiny glass. Nodding her head, Dana signaled to them to stay outside. One of the employees rushed to the doors, mumbling, "I'm terribly sorry." Customers stood frozen in remonstrance; but as soon as they had a firm understanding of the turmoil inside the bank, they stayed out of the way and waited for a resolution.

Barton took off his jacket, folded it neatly and placed it on the desk beside him. The manager gulped twice, his protruding adam's apple rolled up and down his throat. With his hands he played with his belt buckle. The murmur of cars riding by could be heard through the walls, as well as the slight buzzing of the water fountain, which stood about ten feet away in an alcove. Cameras mounted at the corners of the interior did not faze Barton at all. In his state of mind that was the least of his worries. He closed the gap between himself and the bank manager. "Look, Mr. Whoever you are, all you have to do is give me my money and I'll mosey along. Don't opt for a situation you can't handle."

Barton couldn't help noticing the clutter on the desk nearby. Blatant disarray, especially in the workplace, had always maddened him. The girl sitting in front of the desk, a young, innocent-looking brunette with poorly-applied pink lipstick, pushed her chair away after witnessing the puzzled look on Barton's face (his eyes moved back and forth, he ground his teeth). She couldn't quite ascertain whether he was staring at the welter of papers and office supplies, or leering at her with malicious intent. Either way, she wasn't about to ask questions or set him off.

With his hands in his pockets now, the right hand fingering a handful of coins, the bank manager confidently, if not cockily, looked into Barton's eyes. "Here at The Bank of Prosperity, our rules clearly state that—"

Pushed to the brink and unable to restrain himself, Barton snatched a letter opener from the girl's desk, grabbed the manager by the neck, and detained him with the metal opener pressed against his throat. The bank manager tried to thwart the attack but he was outmuscled, his strength no match the brute of an aggressive Barton Williams, a man likely twenty years his senior and twice his weight.

A buzzer, like one heard when opening an electronic door, sounded at the far side of the bank: a car had entered the drive-thru lane and was rolling up to the oversized window. The teller, in the heat of the moment, approached the microphone, waved away the customer, and hit the emergency button under the counter, signaling for help. Had Barton been a random customer the police would have been called immediately. Behavior such as Barton's would never have been tolerated had he not earned repute in the community, had he not been revered by the majority of the townspeople. However, though no one reached out for help at an earlier juncture the teller had an uneasy feeling from the very beginning that matters would get out of hand; she did what she had to do. On a typical day, at this hour of the morning, the police were likely to arrive quickly from a station only three miles away.

The manager in his sinewy clasp, Barton looked around, making sure to keep a considerable distance between him and the bystanders, who remained relatively calm despite the circumstances. Barton seemed baffled by their acquiescence. "Is this what you're instructed to do, Dana? Act like you're in control? I'm unconvinced."

Dana, now standing on the customers' side of the counter, wiped a streak of mascara from her tear-stained cheek. "I'm sorry it's come to this, Mr. Williams. I know you're a fair and generous man. You're just having a rotten day. We've all been there."

A few of her coworkers nodded in agreement; others seemed unsure how to respond, if at all. Dana had shocked even herself: somehow she had remained poised. She had not succumbed to the disorder, as she would have had this incident taken place years ago before she had learned how to effectively overcome her own deficiencies. She had always thought of Barton Williams as a decent human being, an abstemious man, a devoted husband and father. Having passed Barton in town numerous times, with his wife and daughter in his company, she never would have believed that his life could have become this unruly, or that he could have fallen victim to episodes of rage and irrationality.

The drive-thru teller eyed the clock. Less than two minutes had passed since she had called the police and already the impetuous squealing of sirens could be heard en route to the bank. In a desperate attempt to break the tension, Dana mustered her most caring, sympathetic voice, and tried to soothe Barton. "Look, Mr. Williams, why not go home to your wonderful wife and put this day behind you?" She looked at the floor for a few seconds, then at the crowd, and then back at Barton.

A police cruiser had pulled into the lot, its lights flickered against the bank windows, the exterior walls, and leaped hither and thither. With a cursory glance at the lobby, Barton was aware of the arrival of the police—blue-and-red lights splashed the panes of glass in the main vestibule.

"I'll give you the money as you wish," Dana said. "After all, you're one of our best customers and I'd hate to upset you, or lose your business—or your friendship."

"We're not friends, Dana. I'm no fool. I'm just a number to this institution, a statistic." Barton released the manager and pushed him away, then placed the metallic letter opener back on the desk he had taken it from. In a slow, precise manner he sat on the floor and, as if looking at a starry sky, stared at the incandescent lights above him. Colorful spots danced before his eyes. Then he closed them. Ten seconds passed. Through parched lips he spoke. "Was that so hard? To give me what I wanted?"

The officer had come into the building through the side door. He got to Barton, and stood above him. Barton said, "Do I ask for too much from this world?" His question went unanswered.

The officer knew Barton well, respected him, and did not find it necessary to use force or cause further harm. Indeed he was sensitive to Barton's reputation. But now, seeing him vulnerable and scared, he could fully comprehend his helplessness, his loss of sanity, his loss of self. Nonetheless, the officer had a job to do. He took Barton into temporary custody.

Barton opened his eyes and, feeling dizzy but with assistance from the cop, wobbled to a standing position. The police officer cuffed Barton and searched his pockets, and found nothing. The cop held him by the arm and stared sympathetically into his vacant eyes. "What happened here?"

A tear traced Barton's cheek. His eyes, rolling wildly in their sockets, were bloodshot, his face grim and unsightly. "I need to cope."

The cop, with Barton's arm around his shoulders, kept him on his feet. "Don't do this to yourself, Mr.

Williams. Get help."

Barton feigned a smile. "I can do it alone."

"Are you sure?" asked the officer. "You're a mess."

Barton whispered in his ear. "Call Gloria." Before the officer could load Barton into his car, he fainted in his arms.

A month passed. Barton and his wife had been strolling in the park for a while and decided to take a break. They sat on a bench and held hands, shared a few humorous anecdotes, and chatted about life in general. Barton relished the simple pleasures: blowing leaves, chirping birds, the cadence of feet shuffling to and fro, kids playing, squirrels scurrying up the trees. Life seemed good again.

In the distance he noticed a familiar face, one that had left an indelible mark on his conscience. He kissed Gloria on the cheek and stood. "I'll be right back. I see an old friend."

He took a leisurely stroll to a swing-set at the center of the park, where a man was pushing his daughter, and tapped him on the shoulder. The man turned.

"Hello Dylan," said Barton.

The man hesitated, as if waiting for his memory to register who it was before him. "Well…Hello, Mr. Williams. What can I do for you?"

Even though Barton was embarrassed by the way he had treated the bank manager, he was glad he had found him now, in a crowded park on a picturesque day, an auspicious time and place to redeem himself. Barton apologized to Dylan, and his apology was warmly accepted. (Unable to work at the bank after what had happened with Barton, Dana quit her job, making it impossible for him to express his regret for offending her.) "I'm glad you're recovering, Mr. Williams," said Dylan. "How did you do it, I mean, turn yourself around?"

Barton smiled, and spoke in a monotone. "I'm completely clean." Then he pointed at a nearby bench. "Got a minute?"

Dylan shrugged. "Okay." His wife looked at him with a caring face, as if goading him to talk to Barton. She sensed Barton's kindness, his eagerness to make amends. The men sat. Barton waved to his wife in the distance, letting her know everything was okay. He cleared his throat. "First of all, I'd like to thank you for not filing charges. That made a big difference in the outcome. Your willingness to shrug the whole thing off helped me get off easy. I was damn close to getting booked for a whole list of things. Who knows what would've happened had you not been so forgiving."

Dylan warmly tapped Barton's arm. "No need to thank me. Sending you to jail wasn't going to solve your problem, right? You're no criminal anyway." He pointed at his wife, who was attending to the children. "She told me that—and I know she's right." He took a deep breath, exhaled slowly. "Her father's life was no picnic either. That's for another time, though."

"I understand," Barton said. "My wife restored my sanity too… my whole family, for that matter."

Dylan leaned toward Barton, waiting for him to elaborate.

Barton indulged him. "She took me to my daughter's college campus. (He held up his two fingers, as if he were giving the peace sign.) We lived there for two weeks. In an unused room across the courtyard, not far from her room. My daughter and I spoke with the Dean. We convinced him that it would be good PR to help a student's family at a time of need. I think my donation to the college pushed the idea through, though."

"Why would you—?"

Barton interrupted. "Not so fast. The arrangement was the best medicine I could have taken. Her dorm room was the ideal place to confront my problems—it's complete disorder, beyond what I'm comfortable tolerating. The whole situation could have driven anyone with my mentality berserk." Barton shook his head. "It's amazing she's able to concentrate there." He laughed through his nose. "At least she's spending her college fund wisely."

Dylan smiled. Barton, a pensive look on his face, seemed to be gathering the right words, and Dylan could sense the conversation was about to take a more serious turn. Barton rubbed the creases on his forehead. "I had to live with everything not being as it should, and face the truth, the consequences. I found out...that...that life isn't perfect, and neither am I. Whenever I felt myself falling into a trap, losing control, my wife and daughter kept me together."

"I don't completely follow," Dylan said. "You mean to tell me that that was your therapy? No doctors for this one?"

Barton tapped his own temple. "None needed. I

started retraining my brain to accept my patterns…and learned that I *can* survive. In other words, if I'm driven to comb my hair ten times a day, that's normal—for me. If I'm going to be frazzled by the sight of clutter, then so be it. Trying to fight my psychological makeup is futile… unhealthy, you might say."

"Hmm," Dylan responded.

"Why not embrace who I am, instead of challenging it?" continued Barton. "Synchronize my inner world and my outer world, so to speak. These drastic measures showed me the most important part of my recovery: that my family loves me no matter what. They've helped me through this whole ordeal. And any anxiety I had about losing my daughter has been put to rest. We're closer than ever."

Dylan smiled, and gently patted Barton on the arm. "Sounds like you're on the right track. I'm glad you've found a better life."

As Barton got up from the bench, he smiled and looked up at the sky. "Nothing is wrong with me, after all. I just realized I can't change what I've become, but I can manage my troubles on my own—without those *dreadful* pills."

"You've got a great outlook."

"That I do, Dylan. I feel renewed."

"Good luck to you, Mr. Williams." He looked at his wife and then back at Barton. "I'm sorry, but I've gotta go."

"I'll see you around, you fine young man."

The men smiled at each other, shook hands, and Dylan's eyes began to water. "Right back at you," he said.

Barton returned to Gloria and sat down next to her. She stroked his hair. "How'd it go, Barty? How's your friend?"

Barton hugged his wife and refused to let go.

BOUNDARIES

Chris and Evelyn Califon came down the cluttered staircase. For a middle-aged couple they maintained polished appearances. Chris looked fresh and healthy, his hair mud black and gelled in place. His wife's pretty face was unlined; she wore hardly any makeup. Her crisp features did not warrant being covered up by wasteful cosmetics. Short red hair fell gracefully down her neck; her aura was confident and elegant. The Califons were a distinguished couple: great careers, active social lives, parents to a daughter, Krissy. Krissy was a well-adjusted kid, for the most part. She'd been raised in a typical middle-class home. But for a sophomore in high school, she still lacked the ability to be reliable, independent. In the past when she had been left home without supervision, she would sneak out to see friends and had once or twice raided the liquor cabinet.

Tonight her parents had to attend a work function. They presided over a charity organization in the community, and major affiliates were flying in to oversee their progress and present them with a prestigious award. When Krissy refused at the last minute to accompany them, they had no alternative to leaving their little girl alone. Chris and Evelyn had a discussion with their daughter, explaining the urgency of the gala dinner they were obligated to attend. Krissy's mother asked her to be responsible and take care of herself this time. "We'll be back by ten o'clock, sweetness, at the latest. Can you hold things together for us?"

Krissy was sucking on a lollipop. "You can count on me." She threw up her hands defensively and smiled. "I admit it, I've done some stupid stuff in the past, but I'm totally over it."

Evelyn was aglow at her daughter's admission of guilt, accompanied by her confident answer. "I believe you, Krissy. I trust you, honey."

Chris stood with his arm around Evelyn, a sincere smile on his face. "Me too. Don't forget, I got you that Britney tape in case you get bored. And of course, since you love to dance so much, I picked up that club mix from the mall. I pushed it under your door about ten minutes ago. Have fun."

"Thanks, Dad," she said. "You are so cool."

Evelyn walked toward the front door. Chris opened it. His wife leaned on him as she stepped into her heels. "Later, kiddo."

"Bye, guys. Knock 'em dead tonight. Everything's cool here."

The door closed. Krissy secured the bottom lock and latched the chain. She looked through the peephole, watching the distorted images of her parents heading to their car. Her mother and father drove away, their taillights gradually faded into the night. She pulled the lollipop from her mouth. "Freedom at last."

Krissy turned. In front of her, about ten feet away, the stairs led to the second floor. Clothing was draped over the banister. Sneakers and shoes lay across some of the steps; the lowest step in particular was a mess. Her father's golf bag, stuffed with clubs, leaned against the bottom railing. Krissy walked up to the stairway and inspected the clubs. She removed one from the bag; it had a felt boot protecting it. After removing the cloth she saw it was an iron, embossed #3.

Wind kicked up outside; another volatile autumn evening had arrived. Severe storms were forecast to whip through town all weekend. A twister of leaves slapped the front door and peppered the window panes on both sides of the entrance. Krissy stood in the capacious foyer and began swinging the club back and forth. She had never played golf but she liked how the club felt in her hands. She even took a few full, looping swings, chuckling at the whipping sound they made, missing the freshly-waxed floor by only a fraction of an inch. If she were to chip the wood floors she would have much explaining to do, but she continued horsing around anyway.

Across from her, in front of the den wall, a small baroque table held a picture frame, a phone and a fancy phone book. With the club in her hand she walked to the table. Leafing through the book she read some of the names. Some she recognized, others were unfamiliar. The name *Blackmore* shined in blue ballpoint pen ink at the bottom of the B page. She remembered Richie Blackmore, their old handyman. Her parents employed him for years until he got married and moved to the west coast. She thought he was cute. Richie was a professional with perfect references and had, over time, built up a sizable clientele in the neighborhood. He always spoke so highly of his wife and everyone adored him, including her.

Krissy was still sucking on the lollipop when, in the act of closing the book, she accidentally knocked over the picture, cracking the glass. In her clumsiness the lollipop too had fallen from her mouth and stuck to the cover of the book, leaving a blotch. "Shit," she said as she picked up the lollipop. She tossed her candy into a nearby garbage pail, put the club back in her father's bag, and went upstairs to her room.

In her bedroom she scribbled in her diary: *How boring. My best friend is on vacation with her family. It's going to be a lonely Saturday night. Nothing peanut butter can't cure though. Or making out with Ronnie Walters if he was here.* Krissy closed the book and tucked the journal away in her night stand. Bouncing energetically downstairs to the kitchen she hummed a pop song she liked.

In the pantry she found a jar of Skippy and unscrewed the lid. Behind her the kitchen doorknob jiggled. She pivoted toward the noise, eyed the lock, and noticed the dial was positioned upright: the door was secure. Mustard-colored curtains concealed the rectangular windows at the top of the door. Above the sink, just beyond the mini-glass sliders, the branches of an andromeda rustled as the wind spread through the perennial garden. She moved toward the door and placed her hand on the knob. Although she could clearly see the door was fine and there was nothing to be concerned about, she felt more at ease touching the handle for herself—for peace of mind. Outside she watched another spiral of wind-driven leaves hit the porch in a dizzying dance, grazing the siding, the chimes, the screen. *I'm letting some silly storm freak me out. How crazy.*

Krissy dunked her finger in the jar of peanut butter and licked it off, repeated a second and a third time. She grabbed a napkin from the table and made her way into the living room, where she sat on the couch. Using the remote control, she flipped through channels, stopping on an old episode of *Eight Is Enough*. She placed the controller on the floor next to the sofa. She enjoyed mouthfuls of her favorite treat. She twirled her hair, looked around the room, paying no attention to the television. Having finished her snack she sealed the jar and put it down, then draped her legs over the edge of the couch and eased her feet from her laceless sneakers. Within minutes she closed her eyes and drifted off. The cracked picture lay on the floor, the golf club, misplaced in the bag, had its cover fastened incorrectly. Krissy had once again created problems and ignored them.

Krissy heard the gears of the wall clock in the foyer, a car engine moaning in the street, and the insistent bark of a dog in the distance. Then quiet. For quite some time Krissy remained horizontal on the couch, enjoying her nap. She shifted her body and one of her loose sneakers fell off and landed on the remote. The volume of the television soared. Krissy, disturbed and disoriented, quickly searched for the remote. She turned off the TV. She was slipping her shoe on just as the phone rang. It sat on the table across the room next to a bookshelf. She walked over and picked it up. "Hello? Hello?"

Dead silence.

She hung it up, mumbling, "Jerk."

She walked to the bookshelf. A stack of papers

was at eye level. Next to the pile was an envelope. Through the window of the envelope she saw the words *payable to Mr. Chris Califon.* Curiosity gnawed at her. Was this a paycheck? She had never wanted for anything, but she had no idea how much money her parents earned. What could one peek hurt? She would not tell anyone about this. She began opening the envelope to examine the contents.

A creaking came from the stairway, startling her. She put down the envelope immediately. A wavelet of fright rippled through her. Krissy walked slowly toward the foyer. On the far side of the room beyond the foyer she saw the gloomy night staring back at her through the oversized bay window. She licked her lips, took a deep breath and was about to head upstairs. Glancing at the staircase, she failed to detect anything unusual or foreboding. Houses settle and make noises, she told herself. If she listened carefully, she could hear even more trivial ticks eating the silence.

Krissy returned to the living room. She approached the bookshelf and rummaged through several shelves. The first shelf was nothing but technical books that her dad typically read. A few of them had his company name on them: FutureTech. The second shelf had an eclectic mix of reading material: various magazines, Nora Roberts' novels her mother liked, and a few Tom Clancy titles. She hunkered down to get a better look at the lower shelf and spotted last year's school yearbook. She removed the book.

At the dining room table she flipped the pages. She reread some of the comments her friends had left for her. Joshua Pickler wrote: *To the only gal pal I know that doesn't use gallons of hair spray. Have a great summer.* Maggie Armstrong scribbled: *To the smartest one in my class, even though you were only a C student. Still love ya.* On the bottom of the page there was a group shot of the Cougars' cheerleading team. In the back of the group stood her old friend Rose Marie Vitale. She remembered her well. She was the prettiest girl in school with the biggest heart. Rose Marie wrote: *Never be afraid, always be strong, believe in yourself, Rosie.* Krissy smiled. Fond memories were reborn inside her. She turned more of the pages and perused the pictures of her classmates.

Suddenly glass shattered downstairs. The sound came from the basement, a place she rarely went down to. Only her father used it, no one else. The sizable dining room now seemed darker and smaller than usual. Her eyes opened wide, a sensation of doom seized her body. Her heart lurched. She rose from her chair and nervously combed her hair with her fingers, like a girl who imagined being attacked by bugs. Her eyes darted around the room; her hands balled into fists of tension. Hands clammy, she reached for the phone that sat on a table to her left. Clutching it, her heart palpitating more alarmingly now, she considered her next move. If she were to call her parents or the police, what was there to report? Besides, if only a few noises panicked her, how would she face adversity in the future? Run and hide? Call Mommy and Daddy for everything? It *sounded* as if glass had broken in the basement, but perhaps she was hearing things. Maybe it was nothing. She made up her mind: Investigate the noise. Walk downstairs. Take the phone along.

Krissy began moving very slowly through the house, her legs jittery, her knees weak. She left the living room and entered the foyer. Her eyes fell upon the broken picture, the smirched phone book, and the golf club protruding improperly from her dad's golf bag. Her sneakers squeaked on the hardwood floor and echoed in the room. She slipped off her shoes. The wood felt soft and smooth under her sweaty toes. She reached into the bag and grabbed the #3 iron. Now she had a weapon in one hand and a phone in the other. She peeked through the glass panels on either side of the front door. All was normal. A few more paces brought her past the stairway, closer to where the noise originated, closer to confronting some kind of fear that she didn't want to face, nor comprehend. Around the corner on the right was the basement door. Krissy was drenched in sweat and unsteady on her feet. Something tapped the glass across the room. She wheeled. An overgrown evergreen branch had smacked the window. Nothing serious. The steady wind was becoming stronger by the minute. She stopped at the basement door and looked at the glowing phone screen. She scrolled through the list until her parents' number appeared. Again she was overcome with the urge to call them. The sound of breaking glass had to mean something. Krissy had a sinking feeling in her stomach, where knots were forming quickly and unmercifully. She'd been home alone before and had done stupid things: made prank phone calls, had friends over when she was told not to—was caught making out with one of them—and even got grounded once for smoking cigarettes on the roof (a nosy neighbor reported her). But this time, here tonight, she was on the receiving end of a situation she hadn't yet confronted. She had been a bit of a rebellious teen—but never challenged by the unexpected, the unknown. Her parents had always tried to instill trust in her without being overprotective or worrisome. Tonight was the next step in the process: boundaries needed to be established so that respect and trust could develop between parent and child.

Krissy decided not to call her parents. She grabbed the knob and turned it, opening the thick wooden door. She tightened her grip on the iron club and began descending the wooden steps into the dark tomb-like basement. To her right, on the wall, she saw a light switch but did not flick it. She went down a few more steps without being able to see clearly. Faint light spread across the cement floor, rays of moonlight casting a subtle glow. She crept down the last three steps. The ground was cold and damp and grainy under her bare feet. Dust and grime had gotten between her toes and also had irritated the soles of her feet. Anxiety wormed through her, a rash of gooseflesh spread on her arms. She felt sweat tracing her hairline, her palms further moistening, her chest pummeled by her heart's gradual rising beat—a sensation she couldn't suppress. As she turned the corner a cold wisp of wind grazed her, chilling the nape of her bare neck and ears. About eight feet from where she stood, just above head level, she found the problem: a small window was indeed broken. In the vicinity of the broken glass she heard a cat meowing. Hearing the cat gave her some relief. She sighed. Could the cat have broken the glass? She didn't own one but a few of the neighbors did. Krissy approached the wall, searching for the cat and as she got closer, the kitty emerged from behind a cluster of jars—a pudgy, non-threatening little feline. The cat meowed once, twice, and then scampered out through the hole it crashed in from. A string dangled from the ceiling. Krissy pulled it. Bright light deluged the room. She inspected the damaged window, cleaned the mess, and sealed the hole with a piece of spare wood her dad had left lying around. Jars placed against the wood anchored it safely in place.

Satisfied and relieved, she went back upstairs. She returned the club to the bag and walked up to her room. She wanted to watch the DVD her father had bought for her. Confidence washed over her. She felt a renewal of sorts. She had been faced with challenges and emerged victorious. She persevered through heightened circumstances on her own. It wouldn't have been a bad idea to call her parents or the police, but something inside persuaded her to rise above her uncertainty and insecurities and trust her instincts—defend herself, her home. The basement wasn't so bad. Dark, creepy basements only exist in the movies, she thought.

She chose not to watch the video after all. Instead she returned to the first floor, fixed the tattered picture frame, spruced up the black book, and plopped down on the couch with her yearbook again. It was 9:30. Her parents would be home soon. She had much to tell them.

THE MARGIN

It was a hot day, the rush hour traffic brutal and uncompromising. Walter Baxter waited at least a hundred cars deep from the traffic light on Moss Grove Road, a steep incline that connects the two adjoining towns. He despised his job at the textile factory, but for the last ten years had worked double shifts, even braved the skeleton crew a handful of times to fatten his paycheck. This had been an unusual day for Walter. He had worked a normal shift (for once) and now longed to get home. His air conditioner was cranked and he had a CD playing in the deck. The traffic trundled along slowly, horns blazing in unison. The dissonant beeping did nothing though to ease the compaction of three full lanes of traffic. Walter aired his displeasure by rolling the window down and shouting. "C'mon goddamn it! Let's move! What the hell!"

A few heads turned, but no one responded except for a businessman in a convertible with a striking blonde sitting next to him. They were wedged in the left lane about ten cars up. The driver looked back toward Walter and voiced his frustration. "Screw you, man! Just shut up! We're all fucked!"

Walter shook off the man's comments and closed the window. He turned up the volume, deciding a response was pointless. His car was flanked by two lanes, the traffic packed in tightly, each car inching forward a smidgen as the light winked from red to green. The volume of cars was beyond the typical five o' clock commute. The one day Walter had finally been able to leave work on time and there he was, stuck in the fierce clutch of a traffic jam. He started fingering through the CDs on his seat while the traffic stood still. He grew impatient, bored with what was playing and opted for the radio instead. As soon as he hit the button, the tuner landed on WKRX. Blair Johansen reviewed in great detail the summer's heat index, substantially above normal, leaving emergency rooms overcrowded around the Tri-State area. "If you don't have to be outside, stay indoors," Johansen urged.

"What if you have to work for a living, asshole?" Walter said to the radio.

He couldn't take Johansen's voice anymore so he turned the dial to another station. Walter's lane moved forward a few feet. Then everyone advanced a few car lengths. Not much progress, but it would have to suffice for now. A few minutes later he remembered an alternate route home, a detour that began up ahead before the traffic light. It followed back roads that would take him a few miles out of the way but was better than waiting in this mess. If he saw an easy way out of things he always jumped at the chance. He loathed being held up. Walter remembered when he had crossed over the median on Crystal Springs Highway during a snow storm. That day an out of control car had skidded sideways, binding up his lane. He had driven over the grass divider, avoiding the congestion, and had paid the price for it. The police issued a ticket for illegal U-Turn. His wife, Suzanne, was furious over the incident. "When are you going to learn?" she'd said to him.

He'd have to weasel his way into the next lane and ride the narrow shoulder for a few hundred feet if he was going to escape the long chain of cars. Walter signaled to the driver at his right, asking for permission to jump out in front. The driver seemed annoyed, but let him cut in. Walter waited for the perfect time to make his move. At the rate things were going there would be few other chances of freeing himself from the gridlock. Once the vehicle in front of him inched up enough, Walter rolled toward the shoulder, and in doing so too quickly, ended up overlapping it, closing the gap between the right lane and the curb. This wasn't going as smoothly as he had anticipated. Now he was in a precarious position.

From behind him sirens sliced through the air. An ambulance was speeding through the intersection at the bottom of the hill, ascending Moss Grove Road. The driver was moving rapidly, the engine roaring. Walter heard the tires screeching on the pavement as it burned toward him like a locomotive. The ambulance didn't have much of an opening so it used the narrow shoulder. It wasn't possible for the paramedics to fit between the other lanes of traffic, which were in complete disorder. The ambulance's wailing horns alerted the drivers to clear a path. The lights atop the cab were flickering, swirling a prism of red, blue, and gold.

Walter found himself desperately trying to maneuver out of the way. His car was draped across the shoulder with the right front wheel rubbing against the cement curbing. The blaring sirens frazzled him.

Frustrated, he slapped the wheel. "Gimme a minute, damn it!" Walter yelled. He knew these were precious moments for a paramedic. The ambulance was prepared to drive up on the curb in order to avoid a collision, but Walter managed to get back in the lane. The ambulance slipped past him. Walter Baxter took a moment to think; he decided to stay where he was until the traffic cleared.

When Walter arrived home he talked about the incident with Suzanne. "You should have seen the gridlock today, babe," Walter said. "It was bumper to bumper on Moss Grove. It's never that bad."

"Really?" she responded. "That's nasty. I had no idea since I was coming from the other direction. When I came up Route 27 earlier it was smooth sailing. It figures, though, the one day you get out on time and you have to sit in a parking lot for crying out loud."

Walter was sitting at the dining room table with a beer in his hand. "I don't even want to think about that anymore. It was terrible."

Suzanne grabbed the remote control. "I'm going to watch TV before we eat. Do you want to go to Bakers Farm Inn for dinner? Tonight is pasta night. I've had a craving for the stuff all day."

Walter sipped his beer, placed the bottle on the table. "Sounds like a plan. A nice meatball sandwich would hit the spot for me. I'll get showered."

At the restaurant the couple sat in a booth next to a large window. It offered them a view of the vast gardens, enhanced with dreamy roses and a colorful bed of begonias. An expanse of well-groomed grass extended to a beautiful lake, where waves swayed peacefully on the surface. Walter glanced out the window, tapping the glass.

"Check that guy out. He's fishing in this heat? He's nuts."

Suzanne's attention had floated to the crowns of the maple trees that circled the lake. She didn't respond. She was daydreaming, remembering the days when he loved to go out on the lake for the day fishing, even the times when they would wake up early on the weekends and drive over to the bridge on Route 299 and enjoy a picnic at Deer Pond. He was an outdoorsman who over the last few years had seldom found time away from a demanding work schedule. Walter knew his wife had something on her mind. Pulling her hair behind her ears, repeatedly sipping her water, wiping her mouth afterwards—he recognized her nervous twitches. Something was wrong.

"What's up with you, Suz? You're acting funny. Everything okay?"

Suzanne's eyes began to water. "It's nothing. I—"

"Don't give me this 'nothing' business. I know you like a book. Talk to me, hon."

She sipped her water again and took a deep breath. Walter was concerned. He shifted restlessly in his seat, unsure what his wife was about to say.

"Please don't get mad." She hesitated for a moment. "But your behavior worries me lately."

Just hearing those words bothered him. "What?" he asked, his voice elevating.

"Let me finish," she said.

"Go ahead then."

Suzanne continued. Her voice was uneven, shaky. "You've been so impatient the last month or so. What's gotten in to you?"

Walter shrugged. "Don't know what you're talking about."

"Yes, you do," she insisted. She cleared her throat.

"All right, then. Come out with it, Suz—tell me."

She toyed with her hair again. "Well, my father mentioned getting tickets to the football game and you've been hounding me to follow up with him. I told you at least twice that he's out of town on business."

Walter started fiddling with his napkin. "That's the best you can do, huh?"

Suzanne shook her head, sighed. "I've asked you nicely not to walk on the carpet with dirty work boots, yet you do it anyway because you don't want to enter through the garage. *God forbid* it takes a few extra minutes to get inside."

He huffed. "What do you want from me?" he asked

"For you to slow down, be a bit more considerate, that's all."

He rolled his eyes. "You want me to change is what you're saying."

"No, Walter. I don't want that at all. You're a terrific husband and I'm a lucky lady. I've always said that. But yes, the last few months have been touch and go with your impatience." She took a breath. "Look, I know you've been working hard, but it doesn't have to change our life."

Suzanne leaned in toward him, grabbed his hand, whispered. "Even in bed you rush things. That's unlike you. Sometimes that makes me self-conscious, like you're rushing through it for a reason."

Walter stared at the table pensively. "I guess you're right. I'm sorry. I love you."

"I love you too, Walter," she said, drying her eyes with a napkin.

That night when they arrived home Suzanne thanked Walter for listening to her at the restaurant, even though it had been difficult.

"Please, don't thank me," he said. "You're my wife. I'm here for you. I'm past it. We'll look back on this one day and laugh. So…until then…"

Walter smiled, motioned with his head toward the staircase. "Let's go upstairs and be silly. And I promise— I'll take my time."

Suzanne giggled. "Fine by me."

They made love and fell asleep around ten o' clock. The bedroom was dark and cool, the air-conditioner humming. The chime on Walter's watch, which he had forgotten to remove before bed, signaled midnight. He had been sleeping face down with his head just over the edge of the mattress. Suzanne was tossing and turning, becoming increasingly restless. She got out of bed, went to the closet and pulled out a puzzle. She sat on the floor downstairs under a reading lamp piecing it together while Walter was sleeping.

She worked for a while, even stopped for a short time to make a nice cup of tea mixed with a shot of Bailey's liquor. When she returned to the puzzle she continued for a bit longer. Surprisingly, it was over an hour before she grew sleepy, opting to crash on the couch. Then their neighbor Mrs. Dunaway's dog started barking. It continued for a few minutes…stopped…then began again. Mrs. Dunaway was retired, her husband had died a year ago and the Rottweiler kept her company. And sometimes, when she was overwhelmed by one of her many late-night anxiety attacks, she would step outside with her dog and pace back and forth in the street until she felt better. Sometimes, if she knew Suzanne was awake and restless, Mrs. Dunaway would stop by. Hopefully, though, tonight would be a restful night for both of them.

Walter rolled over on his back and tried to get comfortable. The mattress jerked dramatically, forcing him to open his eyes. A slimy hand crimped his mouth, robbing his breath. He was straddled by a man with a buzz-cut and a toothpick in his mouth. The intruder held a scalpel pressed against his neck. Walter tried to push him off and was jabbed by the weapon. There was a pinch in his left arm. The stranger had set aside the blade and injected him with a needle. A rush of heat swam through him. The assailant had madness in his eyes, like rocks of charcoal. They drilled through Walter's. The stranger worked the toothpick back and forth with his tongue. Walter had never seen the man before: he had a square jaw and a prickly beard, both highlighted by the glow of the lamp on the nightstand.

"Make a sound and I'll carve you up," the attacker

said.

Walter was weakening from the drug flowing through his bloodstream. The intruder slid the knife down his pajamas. As the blade sliced into his thigh, Walter's eyes creased in pain. Blood dripped from his wound onto the mattress. He tried to scream but that only forced the man to push down harder on his mouth, hurting his teeth, his jaw. The assailant was biting down so hard on his toothpick that he'd split it in half, and a piece fell just below Walter's eye. He flinched and attempted to shake it off his face. It didn't work. The intruder raised his hand high and brought it down with vicious speed across Walter's face—*smack*. Then he pointed at him. His haunting eyes delivered a warning. Walter's body became intolerably warm. The drug was strong and disabling. He began losing feeling in his hands and arms. The maniac held the knife against Walter's penis. "Your wife is out cold. Methylcybertine is powerful shit."

He bent down and looked Walter in the eyes. "You scream, and I'll kill you both." The man removed his hand from Walter's mouth.

Walter took a few deep breaths. "What, what do you want? Just tell, tell me. I, I don't have much but you can take it all. Let her live and—"

"Spare me, Walter. Don't play dumb with me, man. You know who I am."

Walter was stunned. "What? I...I don't know you!"

The scalpel passed over Walter's wound again, opening the cut deeper, drawing more blood.

"Because of you my mother's dead," the crazy

man said.

Walter was confused. "What?" he cried out. "You've got the wrong guy, all right. I don't even know what you're talking about." Now the blade cut open the flesh on his scrotum. His body tensed and twitched from the pain.

The attacker ground his teeth. "Don't you dare raise your voice—or I'll finish you."

Walter pleaded. "Please, sir. Anything you want. This is a huge misunderstanding. Are you sure it's us you want?"

"You son of a bitch," the man said, a trail of spit squirting Walter in the eye.

"Like I said, anything you want," Walter pleaded.

The lunatic was speaking through clenched teeth, a macerated toothpick still mashed between them. "You fuckin' piece of shit," he said. The veins on his neck were bulging. It was as though air were flowing through them. He pulled out a photo and held it in front of Walter's face. "Is that your car in the picture—HUH?" the insane man asked.

Walter swallowed, nodded. *Yes.*

"Finally, the truth comes out, *Walt.*"

"What have I done? Whatever it is, I'm truly sorry," Walter insisted.

The attacker's eyes burned through Walter's. "My mother died before I got to her. Are you still sorry, you righteous prick? The camera doesn't lie."

"I don't…" Walter muttered.

The killer's voice rose. "My mother was having a heart attack. You blocked the fucking shoulder on Moss

Grove with your car. I was trying to get her to the hospital that day. Go ahead, give me another one of those smug answers. Just try and deny it. C'mon, do it! I dare you! I'll hack you and your wife to bits."

The floor squeaked in the doorway behind them. The intruder spun. Mrs. Dunaway was holding a rifle, the dog at her side. "What's it gonna be?" she asked. "Trust me, man. I know how to use it, my husband showed me." She pulled back the trigger, aimed precisely, and then reached for the phone on the dresser, dialing 911.

"I dare you, you old shit," the intruder said, getting up off the bed. "I'm not the guilty one here, granny. So piss off."

As he took a step toward Mrs. Dunaway, the dog growled. The man stopped, the scalpel clenched in his fist, Walter's blood dripping from its tip. Mrs. Dunaway glanced quickly at Walter, who mouthed "Help me."

A voice came through the phone. "911, what is your emergency?"

In her shaky, raspy voice, Mrs. Dunaway answered the operator. "We got a guy here who broke in and assaulted my neighbor. 221 Chestnut Place."

The intruder smirked then looked back at Walter who was barely conscious, and then shook his own head disgustedly.

"Can you get to a safe place?" the operator asked. "A car's on its way."

"I've got a gun pointed at him, and a dog just waitin' for my command," said Mrs. Dunaway. "That safe enough?"

"Ma'am, just be careful," the operator said. "The

police are nearby."

Mrs. Dunaway hung up the phone. Intruder and old lady stared at each other in silence. The dog too had his eyes fixed on the man; its top teeth protruded from under its upper lip. Sirens were approaching the house. The intruder threw his weapon on the bed and put his hands in the air as if surrendering. "Lady, I'm walking out of here on my own. Don't shoot, crusty. I wanna tell the cops why I'm here." He pointed at Walter. "What he did. The tragedy it caused. He's the guilty one—not me." The intruder stepped forward.

Mrs. Dunaway aimed the gun at his head. "I may be crusty, but I'm not senile. You stay right where you are. Tell it to the judge."

The cops pulled up to the house and ran up the stairs. When they came into the room they saw the ambulance driver standing there, and they stopped in their tracks, stunned that one of their own, a public servant, was the perpetrator. "You?" one of the officer's said.

"Yeah," the intruder mumbled. They exchanged glances, like acquaintances that had a rich history. "Cuff me, Lombardi, I won't resist." The ambulance driver turned toward Walter and spit on him."

The officer grabbed his suspect—a man he knew quite well and who'd saved many lives—and cuffed him. "Hey, knock it off. Let's go."

The ambulance driver grunted. "This asshole deserves far worse."

DESPERATION

For a few minutes on this picture-perfect day, Andre Weston watched the gardener pulling weeds from the flower bed, then he lowered the curtains to shield himself from the overbearing sun drilling through the clean, gleaming glass. Tightening his tie as he plopped down into a leather chair, he pressed the button on the intercom to call out to his secretary.

"Send in the next applicant."

Lila, a twenty-five-year-old wearing cherry lipstick and her hair in a bun, rolled her eyes. "Yes, sir."

Andre Weston straightened in his chair, cleared his throat. In walked a tall striking man, fortyish, black hair combed to the side and dressed in a finely-pressed suit. He extended his hand. "I'm Peter Delaney. It's good to meet you, Mr. Weston."

Weston motioned to the chair. "Please, sit down."

Delaney sat. He glanced around the room, making mental note of the many plaques decorating the walls, symbols of Weston's achievements. Very impressive, he thought.

Weston rolled a fancy pen between his index finger and thumb. "So, what brings you to Weston and Associates?"

Peter Delaney flashed a smile. "I'm looking for a

sales job, sir. I sent my resume in a while back and," he briefly consulted his folder, "your secretary told me to be here at nine sharp."

Weston leaned back in his chair. "Why are you really here, Mr. Delaney?"

Delaney seemed confused. "Perhaps I don't understand the question. What do you mean?"

Weston leaned forward. "I saw your resume, Mr. Delaney, and I'm forced to question your motives."

"Why's that?" Delaney asked.

Weston smiled big, smug. "Because you have next to *nothing* in the experience department and you're applying for a position boasting a six-figure salary. I feel somewhat obliged to interview all of my applicants, which is the only reason why you're here in the first place. I like to cover my tracks. Occasionally...I find a diamond in the rough."

Delaney chuckled. "You're right, Mr. Weston. On paper my work history is laughable for this career path. My last job paid me a third of what this firm is offering, but I believe by applying myself I can show you what I'm made of."

Weston paused, brought his fingers to his chin. "I like that kind of confidence, Mr. Delaney. *However*, selling product takes more than a fancy suit and a programmed answer. It requires aggressiveness that's hard to come by. I've seen business grads waltz in here and never sell a damn thing."

Delaney bowed his head. "I understand, Mr. Weston. I really do." The men's eyes met again. "Your point is well taken. In fact, I agree with most of what you're saying. And that brings me to my next question."

"Fire away."

Delaney winked. "Feel free to call me Peter. We can drop the formality if you're onboard with that."

"Fair enough," Weston responded.

Delaney unbuttoned his suit jacket to make himself more comfortable. "I'm not going to lie to you, Andre. May I call you that?"

"Why of course you can, Peter. I think we're grown men here. I appreciate your attitude—very disarming."

Embarrassed, Delaney's face reddened. "I'm desperate for work. I need a job... *immediately.* You see," he said closing his eyes, "my daughter's extremely ill. The...the medical bills are...well...they're enormous. We're in financial trouble right now. I'm not sure where to turn."

Weston blinked and looked down at his desk, scanning Delaney's resume. Peter tried to fight his emotions but couldn't. A tear slid down his cheek. He swiped it away. "Her illness is in the early stages, it has cleaned us out financially."

"I'm sorry to hear that, Peter. Please understand, your resume is lean, and my staff is well-versed in all facets of my product. My hands are tied here. Why don't you try a company that—?"

"I'll accept half the salary you're offering," Delaney blurted out. "How's that? And...and...if you're pleased with my performance you can give me what you think is fair. If you're dissatisfied you can cut me loose. I won't take it personally. I don't hold grudges. I'm telling you I can do this."

"I admire your tenacity, Peter. But I'm afraid—"

Delaney cut him off. "Please, just hear me out. I have another idea."

Weston shook his head. "And what's that, Peter?"

"Today's Thursday. I will learn your product inside and out by the time Monday rolls around. Give me one week to sell on a commission basis and see if I can't persuade you to take me on long-term."

"I must say that I'm intrigued. Waiving the salary to prove your worth? That's noble of you." Weston considered the proposal. "Well, say that you sell... Hmmm."

Delaney quickly came up with a number. "I think ten thousand will do."

Weston laughed. He had no idea where the sizable figure came from. "Without knowing what we sell? That's a bold number to toss around, Peter. I don't know how you're going to pull that one off—but then again that's your problem, right?"

Delaney reached over the table and shook Weston's hand. "You'd be surprised what someone will do for their sick kid. I need to get a jump on things. See you Monday."

Peter Delaney was on his way to meet his first client. He'd spent the entire four days cramming to learn the company's product while he and his wife, Sally, split shifts looking after their daughter at the hospital. He even brought pamphlets with him during his visits, using every chance he had to get a grasp of the product he would be pushing. Unfortunately, Peter felt as though he didn't have a sound foundation in sales, but he was determined to persevere. Nothing would stop him.

Peter glanced at his wristwatch. He had to meet Steinberg in thirty minutes. On the client list there was a comment next to Steinberg's name: "Impossible to please." *Oh no*, Peter thought. *What did I get myself into? I'm not cut out for this after all, am I? The first stop of the day has me on edge and I'm not even there yet. Weston was right. It takes something unique to be a salesman, something I don't have.* Traffic had come to a standstill. Delaney closed his eyes and envisioned his little girl. She lay in the hospital bed looking pale and weak. Then for a matter of seconds he imagined her healing, clean blood coursing through her small body—a new beginning, another chance. If only it could be true.

Peter would have to focus all his energy on staying positive and keeping in mind his true purpose, never forgetting why he had taken this stressful job in the first place. *Anything for my little girl*, he repeated to himself… *anything. I can't let some job frighten me.*

Delaney pulled up to 41 North Prospect and parked his car in one of the few open spaces in the expansive lot. He looked at the dashboard clock: *Ten minutes and counting until I meet Mr. Impossible to Please.* Those words had haunted him during the commute. Profuse sweating made his shirt cling to his skin. Hands trembling, he reached into his pocket for a stick of gum, maybe chewing it would quell his tension. Peter got out of the car and took deep breaths. That calmed him for now but he couldn't stave off the anxiety forever. A soft steady breeze helped relieve the relentless heat of the day. While walking toward the office he tried not to think about the difficulties ahead of him or the many obstacles awaiting him in the long run. He would have to set aside his insecurities and do what he had to do to help his family. Jobs were scarce nowadays. And his daughter's health had put him in a precarious situation.

He pushed the double-doors and entered the building against a blast of air conditioning, a refreshing cold draft. He consulted the directory between the elevator doors. The name *Steinberg, Martin* stood out from the sign. His office was in B-1, to his right. Peter was glad he didn't have to get on an elevator: After the episode last year when he and four other passengers got stuck between the tenth and eleventh floors of a New York City skyscraper, he loathed them.

He pulled himself together. Then he approached the door with Steinberg's name on it and knocked. A deep, crisp voice responded. "Come in." There was a *click*. An electronic lock was released.

Delaney went through the thick heavy door; it swung shut behind him automatically. He saw a middle-aged handsome man with slicked back dark hair and a thinly-groomed moustache growing beyond the edges of his upper lip.

"Mr. Steinberg?" Peter asked.

"You've found him," the man said. "What can I do for you, Mr...?"

Peter extended his hand. "Delaney, sir. It's a pleasure to meet you."

Delaney took the chair closest to Steinberg's desk.

"I'm here on behalf of Weston and Associates. I'm Andre Weston's newest employee. I'll be here to tend to your needs from now on. You can call me Peter."

Steinberg furrowed his brow. "My first impression: you couldn't sell milk to an ice-cream parlor."

Delaney was taken aback. "Excuse me, sir, but—"

Steinberg smiled. "Don't get your panties in a bunch, Peter. I was just sizing you up—sense of humor needs work. And don't worry, nobody can hear us; place is soundproof. I don't like distractions."

Peter squirmed in his chair.

"Since you're a new guy allow me to end the suspense. Do you know why I've used Weston for all these years?"

"No sir, I don't. But I'd love to. This way I can better—"

"Save me the dissertation, Mr. Delaney. I'll get to the point. I do business with Weston and Associates because they go as far as I ask them to keep me satisfied. That's the secret behind the client getting precisely what he wants: acting like you're never pleased—hence the term 'the squeaky wheel gets the most grease.' In truth, those easily pacified never receive what they truly want—a bit of wisdom for you there, Peter."

Delaney was a bit off his mark, not sure how to counter the comments. Steinberg rose from his chair while buttoning his jacket. "Here's the deal. I believe you would benefit from joining our 'society,' if you will."

Delaney folded his arms. "What are you talking about, Mr. Steinberg? I came here to fill you in on the latest…"

Steinberg bent down, his eyes met Peter's. Peter smelled a recent cigar on his breath. Steinberg winked. "How far are you willing to go to save your daughter's life?"

Delaney's voice rose. "Watch what you say, sir."

"It's a simple question, Peter."

"How did you know about her? I never said a word about her to you."

"Mr. Delaney, a good salesman does his research before the 'big pitch.' Haven't you learned that yet? I guess this is a textbook case of the client taking the salesman to school."

"What *pitch?*" Delaney said, his voice unsteady.

"Look, I know that your little 'pumpkin' isn't receiving top-quality medical care over at Parkersville Memorial. I can change all of that. It's up to you." Steinberg's stare never wavered from Peter's. Delaney wiggled in his chair. His heart embarked on a wild stampede. As his emotions tangled inside him, his lips started quivering. All he could think about was his frail daughter deteriorating, an image he couldn't erase from his mind.

"What are you trying to pull, Steinberg? You fuckin' with me?"

"No need for foul language, Peter. But here's my offer. Keep in mind…I'll only ask once. There are no second chances, and if you so much as shake your head yes or no that is as good as currency here. Do we have an understanding?"

Peter sat in silent contemplation, a doleful look on his face. He was too physically and emotionally drained to do much else. Part of him wanted to get up and leave, but his body wouldn't comply. His gaze floated around the room.

"Mr. Delaney, upon agreement of my pending offer, your precious Rebecca will be transferred to a top-notch facility where she will be privileged to the best care available."

Just the sound of those words filled Peter with a sense of hopefulness he hadn't felt in a long time. Steinberg seemed cocky and secretive but Peter was inclined to listen, especially when it came to helping Rebecca. "How are you going to pull that off?" asked Delaney, wiping his moist eyes with his sleeve. "Who do you know? What do you know?"

Steinberg smiled, displaying his strong white teeth. "Good business is about connections, not integrity." He chuckled through his nose. "Certainly not about going by the book. Do you want me to continue, Mr. Delaney?"

Delaney gripped the arms of the chair. "Please," he grunted.

Steinberg sat on the edge of his desk facing Peter. "Lastly, your medical expenses—past and present—will be taken care of. So?"

Delaney wiped his face. The room fell silent as he dug for an answer. The seconds ticked away. The tension in the room was palpable.

Steinberg, about to expand on his point, was walking back to the chair behind his desk.

Delaney turned pale. "Who...are...you?"

"The same man you met when you walked in here, Peter. And please, don't disrupt me again."

Peter's left leg drummed on the floor like a sewing machine needle.

"Delaney, here comes what most people refer to as the 'catch.' There's always a catch, my friend. I'll come right out with it. All you have to do is go to…"

Steinberg opened his desk drawer and pulled out a legal pad, flipped through the pages. "Here we go. You will go to 2781 Hillside in say…fifteen minutes, directly from here. You'll climb the front steps to the front door. Are you still with me, Peter? I'll only lay out the particulars once."

Delaney nodded, reluctantly. He felt as though the walls were bearing down on him, as though the ceiling was dropping at a slow but deadly pace.

"Very well then, Peter, I'll finish up."

Peter listened carefully, his arms fidgeting on the chair handles, his sweaty fingers stroking the wood.

"From there you will climb the stairs to the second-floor bedroom on the left, next to the hall closet, and enter. There will be a girl lying in bed. All you have to do—is *smother* her to death with a pillow. Of course, you are not permitted to ask anything more about this arrangement. As soon as you're done, our top priority will be to save your little girl."

"What kind of *sick* game is this, Steinberg?"

"This is no game, Mr. Delaney. I'm dead serious. Ball's in your court."

Peter crossed and uncrossed his legs. He felt his body heating up like a furnace. "I don't know what kind of person you are, Steinberg, but I won't commit a murder. I won't do anybody's dirty work."

"Oh yes you will," Steinberg insisted. "Oh yes you will. There's no way a sappy bleeding-heart type like yourself is going to dismiss the best chances at his only child's survival. You know as well as I do…in the hands of some cocky college-grad emergency room doctor, Becca will die."

"You son of a bitch," Delaney said.

"I've been called worse, Peter, and I'm still standing."

Silence enveloped the room. Delaney swallowed. Steinberg remained calm and in control. Awaiting a response, he got up from his desk and walked to the window. He raised the curtain and looked outside. "You see, Mr. Delaney, sometimes there comes a time when we must arrive at decisions on the spot. We don't always have the luxury of time to make up our minds. What I've offered you is true and real, *sincere* you might say. I will see to it that my promises are adhered to. I'm a man of my word. I want to do for you what was done for me when I joined—give back, so to speak."

Delaney's lips parted as if he were about to speak.

Steinberg raised his hand. "Don't interrupt me. You won't like the consequences should you do it again." At the sound of that statement Peter felt a chill curling around his spine. He kept his mouth shut.

Steinberg pulled a handkerchief from his pocket and lowered his head. "About a year ago my wife was beaten to a pulp in a dark alley after a late night at the office. I'll be honest with you. I always disapproved of the extensive time she spent at work. She loved her labors too much. She played too little, with me less and less through the years. Beautiful gal, though: infectious smile, gigantic heart, endless magnetism. She was flawless really; until that night, of course, when some bastard hammered her into a long road of pills and surgeries. Thanks to this 'Death Lottery,' as I like to call it, I was able to have her attacker tracked down. And I must say…" Steinberg turned around and looked at Delaney. "I took great pleasure in hurting that cocksucker's trophy wife. I'm relieved to have exacted revenge. Why? Because I couldn't rest until I had done everything I could to even the score. After much time, effort, and money, my wife recovered—and so did I."

Steinberg came around the desk and put a hand on Delaney's shoulder. "I will ask you this one time. And remember: your daughter's life hangs in the balance. Will you do what needs to be done?"

Delaney nodded once more.

"Good answer, Peter. Your family is counting on you. One day when the smoke clears you'll thank me."

Steinberg sat down at his desk and read from his pad. "Go to 2781 Hillside. The rest is in your hands. I will say this much: Mrs. Holloway is a single mom and a pretty damn good failure at it. She's been divorced for over a year by a waste-of-life husband. Research indicates that both mother and daughter are drug users. Getting into their home may require a bit of ingenuity on your part, but with visions of a healthy daughter in your head… you'll pull it off."

"What if I get caught, Steinberg?" Peter couldn't believe he was accepting this, but there was no turning back now.

"Does it matter? You know what's at stake here, need I remind you? That's a price you'll have to pay."

Delaney stood.

"Mr. Delaney," Steinberg added, "a car is parked next to yours with keys inside. Turn the key and do what is required of you. Return here in thirty minutes and your Rebecca's on the road to recovery. Your progress will be monitored. If you falter one bit…our deal is off, and Rebecca rots in Parkersville. Should that happen, Peter, I won't lose a moment of sleep over it." Steinberg consulted his watch. "Time's a wastin', my friend."

Delaney's world was out of alignment. He left the office and went to the parking lot. The sun was fierce and overpowering. A shaft of light bouncing off a nearby windshield fired into his eyes. He shielded his face with his hand. He felt suffocated by the stagnant air. He got to the car Steinberg had mentioned. As explained to him, the keys were hanging from the ignition. He turned the key and the motor hummed.

Peter peered in the rearview mirror, closed his eyes. *What am I doing? I look like hell—feel like hell. I can still back out. This is going terribly wrong. I'm terrified. Oh my god, what's happening?* He took a deep breath and opened his eyes. A bead of sweat slid into one of his eyes, irritating it. Peter clutched the top of the steering wheel, as if wringing the life out of it, and thought about whether he had the guts to carry on.

He backed out of the space. While rolling through the parking lot he came to a pedestrian crossing where a mother was pushing her child in a stroller. He was only ten feet from them when he lost his focus. Without slowing, he rolled through the pedestrian lane, forcing mother and child to cross hurriedly. The lady gave him a dirty look which had no effect on him. He turned the corner and followed the exit signs. He had one last road to travel before hitting the highway and bringing himself one step closer to the deadly act.

Just before the exit Peter passed a row of overgrown pine trees and a weather-beaten STOP sign on the verge of collapsing. He continued driving. He turned onto the highway. He had that eerie feeling of being watched, under surveillance by some hidden camera. Was it concealed in the vents? Behind the seats? Where the hell was it? Forget it, he thought. There was no time to get distracted.

Having driven no more than a mile or two, he turned onto Hillside Avenue. He double-checked the sign to be sure he had read it correctly. The street was nothing special, rather dull and unpleasant looking. Most of the houses were surrounded by shoddy fences and ill-kept yards. None of the vehicles in the driveways looked new or expensive.

Ahead on his right he found number 2781. He couldn't miss it. The house had shutters on both sides of the second-floor windows, but they were damaged and dangling. The lawn was overgrown and weedy. Even the house number was difficult to read—the metal numbers on the front door were crooked and tarnished. Peter parallel-parked along the front curb, then surveyed the exterior. The coast seemed clear. This didn't appear to be a neighborhood whose residents concerned themselves with unexpected guests. He glanced in the back seat. A dozen roses lay on the floor. *What the heck is this?* A card was wedged between the flowers. This piqued his curiosity. Peter reached over the seat and yanked the card from the clip:

Carry them with you. They're the perfect decoy. If anybody looks they won't think anything of it. Trust me.

Flowers in hand, Delaney emerged from the car. The street was like a ghost town. He couldn't spot activity of any kind. He crossed the driveway and made his way up the front steps. He never imagined he'd get this far. *I love you, Rebecca. This is all for you. I just want my girl back the way she was.* He wrapped his hand around the knob and pushed the rickety door open; it squealed. He kept quiet, listening for the slightest noise. But not a sound impeded the dreadful silence.

Peter went straight to the staircase and began his ascent. His heart drummed against his sternum. He'd forgotten all about the roses. They had involuntarily slipped from his grip onto the carpeted stairs, planks which hadn't been cleaned for a long, long time, their stench indicative of food spills or something worse. The loose banister wobbled under his twitching fingers.

When he arrived at the top of the stairs he heard something on his right. The sound drifted in from the nearby bedroom—a lady was sound asleep, snoring, a hypodermic needle lying by her forearm. Peter ignored what he'd seen and went about his business. He looked at his watch, observed the second-hand ticking away pertinent seconds. With each step he took, the floor boards clattered underneath him. A few more paces put him in the other bedroom—the place where he had to be—where time and determination were of the essence. When he entered, a foul odor assaulted him, a fouler smell than before, a smell akin to mildew. The repulsive air got trapped on his tongue. He could taste the bitterness.

What he found in the bed before him was more unsettling than anything else he'd experienced before this fateful day: a young girl, mid-teens, pale and malnourished, was asleep on the bed. Right away he noticed her wretched features. Her hair was cropped close to her scalp, messy and punkish. Her skin was disfigured by purple blotches of some kind, maybe from using drugs with her mom, he guessed. The blemishes unsettled him. This was somebody's little girl, just like his, and nobody seemed to care that her life was hardly a life at all. The young girl's breathing resembled a wheezing asthmatic's. There were two pillows on the bed, one under her head and one beside her. Delaney thought about his next move. Was what he was about to do really worth the regret that would haunt him for a lifetime? He took a few more steps and stopped next to the girl on the bed. A few feet at the most separated him from his helpless young target. He had no idea who she was. Nor why she deserved to die. He saw an abused young soul minutes away from never waking up again, never seeing a sunrise, never hearing a bird chirping to signal a new day. He subdued the slim chance of her awakening for a split second only to realize that she couldn't breathe and that life as she knew it was all over. Peter looked around the room and saw nothing but squalor. The dresser drawers were overflowing with clothes. The mirror above the dresser was dingy and cracked and tilting forward. That nasty odor was growing stronger with each passing minute. The stench lingered around him, permeated the room. The carpet too was stained in several places, the walls scarred and peeling.

How can anybody live like this? Maybe I can end the suffering? That's what this is, right?

He leaned over the girl and curled his fingers around the edges of the spare pillow, lifted it chest level. *I can't do this to an innocent girl. This is horribly wrong. I may never see the light of day again if I end her life. My conscience can't bear it. What's the matter with me?*

From behind Peter the girl's mother still snored.

Delaney wanted to back out, to run away and hide forever. He was damn close to picking up the phone and calling the whole thing off. But how would he do it? There was no negotiating from this point forward. No number to call. His watch revealed a paltry thirteen minutes remaining to complete the job and get to Steinberg's office. *Will I get a chance like this ever again? Fuck! What on earth am I saying to myself? Chance? Chance to do what? Kill an innocent girl?*

But—But—This will save my child. That's all I care about. I have to act now. I want my princess to have a normal life, like other girls have. Somebody please show me the way!

Delaney held the pillow merely inches from the girl's mouth and summoned all his strength. He couldn't stop himself now. He'd made a commitment. No one would forgive his actions. Peter would have to make peace with that. He would leave a never-ending trail of trauma in his path, but more importantly, repair his own.

How did I get myself into this? Why me? I should've never gone in for that interview. Where will I end up? What will become of me? Terminating one life to save Rebecca's? Is that what I want to do? But there's no alternative, as much as I'd like to believe there's a way out of this mess. I'm here now. My daughter's suffering while I stand here like a failure again—a despicable excuse for a human being, for a father. I'm sorry. My Becca needs me. I refuse to let her wither away.

Peter thrust the pillow against her face—put all his weight behind it, pressed as hard as he could. And before he had the chance to register how far he'd come he began to cry. As he heard the girl choking on the pillow and fighting for air, tears rained down his face. Seconds passed. For Peter it most certainly felt like forever as her body bucked furiously and her lungs crumbled and compressed. Indeed the girl had awakened from her slumber. She kicked her legs like a wild animal, tried to pry away Peter's hands, but he out-muscled her. Sweat from his forehead stippled the pillow. He had applied so much pressure that his knuckles sank into the mattress and the springs resisted and screeched. His forearms began to spasm from the excessive downward force. Peter's eyes roamed around the room, panic guiding them in circles. But the more he thought of Rebecca deteriorating and alone, the more convinced he became that his actions were just, regardless of how horrible they were. He had to protect his own, no matter the cost. Life gradually left the girl's body—her legs fought less…and less… and less. Her half-hearted attempts to draw oxygen were thwarted under Peter's anchoring arms. He somehow found relief in the fact that it didn't last long.

The young girl had no chance of surviving. It was all over.

From the other side of the hall the girl's mother approached the bedroom. She was groggy and almost stumbling across the floor. A stream of blood ran down her forearm where a drug had been injected only hours ago. The veins in her arms were shades of black and blue, the skin had been perforated repeatedly—very little of her flesh had escaped her addiction. She hobbled along using the wall to hold herself up. She peered into the bedroom where her daughter lay dead, an empty shell; Peter had ended her life and left, undetected. Her head was turned to the side, eyes wide open and unmoving, frozen in their sockets, the energy and life gone forever, her skin parchment white.

Mom mumbled to her daughter. "You're still asleep? I'm going back to bed, too…so tired."

Hours later Peter Delaney stood exhausted by his daughter's bed, crying nonstop. He gently stroked her forehead and told her how much he loved her. He was a complete wreck, a lost and wounded soul. "I love you, Rebecca," he said. "This is all going to get better soon—I promise."

The phone on the table next to the bed rang and Peter answered it, his voice drowning in the effects of delirium. "Hello?"

"Peter, it's me. How's our baby doing?" his wife asked.

"She's…she's a fighter," Peter answered from a deep sea of despair.

"I'm on my way over to the hospital," his wife said. "Be there in fifteen minutes or so."

"O…Okay."

"Is everything all right, Peter? You sound lousy."

"I'm just so damn fatigued. My first day was," he closed his eyes, "… brutal. I'll be fine though. Just get here as soon as you can."

"I'm trying. Oh…by the way, I had a call from a Mr. Steinberg. I don't know who he is, but he claimed to know you quite well. He wished Rebecca a speedy recovery, said he hoped the doctors at Parkersville treat her well. Gotta go. See you in a few."

The phone fell from Peter's hand and hit the floor, smashing to pieces. He dropped to his knees and then curled on the floor into a ball of anguish.

CAREFUL WHAT YOU WISH FOR

Devon was celebrating his tenth birthday. His parents, Eleanor and James, threw him a small party with a few friends. They gathered around the table. His mother had decorated the house and was busy in the kitchen. His friends were in the dining room acting rambunctious while his mother added the finishing touches to the freshly-baked cake. James stood by, absorbing it all and remembering last year's party, the way it fell apart before they had a chance to enjoy the meal. Devon was in a weird mood that day. This year James hoped for a better turnout.

The room looked festive. Devon's mom had spent most of the morning tying up loose ends for their celebration. James decided to go out with his son to give Eleanor some space and time to complete last minute preparations; that's how he'd always responded when she was getting stressed. Eleanor wanted to make an impression on her son. Everything had to be perfect, just as she envisioned it. After all, Devon wasn't the easiest kid to please, and when he wasn't he made a spectacle of it. Last month they had gone to a parent/teacher conference at his school. One of the teachers remarked on Devon's inability to concentrate in class, how he occasionally disrupted the group to earn the attention of others who were known for being troublemakers. When he was grounded for his behavior, Devon retaliated the next day by making a fire in a garbage drum outside the school's cafeteria. Upset by his actions, his parents refused to let him leave his room unless it was for a meal or the bathroom. After a week of restrictions—among them no television or friends visiting—he calmed down. Now that his birthday had come they wanted to put those incidents behind them and give him a nice party.

During their morning errands, father and son hadn't said much in the car. Devon stared out the window. His dad focused on the road ahead, only glancing at his quiet son once or twice. James did not understand why his son wouldn't talk, why he seemed so despondent on his special day, a day that comes only once a year. He had an idea what bothered him, but decided not to delve into it until they found a more propitious time. Besides, all Devon wanted to do was get the ride over with so he could go home and have fun. He had waited a full year for a new birthday, just like the one every kid his age usually had. His buddies always had parties in big halls or rented rooms with wall-to-wall friends and gifts aplenty. But not him. Never. *What have my parents done for me this time? Baked a cake? Bought me a few worthless presents like savings bonds or candy, or if I'm lucky a baseball card or two that have no value? Last year Timmy Wilkins got a brand new Playstation with games for his birthday. How come he gets good stuff and I get boring things?*

In the living room, balloons floated high, spreading across the ceiling, "Happy Birthday" stenciled on them. The walls were festooned with colorful streamers featuring some of Devon's favorite sports heroes. Eleanor had bought special paper plates and cups too. She threw herself into creative moments like these. However, the most frustrating part of the day was Devon's failure to appreciate her hard work and dedication. Not once did he comment on the effort she put into delivering him a good birthday. Eleanor had the urge to reprimand him, to lambaste him, to give him a sense of what she was feeling inside, the ache a mother feels because of the ignorance of her own child. James told her to forget about it. "Let it go. It's no big deal. You know how he is. He's just being a twerp," James said.

"Yeah... It's easy for you to say," she snapped back. "You weren't the one slaving all day in front of a hot stove and going up and down a step-ladder." Eleanor walked away, disappeared into the kitchen. James made the announcement that it was time for cake.

Eleanor opened the cabinet underneath the sink, grabbed a lighter and stood immobile for moments. Her eyes started to water. She tried to fight back her tears and her boiling emotions. Devon's inconsideration had irked her beyond endurance; but after calming down, she returned to the party. The boys were becoming rowdier. Devon started being a brat again, poking the gifts, shaking the boxes and predicting what was inside, acting silly. His buddies egged him on. "What is it, Dev? Whaddaya got? A CD? Video game? What?"

Devon looked across the table and noticed his dad wearing a dirty look on his face, telling him with pinched eyebrows to stop being rude. Devon huffed, then put the present back on the table. Eleanor also found it hard to put up with his shenanigans. She bit down hard on her lip, grimacing. For most of the day Eleanor's wrist had been bothering her; she had carelessly touched the oven rack when pulling the cake from the stove and now the burn started throbbing again. She touched the irritated flesh, wincing. She gave everyone around the table a cold stare, especially Devon.

Everybody and everything was in place. She lit the candles. James stood by taking pictures. "C'mon now, son. Make a wish, blow out the candles," he prodded. "Then I'll get a shot of you cutting the first piece. How's that sound?"

Devon leaned toward the shivering flame, got real close, lost himself in its fiery dance atop the wax pedestal. Suddenly and unexpectedly he recalled a vivid dream he'd had a few nights before:

Everything felt terribly odd. At first, Devon was unsure what was happening. He sensed he was under a spell of some kind, but instead of being unconscious, he was fully aware. His friends and family had disappeared, vanished from the party. The cake was still on the table, slices of it were gone. The gifts had been unwrapped as well. What difference did it make? It was the same shit as last year, exactly as he'd thought. There was never a surprise awaiting him, only his pals got those. He wandered from the table, walked into the kitchen. Mom was probably there, he assumed. He opened the swinging door, entered. The room was just as she'd left it. He peered over at the cutting board. Cutlery was missing. To the left, on the kitchen table, the leftover tube of icing lay on the edge of the marble top, remnants oozing from the tip. Devon squeezed his eyes shut, reopened them. His surroundings hadn't changed at all.

He left the kitchen, continued wandering, searching for his friends and folks. Crossing through the dining room into the foyer he discovered his parents' jackets—his first clue. It was freezing outside, the picture window covered with ice. If they had ventured outdoors, the winter coats would not have been left behind. He heard something smack the front door behind him. He turned, facing it. That must have been the wind, he told himself. He heard it whistling outside, its cold slaps rattling the chimes.

Devon shouted, "Stevie? Eric? Michael? Where are you guys? Mom? Dad?" He ran to the front door, peeked through the mesh curtains and saw the branches of a tree bending under the force of the wind's violent breath; the snow-enrobed branches couldn't withstand the heavy layers of snow and ice. Devon was nervous. This bizarre discovery had gotten under his skin. What the hell was this? An out-of-body experience? The *Twilight Zone* theme played in his head over and over again. His dad loved that show. Devon was not allowed to watch TV but occasionally snuck a peek or two at the screen.

From out of nowhere he heard voices: "Devon, snap out of it, snap out of it." But he saw nothing, no one. He scrambled to the window at the other side of the house, just to the left of the couch, and opened the drapes. His mom's car was still parked in the driveway, his dad's alongside it. What was happening?

A creaking came from the top of the stairs. Devon appraised the area, spotted something, a figure, moving swiftly across the top step. He gasped. His heart thundered in his chest, his stomach roiled. He had no way of knowing who—or what—it was. Screams issued from the second floor. Standing uneasily at the bottom step, Devon heard the noises clearly. He stood frightened, shaking as if he were trapped outdoors in the clutches of the brutal winter night. The cries he had heard just moments ago were horrendous, unlike anything he had ever heard before. They became louder, then fell in pitch, rose to a crescendo again, plummeted. A pleading voice mixed with the pain-laden cries, "Please, stop! Damn you!" Devon recognized the voice right away—it was his father's! Although he was petrified, he proceeded to climb the stairs. His body got warm, sweaty. His mouth opened wide, a rictus of horror. Pale light illuminated the staircase, enough for him to ascend. He tiptoed carefully, calves wobbling as he got closer to the second level. Hands braced on the banisters, he kept himself steady.

When he reached the top step he stood, eyes blurred by tears of fear. A long thin feather of light spread like a tentacle across the floor. A light in the bathroom was on, the door ajar, allowing the light to creep out into the hall and pool around his running shoes. The horrid screams subsided. Devon tiptoed toward the bathroom. The voice he'd heard before returned to taunt him. "Devon, come on now. Will you pay attention?"

Where was it coming from? Whose voice was that? What lurked behind the door?

He clutched the knob, turned it, pushed the door in and stepped forward into the room, where he confronted something worse than he could ever have imagined in his worst nightmares. Blindfolded and gagged, his father was bound to a chair by barbed wire. The wire had gouged deep trails into his skin, which was lacquered in blood. Devon was terrified by what stood next to his dad. Someone else was in the room administering these unspeakable cruelties, a person that resembled him. Actually... it was him. Devon was staring at an exact image of himself. His eyes darted to the mirror. Two men were staring back at him—himself and a look-alike. He stood stiff, breathless. The stranger, the ghost, the clone–whatever it was—raised a long jagged-toothed machete above his head and then, with a swift downward stroke, plunged it deep into his father's chest, then into his head, his leg, his arm, and then finally his neck, where it tore through one side and came out the other. Blood thick as paste seeped from the gashes. His father was dead, defenseless, but it didn't stop the deranged Devon from repeatedly inflicting more punishment, ripping open more wounds, deeper and wider than the others. The Devon clone turned and looked at him with intimidating eyes—pupils bright red like lava—and spoke in a scratchy, demonic voice. "Careful what you wish for, Devon. Go play Marco Polo with Mom. See if you can find her."

Devon heard more screams filter in from outside. He glanced through the window by the sink. Below in the yard his friends were running away from the house, heading to the street. They cried out, "Help, help!"

Devon left the room, pinned himself against the opposing wall, and thought about the carnage he'd just witnessed: deep gashes all over his father's body, blood dripping onto the linoleum floor, streaks across the mirror and the tub—an inexplicable blood bath. Having to watch the doppelganger committing those acts affected him profoundly. He was supposed to feel terrible about what he'd seen. And for those few scary moments he did indeed experience fear. But instead of dealing with an emotional disaster he was overwhelmed by clarity, an incomprehensible clarity. He felt…relieved. He was glad he—or someone like him—had killed the bastard. A sadistic smiled creased his face. *Who needs parents like these? They should have done a better job. I mean, they think they can make up for the years of constant screwing-up by throwing me a lame party and pretending to care, especially after last year when all I got was a belt for saying I didn't like my gifts and how Timmy always got cool stuff. Or how about when Mom slapped me good and red for going into her purse for a little cash to get candy at Humphrey's. She's fuckin' next on my list. I felt like slapping that bitch back then. And all she did was whine in that annoying voice of hers. "If you needed the money why couldn't you just ask me for it? Why would you steal from me?" WA…WA…WA. The stupid ass doesn't understand that I would've asked if I knew she'd say yes. But there was always a problem. Well, now it's solved— once and for all. Paybacks are a bitch.*

Devon pushed himself away from the wall, ran down the staircase and moved into the foyer. Up on the right there was a closet door underneath the stairs. On the left hand side of the door stood a wooden coat rack. Various hooks protruded from the post like wormy growths. Devon walked past it and went to the window at the far wall. He pulled back the curtain and stared into the cold, dreary night. The furious weather hadn't let up, perhaps it would worsen. The wind pummeled the house, lashed out violently, snapping a large branch from a nearby tree. It became tangled in the power lines. Devon enjoyed watching the thick branch sizzle, a victim of the powerful electrical charge now left to wither and die.

Behind Devon there was a *thud*. It came from the closet. He quickly spun to investigate. The door separated from the frame, collapsed, with his dead mother crashing down on top of it, her skull mangled beyond recognition, shredded to ribbons. Again he experienced an internal metamorphosis: seeing his parents dead, knowing he or someone else had killed them with his bare hands, was exhilarating. A weight had been lifted. The sons of bitches were finally out of his life. He would start anew; do as he pleased, without rules, without bullshit—whatever he wanted, whenever he wanted it…

Devon's attention drifted away from the candle flame. He sat back properly in his seat, a shitty grin on his face. His heartbeat returned to normal. He wiped the sweat from his forehead, took a deep breath, allowing his mind, his thoughts, to become controllable again. His mom started hassling him. "Don't get so damn close to the candles, Devon."

"Yeah, make a wish for crying out loud, son," his father hollered. "You've been spacing out for the last few minutes, daydreaming, ignoring us."

"What's taking you so long, Dev? C'mon dude," his pals urged.

"I made my wish guys, got lost in a dream I've had

many times before. Taking my time is all. I'm just making sure that's what I *really* want," Devon replied.

He looked up at his parents, then at his friends. "Yeah, it's what I *really, really* want."

Devon blew out the candles.

"I hope you made it count, Devon. It took you long enough," his father said.

Devon beamed. "I sure did. It's the best wish anyone could ever ask for. I hope my dream comes true."

NO REMORSE

For days the public had been captivated by the news. One of the country's most ruthless serial killers was going to be interviewed. Anytime now, Russell Kincade would walk down the long halls of Maratauk State Prison in front of the whole world, wearing an orange jumpsuit, his wrists and ankles locked in a web of chains. The free world was going to be consumed by his story, mesmerized and appalled. This was a man on Death Row, only days from being executed for his killing spree ten years ago. Six feet tall, long blond hair flowing down his back, Kincade was imposing. His eyes were traffic-light green, and the ladies adored him. There had never been another serial killer in the entire universe whose magnetism equaled his. He had received an abundance of cards and letters during his years of incarceration, many of them written by women who wanted to bear his children or just elope and surrender to his needs. Most of the time when he got out of hand it took quite a few guards and sometimes multiple shots from the electric prod to take him down. He was a mountain of muscle that had remained close-lipped until this dreary night, a night when heavy snowfall was bombarding Haledon County, stranding the public indoors in front of the television. The world awaited this murderer's final words.

Thirty minutes before midnight: The young beautiful reporter was escorted through the prison's eerie serpentine halls. The inmates greeted her with a chorus of whistles; they were not shy about making disgusting sounds or gestures. Brittany Landira was an up-and-coming journalist who had written a series of novels about serial killers. She was trying to promote her forthcoming book *Inside the Killing Mind*. She had a January release date scheduled and here she was in December, a week before the holidays, on the verge of interviewing a famous psychopath in front of morbidly curious viewers.

Two heavily-armed guards walked on each side of her. The guard to her right briefed her as they took the stroll from the cellblock down to the interrogation room. Lights and cameras flashed around her. News correspondents chatted beside the door. A man rambled on the phone outside the room where Brittany was headed. The lady next to him scribbled furiously on a pad.

The guard turned to Brittany. "Look, Mrs. Landira. I know you're aware of the rules and capable of doing what you have to tonight. But it's my obligation to warn you, so please listen tight. There will be an armed guard in the room with you at all times. His job is to protect you, plain and simple. He will sit off to the side between you and Mr. Kincade. Do not for any reason make sudden moves. If you feel uncomfortable for any reason, you are to motion to the guard and the meeting is terminated."

Brittany's eyes revealed tension. She never blinked. She paid full attention to the guard's instructions. She rubbed her fingers together and felt the sweat oozing from her palms then she started to play with her wedding ring, rolling it back and forth on her finger. The guard continued. "If he moves at all in a manner we consider suspicious, this meeting is automatically over, no questions asked. I will only allow you to bring a writing implement, a pad, and a recorder into the room. Your purse and other belongings are not permitted inside. Oh, and one more thing… you can swallow now."

Brittany entered the cell and the guard pulled up a chair for her. She pulled out a pair of glasses from her jacket and put them on. This was the first time she'd been in an interrogation room, so she inspected the place with what little time she had before Kincade made his big entrance. Bright tubular lights beat down on her. She made note of a desk behind her tucked away in the corner, and two chairs in front of her. The guard occupied one of them and soon Kincade would occupy the other. Straight ahead of her, behind thick glass, bystanders looked on standing shoulder to shoulder. A small camera crew had set up in front of the glass and their piercing lights made her squint.

The thick, riveted door opened and in walked Russell Kincade. Brittany took a couple of quick breaths and started tapping the pad with her pen, clearly a nervous reaction. The guard rose and pointed to the chair where Russell had to sit. Brittany sat in silent disbelief. She wondered how a man like him, so innocent-looking and seemingly tender, could maim and murder people. His aura and good looks were undeniable. In fact, Brittany smiled at him when he sat in place. He exuded a sexiness she couldn't explain. She hit the button on her recorder.

Kincade spoke. His voice was gentle too, which surprised her. "Hello, Brittany, it's nice to see you up close, if you don't mind my saying so? You're quite attractive."

She was flattered, despite what he was. She couldn't hide her blushing. "Thank you, Mr. Kincade."

He smiled, nodded slightly. "Please, 'Russell' will do just fine. Besides, in a few hours it's not going to matter."

Brittany looked at the pad and then at him. "Well, Russell." She cleared her throat. "I am doing research on a book and it will deal with what makes people kill. What forces a man—or a woman—to cross the line and take a human life without remorse. I was hoping you wouldn't mind telling me some of your story. This is why I am here, sir."

"Of course I will tell you. If you are willing to take the time for me, I can return the gesture. I am going to tell you things as they come to mind, disclosing the details as accurately as I can. All I ask of you is this: If you write a book about me, represent what I say with regard to the truth only. What I tell you is nothing but that. Do not put your own spin on what I reveal. Don't butcher my story." Russell smiled. "No pun intended."

He continued. "Take the information I give you and try to learn something from it. I've sat through countless mental examinations over the years and all that's come of my sessions is wealthier doctors. I'm not a sick man, Brittany." He looked up at the ceiling, then focused on her, looked right through her beautiful brown eyes. His own eyes were like a set of powerful green torches eating their way through her. "I just stopped caring about my species and what they stand for. For the first thirty years of my life I was just like everybody watching us right now all over the world. The only difference between them and me… is that I acted on my impulses. So, if you don't have any questions—I'll begin."

Brittany shook her head. "No, sir…sorry—Russell."

"It all started when I was a teenager. My father was a hard worker and he made a decent living. We had food on the table and a roof over our heads. Where I come from that means you're doing pretty damn good. He was a salesman and spent most of his life trying to close the deal, hustling to keep the family afloat. My mother worked in the beginning and the two incomes helped make life easier. There was a time when my father's business really skyrocketed and my mom decided to stay at home. I was an only child and there were no others to take care of. What I gathered at the time was that Mom wanted to sit on her ass and contribute nothing. She always wanted that and the old man caved in to her desire.

"For a while it seemed to work, but it wasn't long before he started to change. He became a different man: bitter, angry, pushing harder to keep their lifestyle up to what they were accustomed to. When my mother was working it took the edge off him. But when it was him alone, the workload wore him out and his life started to deteriorate. I saw the signals flashing before my eyes that there was trouble down the road and we were headed straight for it. My dad would come home from a long day at work trying to push products and he'd toss his briefcase onto the kitchen table, disgusted, defeated. He was exhausted just about every day, and more than a handful of times he even fell asleep at the table. My mother would usually prepare a meal for him and he would have to struggle to eat he was so damn burnt out. But for a stretch of who knows how long, my mom had the life she always dreamed of, and meanwhile my pop worked his ass off to try and keep it that way. I never saw the point in any of it. They rarely spoke, and on a good week they spent a few hours together in front of the television where he would eventually doze off anyway. That was the first time in my life I asked myself how my mother could sit back and watch him kill himself without jumping in to help the sorry bastard. For some reason nobody saw it my way. Needless to say, my parents became strangers living under the same roof…and I watched from a distance. Nothing changed for a long time, when suddenly shit happened.

"The old man's business took a hit and the family, if you want to call it that, was struggling to keep it together. My father felt like a shit, like a failure. He had to swallow his pride and surrender his nuts when he asked my mother to find work before they drowned in troubled waters. That didn't go over well and the gloves came off. I recall a few demeaning comments she made to him. Who knows where her venom came from, but she poured it on like a real beast. If there was one thing good I could say about my dad it would be that he was resilient. He powered through the obstacles. But his doing so really irked me. I thought his actions were despicable actually. I told him to speak his mind—tell her to get a fucking job!

He just looked at me with a puffy set of purple bags under his eyes and said flat out, with his voice drained of life, 'What's the point? It accomplishes nothing.'

"Do you know how that sounds? I couldn't help it. I viewed the man with contempt. I mean, to not even defend your manhood, to let her shatter your humanity to bits. I sure as shit would have made some different decisions, some really drastic ones. I'd fix that crap in a heartbeat. Shortly thereafter my mother spent hours each day at the church asking the Lord and the priest for a better life, squandering cash each week in the baskets, hoping that the ghost upstairs would answer her prayers. One day after she came home from church, she and my father had an argument about the financial straits they were in. She asked coldly what happened to the money he had made in the past. My father had an empty look on his face, staring at nothing, like a lost soul. The dilemma left my mother no choice but to find work or risk losing the house. With much prodding she went back to work. Her disappointment only fueled my father's humiliation, made him feel less like a man. He kept plugging away and ignored her constant jabs. She found work at a dry cleaner. All she did was bitch about the pay and the early hours. Dad told her to just hold onto the work until something better came along. It was desperate times then, Brittany."

Brittany placed the pen between her teeth, deep in thought. "So, tell me what happened after that."

Kincade clucked his tongue. "I was getting there. Maybe you should reserve your questions until I'm done."

Brittany smirked nervously, but said nothing.

Kincade continued. "She worked for a few

months and then swiftly jumped ship to work as a secretary in a real-estate office. The pay was substantially more but the job had its drawbacks. The worst one being that she had an affair with one of the partners. It wasn't long after that when she walked out on my dad and never looked back. That's no bullshit. Everything happened that fast. When they split up I was already on my own. I had to find my own way in the world. What's a man to do with such pathetic role models in his life? Then I recall vividly that it was somewhere in my twenties when my life changed. There was no warning. It just hit me out of the blue like a left hook. I met someone. It's hard to believe, I know. We shared a few good years before she evolved into a real nutcase too. What luck I had. She questioned everything. Her name is not worth mentioning. She deserves to be strapped to a pole and beaten to death. I thought about doing it, believe me.

"Our relationship had some good times mixed in with the misery. I remember when we started out she used to be so into me. She was insatiable. Then after a short period of time we confronted the once-a-month plan, twice when I pushed hard enough for it. I never understood her problem, why she played games for no reason. I was decent to her too—tried to keep her happy—but she transformed into a jealous freak. And I was never a cheater, mind you. You must understand, I was a witness to what my gutless old man went through with my heartless bitch mother, and I still made every attempt at showing a little niceness with the ladies in my life. My ex was no different. But lest you wonder, she planted the seed that soon germinated into a thriving crop, my insanity.

"I'll never forget the day when the wrong wires crossed in her head and I started down this path which soon will lead me to thousands of volts coursing through my body until it's fried to a crisp. I came home that day and she was in one of her moods. She had them often and they always flared up unannounced. There was no warning or special distress signal. When it happens—a man's got no chance. Ask any one of the men in this room, or even your husband. He'll tell you all about the mental scars, and the indelible mark that's left on the male psyche when a woman separates at the seams."

"My husband wouldn't share your insight," Brittany said.

"Keep dreaming, honey," Kincade responded—then he continued.

"She was one of these high-maintenance cun... Sorry. I won't use that word in front of a lady like you, Brittany. Pardon my almost French, but that's honest, direct language when talking about her. They are the sole reason that domestic battery crimes have risen during the last ten years. I walked in the front door and she attacked me with a mouthful. She went on and on about pressures in her life and the stress she was under. I'm not going to lie to you at this point. It wouldn't serve my purpose here. She didn't know what pressure was and I didn't give a fuck about her outburst or what was going on inside that pea brain of hers.

"One of my best friends from way back was in the military. He told me stories that blew my mind: tales about the sound of explosions and bombs, about dead bodies and charging enemies, about holding a dead nurse, or even a bunker buddy in your arms as they take their final breath, about seeing a missile coming straight for your head and realizing that your life is about to end in a flash of seconds, and telling your loved ones back home how much you loved them although they'll never hear it. So forgive me if that little pain in the ass's outburst didn't concern me.

"Anyway, I stormed out of the house to get some fresh air. I had to clear my head. I walked down the road and found my way to the park where I strolled along the edge of the woods taking in the scenery. I needed time alone, or I think I might have killed her right there. Suddenly I heard a girl whimpering in the distance and I turned to see what was going on, who it was. There was a young girl, maybe thirteen or fourteen tops, sitting on the bench crying her eyes out. I felt horrible. The sight of her hands cupped over her face and the sound of her weeping just crushed me inside. She was all alone and almost looked abandoned, lost—helpless. I was curious so I made my way over and sat next to her. I asked what the problem was and she lifted her head from her palms. Her face was redder than an apple. Her eyes were engorged with tears and there were lines of saliva scaling from lip to lip. She started to talk but what I heard was mumbling through her distorted attempts at speaking.

"Eventually she revealed to me that her father had slapped her mother in the face right in front of her, and she ran out of the house while they were fighting. She said she never once saw her dad snap like that and it really terrified her. All I remember her saying after that was

'How could he do that?'

"After her little revelation she wept more and then placed her head on my shoulder. I wanted to comfort her so I put my arm around her and pulled her closer. I assured her that none of this was her fault and that sometimes adults get out of hand. All of which is true, by the way. Don't tell me you and your husband never locked horns, Brittany. Violence is inbred in our culture, just as much as male chivalry. But I digress."

"My husband is not a brute, Russell. But my personal life is irrelevant."

"A little defensive are we?"

She licked her lips, pushed the interview along. "So what happened with this little girl?"

"A few minutes later she composed herself and thanked me for my help, then hugged me and kissed my cheek. It was at that precise moment that my life hit a road block. My woman drives past and sees that innocuous episode transpiring. She went ballistic and sped away. Later that night she ripped into me, tore me a new ass. (That's a better way of putting it.) She wouldn't hear me out, wouldn't listen to my side of the story. She asked me if that's what I always wanted, some hot young thing? I know if that kid were a fat crap she wouldn't have went crazy on me. She walked out on me and stole some of my money. She weaseled her way into my private stash somehow. I don't want to talk about her anymore, Brittany.

"I turned into a bitter man after that. That's an understatement actually. I started to despise... no, in fact, hate women. I thought of terrible ways to harm them. I slowly felt something…happening…inside me…that I didn't want to resist. There was this one Friday night that I came to grips with the fact that I had permanently and dangerously crossed over into madness and that I needed to lash out at will, let go of my pent-up anger. I went to a bar that evening and started chatting it up with some chick. From the second we made eye contact she wanted me, and we both knew it. We sat at a table, and she discreetly but purposefully hiked up her skirt allowing me a better view of what was hidden beneath. What she did aroused me and that was why she did it. Women and their games… it's unbelievable. I kept my cool and we had a few drinks. The vibe we shared was undeniable. She kept looking at me like a fatso staring at an ice-cream sundae. All this from a girl who was drunk, flirting, and had a Jesus cross dangling from her neck and a cross ring on her finger. We got back to her place and I made a move. She retreated and it pissed me off. I told myself then and there that I wasn't leaving without getting a shot at her prize. My balls had swelled to the size of softballs. That's how they felt to me. Go ahead, Brittany, ask any guy in this room how that feels." Russell laughed. "They'll tell you the truth.

"The situation got out of hand and I grabbed her by the hair and forced myself on her. She tried to push me off but I was too strong for her. My desires outweighed all logic and reason. I entered her and she played into it, and I fell for it. She was moaning and pretending to enjoy it, and I was too stupid to realize she was suckering me in. Why couldn't she be civil before and just give it up instead of forcing me to get violent. She ended up on top and swiftly yanked my pecker so hard I was shocked she didn't detach it. Well, my night concluded in handcuffs, but much to my surprise the whore dropped any charges. I was soon released. My record was clean. I had no priors. Plus she knew if they investigated further they would uncover that she permitted me to enter her. She had no bruises or cuts on her body, no evidence of a real struggle for her life. It was all a game…like I said.

"I remember walking down the street after I was set free and going into a store to buy cigarettes. There was a young guy there, an off-duty cop, looked like some twenty-year-old to me in street clothes. He put his finger in my face and told me how lucky I was that he didn't catch me in the act with that girl because he would have roughed me up. I grabbed his index finger and nearly fed it to him. I clamped his other hand at his belt just to show 'Mr. Tough as Nails' that if he had a gun he was too slow and not strong enough to take me down. I wanted to show him that without it he was nothing. He was overpowered. As I walked away from the store I thought to myself, if he was in my shoes I guarantee he wouldn't settle for a cold shower. It was then that a sick feeling washed over me. I needed another rush, and soon.

"Any goodness in my heart was long gone, drained clear. Fuck people, I thought. Humans live in a very cushy society, and all I wanted to do was completely disrupt the flow and infuse chaos into the box they've built for themselves. I wanted to rattle their cages, do what was done to me, and teach the world a painful and powerful lesson, one they'd never forget. It didn't take long for me to commit my first murder. And once I developed the taste for it, I knew that's where I belonged. You have to be willing to pay the ultimate price if you want to be a serial killer: to never look back or second guess yourself, no matter what the cost.

"That night we had nice summer weather. The sun was setting and I was off to my night shift at the factory. I drove a Ford two-door at the time. It was nothing fancy but it got me from point A to point B. When I came to the intersection of Dwayne and Hamilton I had the right of way. To my right, at the last second before I cleared the intersection, I see a Lexus ripping toward me. The fucker was talking on his cell phone and had no plans on slowing down or stopping. Whether we collided or not was in my hands. I used evasive action and steered away to avoid an ugly incident. The guy, this asshole, kept on going. Our vehicles didn't clash but I was forced into a spinout and I hit the curb and came to an abrupt stop. The anger I felt consumed me. I was seething, Brittany. It was a state of mind that I tried to wrestle down to the ground, but it latched on and persuaded me to do something I'd never done before. I backed away from the curb and followed the man. Getting to work no longer mattered. Seeking payback was what I had in mind. There was no turning back. One thing that sorry ass didn't know was that he was about to experience his worst nightmare and I was more than eager to rise to the occasion. I trailed him for about ten minutes, never letting him out of sight. I was mentally preparing for my first kill, a well-deserved one too... You know, I have to say something. It's even easier to bring this up now, being that I'm moments away from being juiced to death. But the truth is that some people deserve to die. Most of the world is full of pussies too afraid to explore that notion. Everybody's always crying about being an innocent victim. What a crock. There's evil inside of everyone, and it finds its way out sooner or later. Think about that while the voltage is screaming through me and you're selling tons of books, Brittany."

Brittany lowered her glasses. "With all due respect, Russell, I'm not trying to sell books. Don't misinterpret my agenda here. The world wants to get into your mind, and working for the media provides a conduit. As far as everyone being evil is concerned, Russell, I beg to differ. I'm far from what you've suggested, but let's not get off track. Please continue. What happened with the man who drove you off the road?" Brittany put her glasses on again.

"That man in the Lexus made the biggest mistake of his meaningless life. People don't understand common courtesy. They don't give a damn about respect. They don't like being inconvenienced. They don't understand how one stupid mistake ruins another's life. But…they do understand pain, they do understand revenge, they do understand fear, they do understand retribution. They understand all of those human emotions…but they're deathly afraid of them. Human beings put on a strong front, but each and every one of them is so fragile inside. They walk around all day like zombies, easily frightened about everything, afraid that their little nest they built for themselves will be shattered to pieces. What a pointless existence. Don't you think so?"

251

Brittany uncrossed her legs, and crossed them the other way. She looked away for a second then returned her focus to Kincade. "No I don't. Frankly, I think *your* existence is pointless. You are the weak one, sir. You're the one who couldn't control his urges and deserves what he's about to get. I think you're the—what was the word you used before? 'Pussy' was it?"

Russell laughed through his nose. "A lady using the word 'pussy'...I like that."

"Please, Russell, go on," she said.

"Fortunately the Lexus took a pit stop for a cup of coffee. I pulled into the parking lot and turned off my car, watching and waiting carefully for him to enter the store, eager to make my move. It was the perfect situation for a crime, the ideal situation to embark on my first kill. The idiot got out of the car and went inside, only to wait in a line that was roped off from the register to the front door. I slipped into his spacious car and nobody noticed my little maneuver. Either that or nobody cared. I found humor in the fact that here I was, just minutes from maiming this guy, and he's rushing into a Starbucks for a three dollar cup of tar.

"How pathetic. He left the store with a coffee in one hand and a newspaper in the other. Wedged in between his shoulder and his ear was a cell phone. The ignorant bastard didn't see me or hear me. He was too self-involved, clueless as hell, the way us crazies like them. The ride lasted five minutes or so. We pulled into a parking garage that was dimly lit and had lots of levels. He parked in a corner and my palms were sweating from a rush of adrenaline. I had been wedged the whole time on the floor between the front and back seat, and he never picked me up in his vision. I never faded into his attention span. I thought about just stealing the car and dumping it in the river, but then I thought: it's better that he learns what the consequences are of being careless and dropping his guard.

"He opened the car door and got out, leaving his coffee behind. I was so anxious to strangle this prick right then and there, but at the last second good ol' Russell had a change of heart. I wanted to make an example of him, not just waste him in a parked car. That's no fun. So I got out of the car. He clipped this mini-receiver to his ear and carried on with that usual business-pig attitude. 'I want it a done deal by the end of business today, got it?' That's what he said. As we walked toward the elevators I kept a safe distance behind him so I could carefully measure my chance. It was hard to control myself, I was so psyched up. I inched up closer behind him. Five feet and closing in. The schmuck was still oblivious. Three feet... Six inches... By the way, in the back seat of his car I found a pocket knife that served a valuable purpose. You'll find out later what that was. I tapped his shoulder. He looked back and held his hand up and said, 'Just a minute. This is important!'

"I was pissed. I didn't appreciate being delayed by some suspender-wearing cocksucker. I scoped out the hallway where the elevators were. It was a quiet place. There were vending machines at the end of the hall. There were a few nice plants standing in huge ornate pots and a directory of offices hung on the wall to my right. The man paced back and forth, never breaking stride, never hitting a button to call an elevator. But I went ahead and did it. You'll understand the reasoning behind that in a minute. Finally…I got my chance.

"Into the phone he said, 'Hold on a sec…' He looked back at me again and in the rudest tone known to man asked, 'Whaddaya want, guy?'

"I gave him an ice-cold stare and responded in my best genteel voice. 'You should learn to be more considerate when you're driving, sir.'

"Then I drove the knife into his temple and the man shrieked in pain. He hit the floor like a box of rocks. Blood shot out of his head. His whole body trembled as if he had been cattle prodded and filled with electricity—kind of like how I'm going to look in a little while. Afterwards I ran to the car and grabbed that cup of coffee he never touched and hustled back to his lifeless body, poured it all over him. He was dead before the cup emptied. I disposed of his body in the stairwell. Let some other corporate-criminal asshole clean up the mess and tell his family. Murder made me hungry so I rammed my fist through the glass of the vending machine and helped myself to a snack. I fled the scene in his car. So at that point I was baptized in the killing game. It was my first gig. My attempt at leading a peaceful life gave way to a thirst to spill more blood."

Brittany was writing on her pad. "Russell, it seems strange that a man was your first victim. I'd think that…"

Russell cut in. "Very perceptive, Brittany. But I don't choose the order, my dear. I've always killed in the moment. It's more fun. The thrill of the hunt is tedious work, a bit overrated too. But the excitement of a sudden, unexpected killing is a powerful tonic that lasts forever."

Brittany was fidgeting with her pen. "To backtrack a bit, after all those years what happened to your parents?"

"I never heard from them again. They seemed to vanish from the face of the earth. I'm sure Mom ended up with the realtor and Dad sure as fuck hung himself. Who cares anyway? I went on to slaughter much more human scum—upwards of thirty victims—the vermin that most people want to murder but are afraid to take the next step. Don't be afraid. Take matters into your own hands, my friends. That's been my philosophy during my darkest years. If there's a will, there's a way, and I found it, lived by it. When you step outside of the hideousness of it all, everything clears up. The law fell asleep at the wheel on this one a long time ago. The game is fixed and everyone knows it. Lawyers get rich and famous off people like me, never solve the problem though, because you can't, and society is too god damn stupid to realize that. You are no safer now because of this interview; or because of some silly book you'll write that'll probably become a bestseller and make you ridiculously rich. All the profilers, the experts, the shrinks—it's all a waste of time...but everybody tunes in like they might learn something new, unravel the layers. The television coverage is incessant. Frankly, it's more entertaining than a day at the ballpark. It's captivating really, and every single so-called law-abiding citizen gets off on it.

"Bundy, Gacey, Dahmer, Ramirez...all of them. Their stories are all bestsellers and Hollywood cash cows. If you do a little research you'll find that factoid to be undeniably accurate. Allow me to offer perspective. On the outside, my life sucked ass. You need to do lots of maneuvering and fake a smile to get through the days. People are their own worst enemy and they create land mines to walk on. I, on the other hand, sat in a prison cell with access to privileges the public wouldn't believe. I acted out my murderous impulses…and it was intoxicating. I ate three meals a day. I pumped weights like a madman and got stronger by the minute. I've done some ass-kicking around here and it's garnered me the respect I had never obtained out there among the civilians. I received three ice-cream cones a week, watched movies every night, smoked stogies, read books, listened to music, and screwed women who wrote to me and fell in love with me. They gave me a love that no woman in the outside world ever gave to me when I wasn't a monster. The most compelling part of all this is that when I'm good and charred to death, there is just another one in line ready to take the world by storm.

"Look, Brittany, what you have heard is the truth, every word of it. The real demons in this world are those of you on the outside. As I've stated before, I am about to pay the ultimate price for what I believed in. I have not one regret, can you say the same for yourself? I think not. My name is Russell Kincade and that is my story. I'm sure one of my heroes out there is picking up where I left off, and if you get lucky enough sooner than later, you may get to interview him too."

Russell licked his lips. "I have nothing more to say. You can take me away…I'm ready to meet my fate."

Brittany motioned to the guards. One of them

escorted her out of the room, the other stood by Kincade. Brittany removed her glasses and wiped the sweat from under her eyes, turned toward Russell. "Thank you for your candor, Russell."

Kincade smiled, blew her a kiss.

Brittany walked to the front entrance taking deep breaths to compose herself. Once she got to the lobby her agent met her, smiling. "Brittany, you're not going to believe it. *Modern Crime Magazine* wants an exclusive tonight about your book. I have them on hold. It's so great, isn't it?"

Brittany dried her face with a tissue and put a hand on her agent's shoulder. "Thanks, but tell them some other time. I've had enough for one night. I'm going to bed."

BEHIND THE CURTAIN

When Otis was faced with his wife Madeline's illness he was absolutely terrified. It was extremely challenging for him to confront her emotional and physical deterioration. He had never imagined tragedy coming between them. They had been inseparable for ten years. He'd met her just after his fortieth birthday (she was only thirty-five then) after a lifetime of being a loner. He and Madeline shared many things including a wonderful sex life. Far from a prude, she was usually the aggressor and that pleased him. Otis Wilcox had an insatiable sexual appetite and boundless imagination. Marrying Madeline not only completed him emotionally—it fulfilled the darker, more erotic elements of his personality.

Otis had spent most of his life harboring unusual sexual urges. Often he would push Madeline into acting out his wildest fantasies, many of which he had kept hidden deep in the past before their union. Madeline never refused him. She loved him. She had fun role-playing with him. During the last year of their marriage (which ended due to her death from cancer) Otis approached her about engaging in a rape fantasy he'd had since he was a teenager. She obliged. They trusted each other and entertained the scenario once or twice. Otis's obsessions had become part of their sexual regimen, and Madeline consented even when she thought they were going too far.

That was the kind of person she was and what Otis loved most about her—she was daring.

The cancer shook their marriage. Otis spent almost a year taking his wife back and forth to treatments, shuttling her to doctors, administering medication, and still managed to work full-time as a roofer. He didn't earn much, but between his income and Madeline's insurance he'd had enough to pay the bills.

Six months ago he had come home from a night of playing cards and found Madeline dead in the basement. She wanted to be alone for a while that evening so she encouraged Otis to go out. He had agreed, and went to a friend's house down the street. Madeline had been watching television and she'd passed away upright on the couch. Something in Otis snapped. He had a hard time coping with the loss. Soon thereafter he had embarked on a dark journey that twisted his world into troubling knots. Some days were better than others. He tried to ignore the disturbing thoughts that consumed him. It only became harder, though. His insidious addiction was getting tough to control.

On a sunny afternoon Otis Wilcox stood at his living room window. Knowing he could possibly be seen didn't faze him in the least—actually he got off on it, and no one could do a damn thing about it. This was the third time this week. It had happened so much lately that he'd lost track of when and who. This girl he would remember: every last detail down to the color of her socks and the pretty choker around her neck. She walked past his home the same time every day, at three o'clock in the afternoon, from September to mid-June. He greeted her in his own way, from where nobody knew he was lurking. At least he thought that to be true. This was his home and he had rights as an American citizen. No one had the power to take that away from him. He'd watched every fascinating move she made: the sway of her hips, the way her hair bounced over her pretty shoulders like delicate, delicious springs. He had imagined himself nuzzled up against her shapely body, enjoying a nose full of her sweet breath and perfume as they fused together into an erotic package.

The laws didn't allow him to act on his urges so he leered at her from the window on the second-floor balcony, masturbating behind the curtain. He wanted her badly. He knew if he was inside her it wouldn't last long. His fantasy would be fulfilled and he could move on to the next young specimen. Little Daphne Samuels was looking mighty appetizing. Otis was concealed by a fold of light-brown silky curtains. His chestnut-colored hair was impossible to distinguish alongside them. With his left hand he braced himself against the window and used the right to manipulate his cock. God, she was sensuous. He craved the innocence she exuded. That's what really turned him on. If only he could fuck her once it'd please him enough to keep her out of his thoughts—bring him back to normalcy again—if such a state existed. He ejaculated on the floor and pulled up his pants. As she walked around the corner and out of sight he thanked her—as he always did afterwards.

See you tomorrow. Same time. Same show.

Later that afternoon Otis paid a visit to the grocery store. He was browsing the shelves and heard shoes clicking on the floor behind him. He looked up and saw

Marcy, the Timmins's fourteen-year-old daughter coming toward him. He had fun hanging out with them at bingo games. Marcy's mother saw her daughter approaching him. Otis was stricken with more erotic thoughts—noticed her succulent tits and the way she wiggled.

"Hi Otis," her mother Lucy said. "Marcy spotted you and wanted to say hello. Getting some shopping done?"

Otis smiled and grabbed a can from the shelf, showed it to her playfully. "Just picking up a few groceries. The cupboards are bare. Soon I'll have to snack on the ants."

"Yuck," Marcy replied. "That's gross."

"I'm only teasing, Marcy," Otis joked. "You know I'd rather snack on that cute little nose of yours," he said as he poked it with his index finger. Mother and daughter giggled.

"See you at bingo next week. Gotta go, young ladies. Lots of errands to run today."

"Take care, Otis."

When Otis arrived home, he went directly up to his bedroom. He threw the groceries on the bed and they scattered on the mattress. In the closet he had a shoebox full of photos. He'd been compiling them since falling under Katie Winston's charms. He had watched her many times while fixing the Mulligans' roof next door. He pulled them out, sorted through them. Sometime in the past he'd managed to snap a few long-range shots of her coming in and out of cheerleading practice too, even snapped some of her taking a bubble bath. Each day his collection continued to grow. Soon he would add Marcy to the pile.

Marcy sat with her mother in front of the television. Her father was away on business for the week. He traveled often for extended periods of time depending on the frequency of his commitments. She got up from the living room couch and went to the kitchen, opening the refrigerator. A set of headlights skimmed across the windows and poured weak light into the room. Marcy was thirsty from her evening dance class. She reached for the juice, pulled a glass from the rack and set it down on the counter, filling it. Suddenly a series of flashes from outside caught her attention. She put the juice container down and peered through the window, but saw nothing out of the ordinary except for a cat running across the front porch as it passed under the glowing motion light.

Marcy went upstairs and began winding down for the night. Following her snack she wanted to settle in. So she began getting undressed and decided on watching some television in her room. She went over to her dresser and pulled out a shirt and sweatpants and began disrobing. A garbage can rattled outside. Marcy snapped her head up and peered through the window. She studied the yard and the street. "That damn cat," she mumbled. The little bugger was always making noise outside her window, especially at night.

The next day as usual, the kids on Valley Street gathered at the bus stop. Typically a crowd of six met at the street corner, but today a few of the students, including Marcy, were late. Otis snuck his head through the curtains and stared intensely at the corner of Valley and Muldoon. Otis knew the exact time the youngsters arrived. What he knew even more about was the girls' clothing. For each day of the week, and for the last year—without fail—Otis had kept meticulous notes on what each girl wore, especially Marcy.

Marcy was his favorite—she excited him the most—aroused his darkest and most disturbing sexual curiosities. He couldn't fight it. Even when he tried to dismiss these feelings there was a part of him that longed for young girls. He had tried many times before to seduce women his age and had failed miserably. What's a man to do? He would stare in the mirror every day and ask himself that same question—never getting a relevant answer. On an ordinary day he'd look at his reflection and wonder where his muscular frame had disappeared to, or where the extra fifty pounds came from. The days of a hundred seventy-five were long gone.

Otis hid behind the thick curtains in his bedroom and watched the intersection. Finally, much to his pleasure, the rest of the girls were making their way around the bend, book bags swaying from their shoulders, sweet little skips in their steps, their short dresses rising up their firm legs. Otis wrapped his hand around his penis and gently squeezed. Marcy had given him so many mornings full of pleasure, and filled quite a few lonely nights when the porn magazines and the skin flicks didn't suffice. He had planned on using her again, watching her and getting off. Otis considered another means of feeding his sexual fires. There was only one thing left to do. He would try an older woman again. Pursuing a prostitute never entered the equation for Otis. It wasn't even a consideration. He would discover on his own what was required to feed his needs and nothing would get in his way.

For a Thursday night the club was relatively busy. Otis frequented Sizzle, and since he wasn't the dancing type he had always come alone and enjoyed himself. Sometimes he would sit at the small table in the corner by the dartboard and nurse a cocktail while the music pounded from the speakers. He loved watching the main entrance, the steep flight of wooden stairs where the patrons entered the club. He was able to watch many fine pairs of succulent legs parading down the planks in sexy high heels.

As he looked around the place his eyes fell upon a near-perfect specimen. She stood at the bar. From his vantage point she appeared to be in her thirties. He was attracted to her. Everything about the lady sang beauty and perfection. He gathered the courage to move in. A few deep breaths and the final sips of his drink had him primed and ready. Otis walked toward the bar. The bartender made eye contact with him and smiled, knowing he'd be able to watch another attempted pickup. Otis gestured to the man, bought her another round of wine and then politely tapped her shoulder. He smelled her sexy perfume. It reminded him of how it would smell if he was among a garden of roses on an impeccable spring day: profoundly sweet and intoxicating. The lady turned and looked at Otis. She didn't frown–or smile. Her face was neutral. Otis's eyes darted toward the drink, then to her. He extended his hand and she took it.

"Name's Otis. That one's on me, young lady."

She smiled confidently then pushed away the glass. "No thank you, I'm spoken for."

"Fair enough," Otis responded. "Will you at least give me your name before I finish that drink myself?"

"Sabrina," she mumbled.

"Well, thanks for the delightful conversation, Sabrina," he said dryly. "I just wanted to tell you how beautiful you are, and how not one of the girls in this place can hold a candle to you."

His comments stirred her attention. She resisted smiling. "Thank you for—"

"Please don't thank me," Otis said. "I speak the truth. I just wanted somebody to talk to. Somebody who had more going for them beneath the surface, if you know what I mean?"

The comment piqued her curiosity. "What are you trying to say, Otis?"

"Nothing really, I meant it as a compliment. I've been here many times, you know, over the years. There's something more interesting about you that these other gals don't have. It's why I talked to you in the first place. Sorry if I—"

"It's okay. I'm sorry if I came off harshly. You seem nice and all. It's just that—well—I do have a boyfriend. Been together for a long time, plan on getting married soon."

"What are you doing here then, if you don't mind my asking?"

"My boyfriend's out of town for the night and I

love to dance. Normally he takes me here when I want, but my friends are meeting me here later."

Otis glanced down at her shoes. Man, she was a looker. She had a body that was well-earned by sweating for hours at the gym. He knew the type well. "Don't you think you should have worn more sensible shoes for dancing, Sabrina? Those have to be a good four inches."

She shrugged. "They're comfortable. Besides, I'll take them off before I dance. I love heels anyway, they make me taller. If you were a girl you'd understand."

"Anyway they're nice. I guess I'll be going." He turned away from her. "Take care of—"

Sabrina interjected. "Hey Otis. Answer one thing before you go?"

She got his attention. "Sure. What is it?"

"How long have you been married?"

"Excuse me?" he said.

"What's with the wedding band?"

Otis stared at the floor for a moment, and then back at Sabrina. "I was married up until a couple years ago. Her name was Madeline. She died of cancer. I still wear it occasionally when I'm feeling, you know— lonely."

Otis walked away, waved goodbye to her. She looked stunned as she watched him climb the stairs.

On the way home he roamed the streets for hours, overwhelmed by thoughts of Sabrina. He wanted her. She was his age—his type. Over the years, Otis had been turned down by many formidable women; this was no exception. When he returned home he couldn't fall asleep.

He'd hardly drunk anything, spent his time sipping a screwdriver on the rocks. Now he was tense, fighting pent-up sexual energy that needed to escape. He went into his basement and turned on the small lamp. It burned on the lowest setting, just enough light for him to see what he was doing.

Otis removed his pants and sat on the floor. He liked the sensation of his naked body touching the carpet. Faint light grazed the walls. Pulsating shadows lulled him into an abyss of concentration. His imagination blended images of the girl at the bar with the others that he had watched parading down the stairs in their hot outfits. He reached down and began rubbing his shaft, and not surprisingly, became erect in a matter of seconds. His brain offered him fantasies he couldn't resist: Sabrina seducing him, being naughty and rebelling against the binding moral threads of her relationship—the thought of her risking everything to be with him intensified his pleasure. Otis was deeply engrossed, lost in a valley of streaming thoughts.

While Otis was sprawled on the carpet, something scratched the basement window, a scratching that occurred again, and again, and again. He was unfazed. Jeffrey Baylor, a young waiter who lived next door, had been up late since working a long shift at a restaurant downtown. His dog, Barnaby, was clawing at Otis's basement window. He'd been carrying on now for several minutes. Then Barnaby barked—for a small dog he had a loud mouth. The noise woke Jeffrey. Jeffrey pried himself out of bed to investigate. When he opened the porch door he glanced left and saw Barnaby with his snout nuzzled up against Wilcox's window.

Jeffrey patted his leg. "Come on Barn, let's go back to bed, it's late." The dog didn't listen. It clawed the window again, turned back toward Jeffrey and whimpered. "For crying out loud, Barnaby!"

He ran across the yard and pulled on the thick collar around the dog's neck. "What the hell is so interesting here, Barn...?"

Jeffrey bent down and looked into the basement. He was appalled by what he saw. He had a perfect view of Otis in the midst of masturbation. Repulsed and quite horrified, Jeffrey's eyes gaped. But what could he do about it? He grabbed the dog, went back into his house, and sat at the kitchen table staring around the room as if what he'd seen wasn't real. He'd never look at Otis Wilcox the same way again.

As the week went by, Jeffrey Baylor kept his distance from Otis. Even when Otis extended a hand for a friendly shake in the driveway, Jeffrey backed away. His actions forced Otis to wonder what he had done to deserve such a brash reception. They'd always chatted when their paths crossed—Jeffrey Baylor usually initiated their exchanges. Otis brushed off his behavior and moved on.

When Bingo night came around again Otis was excited to meet Marcy and her mother at the hall. They had always met at the church auditorium on Drexel Way. Marcy eagerly awaited these events, especially since Otis was good for a few laughs. He frequently had them in stitches from his cleverly-delivered jokes. The church was a full house. Marcy, sitting across from her mother, noticed Otis coming toward them. His appearance spread a smile across her face. He came up behind Lucy and gave the *shush* sign to Marcy, then covered her mother's eyes and said "Guess who?"

Lucy laughed. "It's got to be you, Otis. Who else?"

Otis laughed. "What can I say? You're quite the little sleuth."

He sat in the empty chair next to Marcy. He knew they were happy to see him. There had to be about a hundred tables in the room, all of them occupied. Each was decorated with long flowing tablecloths. They were red with white ruffles at the bottom, dangling an inch from the floor. Everyone sat on folding chairs packed close together. Otis inconspicuously looked down at Marcy's legs. She was wearing a denim skirt with black stockings. He couldn't take his eyes off her shapely legs. Instantly he felt his cock engorging with blood. He had watched her from his bedroom many times, but being so close to her now fed his untamable sexual need. Otis carefully lowered his hand to within an inch of her shiny stockings. He surveyed the room, made sure no one was aware of his actions. Otis maneuvered his hand farther down, inches from Marcy's knee. His fingertip grazed her pantyhose. She didn't realize where his hands were. She had no idea that he was boiling over with lust for her. Otis was desperate to sample her once, just to know how it felt to grope a young ripe body. He craved her reaction—her attention.

Otis licked his lips and then guided his eyes down

her blouse. Still no one suspected a thing. Her cleavage was remarkable for her age, her breasts round and perky. He was tempted to suck on them right now. She began kicking her leg under the table, combing through her silky hair with her fingers. Everybody was still clueless to what he was about to do. Marcy's leg rocked back and forth, the scent of her perfume was driving Otis mad. He was anxious to feel her leg. His whole body felt as if he were locked in a steam room. His hands were moist, trembling. Otis glanced toward the other side of the hall where his eyes met another woman's. She appeared to be in her mid-forties. She winked at him; he politely reciprocated by smiling at her.

Otis touched Marcy's leg. Then he dragged his fingers from her knee up to the fringe of her skirt. Marcy didn't seem to mind. He was absolutely positive that she had felt him there, wanted him there, needed him there. Her mouth was slightly open, and he watched her tongue wiggle behind her impeccable teeth, her glossy lips. She smiled innocently at Otis as he rose from the table. "I'm— I'm sorry. I have to be going. I forgot that I have an important phone call to make."

He hoped they believed him, wondered if they saw the sweat glistening on his face. He felt the perspiration sliding down his forehead and the back of his neck. He wanted to go home and be alone. "Good night, young ladies," he said as he left the room.

"Have a nice evening, Otis. Thanks for stopping by," the ladies said.

Otis was roaring down Route 71. It was just past nine o'clock. The traffic was light and he had the road to himself. He tried to concentrate, tried to erase Marcy from his mind but couldn't. The thoughts running through him were vivid and undeniable. He picked up speed, repeatedly glancing in the rearview. His car, motor groaning, was pushing seventy-five in a fifty mile-an-hour zone. The sooner he arrived home the better it'd be. Now he wished he had never touched Marcy. Not for reasons of guilt or any wrongdoing, but because he felt his obsession festering—, and worse, he feared the rational parts of his mind were splitting at the seams. He had seen the way her eyes met his when he touched her. That wasn't a look of disgust—rather of endless possibilities and a future of clandestine passion. Perhaps the heat of desire was flaring up in her too. The mere thought of that turned him on. He pulled the car off the road and drove into Mulberry Park, hung a right onto the old gravel trail that chiseled a path into the woods.

Nobody ever passed through there at night. It was commonly used by the Park's Department to dump some of their used gardening materials and waste like leaves and brush. At this hour Otis would have no interference. He pulled up behind a row of spruce trees and parked, shut down the engine and killed the lights. He shoved his trousers to his knees and played with himself. The vision was there in his mind: Marcy's firm body hidden underneath tight pantyhose had his heart jack-hammering. Completely aroused and tingly all over, it wasn't going to take long to reach orgasm. Five more minutes to get home was too long for him to wait. This is what Marcy did to him. Seconds passed. He climaxed.

As Otis pulled into his driveway he saw Jeffrey

Baylor leaning against his car smoking a cigarette. Otis waved. Jeffrey halfheartedly raised his hand back. Otis wasn't in the mood to make small talk so he went straight up his walkway toward the front door. He got to the door and unlocked it. Jeffrey spoke to him. "Don't worry, I won't tell anyone. Next time… turn off the lights."

Otis never cared for Jeffrey's snide remarks. He and his other restaurant buddies were smartasses sometimes. Otis turned and saw the glowing embers of the cigarette bleeding through the darkness, the flame brightening as Jeffrey took a puff—then another. "Excuse me? Did you say something?" Otis asked. He had heard him clearly, although he was astonished the kid had the balls to broach such a topic.

"You heard me. Oughta be more careful. There are kids in the neighborhood, you know."

"Don't know what you're talking about, young man, but I don't care for your tone. What's gotten into you lately?"

Otis approached Jeffrey, stood a few feet from him. The kid took another drag of his cigarette—a deep one—then dropped the butt on the driveway, stamped it out. He turned his head, exhaled a cloud of smoke. "We all do it, man. You should just be more aware of *where* you do it."

Otis was uncomfortable. "So what? Do you like staring in people's homes? What're you, some neighborhood watchman? This is my home. Mind your own business."

The kid walked away. "I was just busting your balls, man. Your secret's safe with me."

Otis went inside, his mind racing, spinning. He felt violated; his sanctity breached. He ran to the laundry room and disrobed, threw his grimy clothes into the basket and jumped in the shower. He thought about his and Jeffrey's exchange. He was upset that Jeffrey had seen him. *Was he spying on me? Why was he looking in the window? He better keep to himself.*

The next day Otis woke with a maddening hunger to see Marcy again. He sat on the edge of his bed and tried to discard his bad thoughts. But he couldn't. He got dressed and walked over to his dining room table. In the center sat a beautiful plastic flower arrangement in an engraved bowl that read: *"A flower is as good as a smile."* He removed it from the table and hurried to his car.

At Marcy's he rang the bell and waited patiently. Anxiety and expectation had his mind whirling. The door opened. Marcy stood in the doorway, much to his surprise. Otis smiled, his sweaty face gleaming in the morning sun. He felt his clammy fingers losing their grip around the bowl.

"Hey Otis! What brings you here so early?"

"Is it okay if I come in? These are for your mom."

"Sure. Why not? She's out running an errand but she'll be home in about ten or fifteen minutes. Would you like some juice? I was about to have some."

Otis smiled bigger. "I'd love some." She filled two glasses of juice and handed one to him. He held it in his hand for a moment, watched her lips meet the glass. She put down her empty cup and looked at his.

"Aren't you gonna have some? Stuff's not cheap you know." She giggled. He liked that about her. Her bubbly personality sparked his naughty imagination. Otis drank his in one shot, then walked past her to the sink and rinsed out the glass.

"Can I ask you a question, Marcy?"

"Sure."

"Do you have a boyfriend these days? Anyone *special* in your life?"

"Yeah. Evan O' Connor. He's really sweet."

Otis furrowed his brow. "Does he treat you right?"

"Of course he does, Otis. Why do you ask?"

"No real reason. It's just that your mom speaks the world of you. I think of her like the sister I never had sometimes. You're a friend too. I care about you. The thought of the two of you not enjoying happiness upsets me. That's all."

"Ahhh. You are so sweet." Marcy walked over and gave him a hug. He wanted to take her right there. Her wet hair flopped down his neck, tickling it like a clump of feathers. The smell of her skin was sensational, exotic. It had an inviting odor, a fruity smell. His eyes met hers. He wanted to force his lips on hers and roam her mouth like Evan O' Connor had done—give her what a young man lacked and what a grown man mastered.

Marcy's mother pulled in the driveway. They broke their embrace. Otis left the house and crossed paths with Lucy. "Otis, what brings you here? Everything okay?" A shopping bag dangled from her hand. "I stopped by and left a little something with Marcy for the house. Nothing special. Thought you might like it. Anyway, I have to go," he said. "I need to take care of a few things myself. Have a good one."

"Bye, Otis," Lucy said.

Otis stood in his basement staring at the walls. The sun was completing its descent, darkness shadowed the block. He wondered how long he would carry on this way. He had forgotten where it all began. Why it began? He remembered his wife's illness. It invaded their life and stole away their dreams, infected him permanently. What he wanted was young girls and there was no hiding from it anymore.

Otis walked to the couch and peeled off one of the cushions. His private stash was concealed there. They were always there when he needed them—in his favorite place— always reliable. He picked up the pictures, studied them. Each one of them showed Marcy in a different outfit she had worn to school. His favorite was still the dress with the ruffles and the tight white shirt underneath the shoulder straps, white stockings and shiny black heels. He had beaten off to that picture more times than he could remember and he wanted to do it again, right now.

Otis decided on a change of scenery. He went upstairs into the living room, raised the thermostat and closed the curtains. He dropped his pants. For a minute or two he lost his thoughts in the splendor of Marcy. He imagined being her dream date, picking her up from school, leaning across the seat of the car and offering her a deep sensual greeting with his tongue. He went at it again. The sweat was dripping from his forehead. Otis was in deep now, drawing the most perfect scenarios his mind was capable of. God, she was gorgeous. No woman his age could deliver the pleasure he was experiencing now. In fact, he had been turned down by so many double her age and half her caliber. From now on he would stay with the young meat—no attitudes, no sagging skin, no image issues, no personal baggage, no nosy kids. They were perfect. In his own twisted world he could have as many as he wanted, whenever he wanted them.

As he stroked himself the doorbell rang and broke his rhythm. He was close to orgasm and wanted to finish, but not answering the door wasn't a wise move. Everybody knew he was home. Ignoring the door would draw unnecessary attention. He pulled up his slacks and wiped the sweat from his face, then dried his hands on his shirt. Otis walked toward the door, looking back from the halfway point. The pictures were sitting on the cushion out in the open. He nervously grabbed the photos and stuffed them under the seat cushion, then went to the door and opened it.

Lucy stood there with a big smile on her face. "Hi Otis," she said. "Is this a bad time?"

Otis swallowed. "No, not at all. Please come in."

She stepped into the living room. "Are you sure this is a good time, you're really sweating."

"Everything's fine. I just came out of the attic, got a few boxes to go through yet." The lie escaped him rather easily. "Don't sweat it."

Lucy laughed. "That's a funny one."

"Can I get you something to drink, Lucy?"

"Oh no, that's all right. I won't keep you. I just

came to thank you for the wonderful bowl of flowers. I felt like thanking you personally since you went out of your way with such a nice gesture."

"Please, don't mention it, Luce—I enjoy doing nice things for wonderful people."

Lucy put her hand on Otis's arm. "We think the world of you, Otis. Marcy thinks you're as sweet as pie, and so do I."

"That's really kind of you. I appreciate the sentiments, really. I know I stay locked up in this house a lot thinking about what I had with Madeline, but I'm getting better with each day."

Otis took a step backwards and accidentally nudged the seat cushion, exposing the corners of the pictures. Marcy's legs were out in the open, the rest of her portrait hidden underneath the cushion. Otis's heart started to palpitate, his sweating intensified. He was careful to obstruct Lucy's path, blocking the view of the photo. Now the trick was getting her to leave, and it wasn't going to be easy. She had a tendency to become a chatterbox. Lucy looked toward the dining room and beamed. "I like what you've done with the curtains, Otis. You have an eye for good decoration. Just ask any woman, she'll agree with me. Marcy would appreciate that too."

Otis's face turned to stone. He was starting to feel a little edgy and Lucy wasn't moving along as quickly as he would have liked. For a second he considered a better approach, a means to push her on her way. "I'm sorry to do this to you, Lucy, but I want to be alone for a bit. Please don't take this the wrong way. It's just that...well...in the attic I was going through some of Madeline's belongings and it was bringing back many fond memories." He found lying was becoming easier. "I'd like to be with her, in a sense—alone. Hope you don't mind?"

Lucy kissed his sweaty cheek and walked toward the door. "I'm so sorry about this, Otis. Sometimes I don't use my head."

He responded calmly. "Don't mention it. It's not your fault. Stop by this evening if you'd like. You and Marcy are always welcome here."

Lucy was glowing. "Thank you, Otis. Take care."

Otis waved. "Goodbye, Luce—"

When Lucy shut the door, Otis breathed a sigh of relief. That was a close call, closer than he was prepared for. He went upstairs and took a cold shower. After he cleaned up, Otis took a ride to the shop to check on the week's pending jobs. He was excited to discover only a few jobs were planned. That freed up time for him to be alone, maybe get out of the house for a bit.

Evening had set in. Otis took a long walk around town. The extended summer day had come to an end and a refreshing breeze swept the air. He walked up Mercer Street and saw a young couple (high school kids) kissing in the shadow of a house. He stopped walking and stared at the couple, aroused by what he was seeing. He spotted a sizable tree and hid behind it. The kids had no idea they were being watched. Otis fingered his genitals. He'd never had an experience like this one, never thought he'd enjoy the sight of two youthful strangers groping each other. He found it deeply fascinating. Perhaps in the future he would seek couples who enjoyed being watched and he'd pleasure himself. As the couple's exchange continued, Otis imagined how it would feel to be sandwiched between them. He had absolutely no feelings toward men—none at all—in fact he was confident of that. But the idea of a woman taking on two horny men awakened something in his psyche that he couldn't ignore.

The two of them had paused, whispering to each other, and then went back at it again. Their passion for each other was absolutely sizzling. They were just like him, Otis thought, innocently exploring their sexuality. A subtle stream of light from the driveway's motion light grazed their figures in the dark, showcasing their young toned bodies. Otis was close to having another orgasm. He came out from behind the tree and started walking home, desperate to relieve himself.

The boy heard a noise—Otis's shoes had scraped the ground, capturing his attention. "Who the hell is that? Wait here, Amber," he told his girlfriend.

Otis already was quite a distance up the street when the boy caught a glimpse of his silhouette under a street lamp and decided to follow him. His girlfriend went along. "What is it?" She tugged at his arm. "I don't remember asking for an intermission. Where did we leave off?" she asked, pulling at his arm again.

He shook his head. "I don't trust whoever that is. Don't know why. Stay with me for a sec. Afterwards we'll get back to business," he said, smiling playfully.

The girl tossed her hair. "Fine."

Crickets randomly stirred within the darkness, from places near and far. The sounds bounced from corner to corner, bringing to life a typical summer night. The kids followed Otis, using shortcuts, keeping a safe distance. The two of them snuck into the Watsons' yard and tiptoed around the side of the house. That put them closer to Otis but hidden behind a wall of dense, flourishing rhododendrons. They kneeled in the flower bed and peered through the bushes, watching Otis carefully. He went two more blocks and then made a left onto Valley Street. The lovers emerged from behind the bushes and remained on Otis's trail. They came to a wooden fence that adjoined two properties and saw Otis entering his home. The boy whispered in his girlfriend's ear. "I've seen this guy before. I think I saw him one day at my mother's church. Everybody loves him, thinks he's such a great guy."

Otis entered his home. As he walked into the living room he switched on a lamp.

The young boy Dennis refused to leave the situation alone. "What're you doing?" Amber asked. "Let's be done with this. We have no right being here, and you know it."

Dennis shot back, "Just one peek inside. Then we leave, agreed?"

She nodded, reluctantly.

They snuck around the back. The neighborhood seemed relatively quiet. Nobody would know that they were spying on Otis, as he had done to them. The air conditioner groaned in Otis's window. The kids braced themselves on the air conditioner and looked inside. "Sick fuck," Dennis whispered.

Amber raked her fingers through her hair. "Oh my god. This is so wrong. Let's get out of here."

Otis sensed something outside, turned and gazed through the glass. Nobody was there.

Ten minutes later a mass of swirling red lights brightened the night—a police car rolled along Breyerstone Street. Dennis and Amber stood at Dennis's parents' picture window watching the patrol car drive past, en route to Otis's home.

Otis's doorbell rang. He quickly pulled up his pants. The bell rang again. He fastened his belt, his hands shaking as he worked. Becoming impatient, the policemen knocked. "Please open up, sir. This is the Halloway Police Department. We just want to ask a few questions."

Nervous and confused, Otis's face was slimy with sweat. He peeped through the hole in the door, saw two cops on the porch, their heads cleanly shaven, pencil-thin moustaches punctuating their complexions. It had been a long time since he had felt the kind of fear that was rushing through him, at least not since his wife's final days. He knew why the officers were there and knew the series of questions that would comprise their interrogation. Otis reached out, loosened the chain, and opened the door.

"Good evening, Mr. Wilcox. We're from the Halloway Police Department. May we come in?"

Otis's eyes were wide with paranoia. He fought to control it, to act normal. "Yes...yes of course."

He stepped back, giving the cops enough space to enter. The officer to his right, the taller and more muscular one, spoke first. "I'm Lieutenant Bradke and this (he pointed to his partner) is Officer Monroe. We have only a few routine questions and we'll be on our way."

"Okay," Otis responded, his voice unstable.

"We are responding to a call about a strange man spying on a couple of kids. Where were you during the last thirty minutes?"

Fidgety, Otis fingered a nearby magazine on the table. "Been right here, officers. Chilling out."

"What were you doing? I mean it's pretty dark in here," the cop remarked. His partner, Monroe, had his eyes locked on Otis.

"Just watching some television, got bored, so I closed my eyes for a bit."

Monroe turned toward the television, studied it, and noticed it was unplugged, spotted a white hand towel draped over the couch cushion.

The Lieutenant continued the interrogation. "Look, Mr. Wilcox, this may make you uncomfortable but it's our job to address certain concerns. It's our duty to the public as law enforcement officials. So I'll get to the point."

Otis felt his heart firing non-stop in his chest. It was off and running like a runaway train. He had been nervously fiddling with the magazine on a nearby table but couldn't stop himself.

"Are you exposing yourself to the public, Mr. Wilcox?"

The magazine fell off the table. Otis bent down to pick it up.

"We don't mean to embarrass you," the officer said.

Otis let out a nervous chuckle. "Why would that embarrass me? I've never done anything like that. Why would you ask me such a preposterous question?"

The officer clutched his belt and straightened, got into Otis's face. "Because we've had a complaint about you doing things...fondling yourself, Mr. Wilcox. That's indecent exposure, sir."

"Well I assure you, officers, I've done nothing of the kind. And last time I checked an American citizen can do whatever he wants in his own home as long as he's not hurting anyone else. Doesn't the law protect those rights too?"

The neighbors were peering through their windows—some came out of their homes to investigate the commotion. A few bystanders seemed surprised that the police were at Otis's place, an upstanding citizen, a good neighbor. A few minutes later Lucy came from around the corner and across his lawn. "Is everything all right?" she asked. "This man is a dear friend of my family."

Smiling awkwardly, Otis waved his hand to send her away. "Everything is fine, Luce...just a misunderstanding."

From the other side of the driveway Jeffrey came out of his house, a cigarette hanging from his lips. He strode along his front walk, smirking at Otis, smoke rising into his face, his hair uncombed. He had an idea what this was about. He went in Lucy's direction. Otis looked over the officers' shoulders. Jeffrey had entered his field of vision, standing a few feet from Lucy but focusing on him. Otis stiffened, put his head down. Lieutenant Bradke reached for his pad and began writing on it.

The police had left Otis's home and now stood in the street amongst the people, ordering everyone to go home. Lucy was the last to leave the scene; she spoke with Otis for a minute or two. "What was that all about?"

"Oh nothing," he explained. "Someone complained about my music being played too loud and I was given a warning. Next time they are going to issue me a summons."

"Glad you're okay, Otis."

"Sorry, but I've got to cut this short. Goodnight, Lucy. I'm going to bed."

"Oh. By the way, I have a quick question for you, Otis," she said.

"Shoot."

"Can you show Marcy your curtains tomorrow? I told her all about them and she'd love to see them for herself. She's been bugging me about it. I promised her."

"No problem. Send her over. I'll be here."

ACKNOWLEDGMENTS

AuthorMike Ink/Dark Ink (Michael Aloisi and staff): Thanks for taking a chance on me, for making me feel like part of your family, and for placing me in the company of extraordinary talent. You guys are first-rate! Let's do it all again soon.

Gina Petrone: Thanks for lending me your keen editorial eye. Your critique was honest, direct, and respectful, your suggestions invaluable. I couldn't have asked for anything more. You give editors a good name.

My family: You have been an integral part of my growth, a driving force behind my success. Ever since I started writing you've been sharing words of encouragement, patting me on the back and nudging me in promising directions. Your unwavering belief in my craft gives me endless strength and happiness. You deserve a heartfelt round of applause. Much love!

My wife's family: You have always applauded my various works. For years you've been sending your good cheer my way. Thank you kindly for your support.

Friends & neighbors: You've never stopped cheering me on. You are dedicated fans who treat me as though I'm a celebrity. I'm fortunate to be surrounded by such caring, nurturing, enthusiastic people.

Ed Minus: I wouldn't have been able to write the stories in this collection without your friendship and guidance. Much of my success I owe to your teaching. Your patience, your selflessness, your ability to educate without preaching, and your hard-earned wisdom have reinforced my passion for writing. You have my everlasting gratitude. Not only have you made me a better writer, you've made me a better man.

My dogs, Murphy and Madison: Thank you for keeping me company at 5:00 a.m. when the words are coming out of me. I like it when you poke your noses through the door and give me that "Whatcha doin'?" look, and then curl up next to me, comforting me in my labors.

My grandfather, Frank Boyle: He spent most of his life writing stories and songs and anything that inspired him. Unfortunately, during his long life of investing countless hours and effort (and money) in his craft, he never got any of his work published. Well, Grandpa, let's enjoy this book together. Rest in peace.

Readers: You keep my work alive. Your unflagging support stokes the fires of my imagination. From the depths of my soul, thank you for participating in the scenarios I create.

Editors: I would like to thank each and every editor who has allowed my work to be in print.

Writers: Thank you to the writers—past and present—whose work instilled in me the desire to explore my passions, the responsibility of respecting my craft, and the maturity and the tools to continue my literary quest.

Diane Sebastian & NJ libraries: Thanks for giving me the privilege of speaking with others about the written word. These sessions have given me the opportunity to meet talented artists in communities throughout New Jersey. And thanks also for putting my work on the shelves among authors whose fine accomplishments we all celebrate.

Bookstores and anyone else who's had me as a guest over the years: Thanks for giving me a forum to interact with readers.

Myspace: Even though many networking sites have gained more popularity on the worldwide web, Myspace jumpstarted my journey as a writer. Through this platform I developed friendships, found my first fans, and shared my work with readers, editors, and fellow writers I never would have met otherwise—all these conveniences at no cost.

John Carpenter: Of all your masterpieces, Mr. Carpenter, "Halloween" was the film that made me eager to discover my own creativity, to explore my own darkness, and to begin to write with passion and great pleasure. Your storytelling ability, your vigorous imagination, your breadth of technical savvy—these talents which you have used so skillfully over the years are precisely what drew me to horror cinema as a whole, exposing me to an infinite range of artistic expression that never ceases to inspire me.

Saving the best for last—my devoted, intelligent, ravishing wife, Elizabeth: Thank you for over fourteen years of joyful marriage. Often I take time away from our life to put ideas on paper yet you've never uttered an unkind word or dissuaded my creativity. Since we first met, almost twenty years ago, we have shared an interest in all things horror-related. When we discuss the world of scary make-believe we become childlike, energized and imaginative. The two of us share the same sensations for the stories in this book. For me, writing these stories recaptured the old days when people told creepy stories around the campfire, everyone captivated by listening to one chilling yarn after another. You've read the stories in this book with equal enthusiasm and pleasure, demonstrating how proud you are of me by having that sparkle in your eye. Needless to say, as a writer I have endured much rejection and harsh critiques, faced my share of disappointment and dishonesty, but you've always held me close and reminded me what's most important. I love everything about you. You are my special lady.

ABOUT THE AUTHOR

Inspired by his ravenous appetite for movies, David Boyle began telling stories of his own in 2007. His breakthrough in 2008 came with the publication of his first book, *Blood Works (*Arctic Wolf Publishing*)*. In the same year, one of his stories, "Blindsided," was adapted to film in Canada by Jack Action Films. Among other credits, David's work—stories, essays, articles, aphorisms—has been published in several online and print periodicals. He enjoys a quiet life with his wife, Elizabeth, and their dogs, Murphy and Madison, in Denville, New Jersey.

www.AuthorDBoyle.com